CH00846994

Mallmoc's
Castle

The Knights of Liöfwende

Mallmoc's Castle

Book Two of The Knights of Liöfwende

Garry Kilworth

www.atombooks.co.uk

A paperback original from Atom Books

First published in Great Britain by Atom 2003

A CIP catalogue record for this book
is available from the British Library.

ISBN 1 904233 12 0

Typeset in Cochin by M Rules
Printed and bound in Great Britain
by Bookmarque Ltd, Croydon, Surrey

Atom
An imprint of
Time Warner Books UK
Brettenham House
Lancaster Place
London WC2E 7EN

CONTENTS

PART ONE

A boggart's homecoming

ONE

'Where are we going?'

It was the young mortal youth who had spoken.

Spiggot, the boggart knight, answered, 'Home. To my home, that is, not yours I'm afraid, Jack. I need to pick up some things.'

They were trudging over hill and dale, across fen and moor, through woodland, around bog and marsh.

'If we get there alive' muttered Kling, who was as usual harnessed to the cart which held Spiggot's wonderful suit of fairy armour.

Rosamund, the only other mortal in the party apart from Jack, remained silent. The daughter of Baron Guillaume de Arundel was a maiden from the medieval era of Britain and the gulf between her and Jack was considerable. They each spoke about matters which confused and often distressed the other.

Spiggot was an unlikely leader even for such a party –
a short, stocky, muscular boggart who came from a long
line of faerie metalsmiths. He had a shock of dark hair on
his head and there was good deal left over for his arms
and legs. His features, however, were pleasant and
simple, with little hostility in them. Spiggot's culture was
firmly embedded in Liöfwende, the faerie name for
Faerieland, and sometimes he was more a hindrance than
a help when sorting out the differences between the two
mortals. Only the rat, Kling, had a reasonable grasp of
universal knowledge and Kling was not inclined to assist
the others when they became confused. In fact, he rather
enjoyed watching them wallow in misunderstandings
and misconceptions.

The group of four travellers were a little more grumpy
with each other than usual this fine Liöfwende morning.
They had just been through a wide valley where thousands of faerie weapons lay scattered amongst the grassy
knolls. Great white feathers from elven hats littered the
ground. A rare pixie cannon, its barrel etched with
curlicues and fleur-de-lis, was buried snout first in the
blackened earth, having coughed its last. A fairy musket,
the like of which were few and far between, was twisted
around the stem of a gorse bush. Bolts from fairy crossbows, long thin pikes, breastplates, helmets, all were
cluttering the turf. It had been an amazing sight.

A great battle had recently taken place there, between
pixies and elves on one side, and ulcugga fairies.
Ulcugga, fair of complexion and foul of heart, were the
most numerous and certainly the most vicious fairies in
Liöfwende. The pixies and elves had lost. Their armies

had been routed. They had fled in all directions. The ulcugga had returned in triumph to the north, where the sorcerer Mallmoc's iron castle held sway, boasting of their victory. They had slaughtered valorous West Country pixies and the Southland elves and had sent them crawling into rabbit holes and under the thorns of heathland shrubs. It was not a result which had the four travellers hopping around in glee.

'See, this is why we have to enlist other fairy nations,' said Spiggot. 'You have to fight fairies with fairies. Elves and pixies are all right, but they haven't the flair for fighting that fairies possess. And Mallmoc has been increasing his ulcugga army for ages and ages.' Spiggot was always vague about time passing, as it almost seemed to stand still in Liöfwende. 'There's thousands of them. There didn't used to be.'

If Spiggot was unsure about the passage of time, it was nothing to Jack's ignorance of procreation in Liöfwende. He knew that boggarts and possibly most goblin families were born much in the same way as mortals, but fairies, the highest order of aerial beings and supernatural lifeforms, seemed to come out of thin air. He now made the mistake of asking Spiggot where Mallmoc got his ulcugga fairies from.

'Why, they're there, aren't they?' said Spiggot.

'He conjures them up by sorcery, does he?' asked Jack.

'No, he just calls them forth, and they come from their sleeping-lairs, from their jars and pots, from their holes in doorposts, from green wooden bottles, from amongst the fallen ash branches and flinty rocks. They are disgorged from the lips of trout, they fall from the nests.'

'All right, all right.'

It seemed there were secret places where ulcugga without number lay dormant. Or perhaps where the ingredients which made an ulcugga were to be found? Mallmoc apparently knew the cryptic ways of drawing these malicious and nefarious creatures forth, multiplying them, until he had vast armies that were spreading across the plains and hills of Liöfwende.

It was also believed that the sorcerer had stolen a keystone to a Scottish cairn. The theft had freed dread underworld creatures – skaggs and thrum of Gilscipe – who were now pouring forth in great numbers to ravage the land. King Cimberlin of the Northumberland fairies, whose standing stone city of Xuagguaqac had been surrounded by the ulcugga after the pixies and elves had been defeated, had given Spiggot the authority to go out and find the locking-stone to the magic cairn. A quest. Spiggot, however, had been thinking about this and decided that if the stone was indeed with Mallmoc then it was not enough simply to look for the stone. He had decided to sound out faerie clans on the way, to see if they would follow him into battle against the ulcugga, should it be necessary in the end.

To aid him, the King had allowed Spiggot to keep the magical armour which Spiggot's father, Gnomon, had fashioned for the northern monarch – armour which Spiggot was supposed to deliver to the King, but had worn without permission during various emergencies on the way. The boggart was thus armed as a faerie knight and he had his father's domestic giant rat to help him in his quest. Kling was wise in the ways of Liöfwende and

Mortaland, and was an invaluable source of information. And Jack and Rosamund were tagging along in the hope of finding a way back to their own time.

The group were tired after the long day's march. As the sun began to descend in the west, Spiggot threw off his pack. 'We'll camp here,' he said, pointing out that there was a beck nearby with fresh clean water tumbling over its stones.

'Kling wants to get out of the harness,' said the giant rat. 'Kling is weary from his teeth to his tail.'

'Aren't we all?' said Jack, falling to the ground and laying on his back, to stare up at the emerging stars. 'I'll help you in a minute.'

'Now, please, Jack,' Kling ordered. 'Look at the sweaty stripes the leather has made on Kling's poor back. Kling needs to wash in the stream. Kling needs his coat brushing to its usual glossy form.'

'What do you think you are, a sable?' Jack grumbled. 'You're a common rat. Rats don't have glossy coats.'

'I shall brush thee, dear Kling,' Rosamund said. 'Thou shalt have a shining coat, rat or no. Thou hast worked thy right to be cossetted and coddled. I shall groom thee as I would my jennet, my dear sweet horse whom I shall never see again.'

'Well, I'm glad someone appreciates Kling.'

'That's right,' said Jack, getting up reluctantly and loosening the buckles on Kling's harness, 'spoil him.'

'He deserves spoiling, Jack. Rosamund would do the same for thee, if thou wast in harness. Or mayhap you would prefer your gadfly, *Jenny*, to do it?'

Jenny was Jack's ex-girlfriend back in Mortaland.

Their break-up had been recent and try as he might, Jack could not help talking about her some of the time. He hated himself for it, and knew he was acting like the dumped, pathetic, whining creature he was, but one couldn't simply forget someone like Jenny overnight. They had been childhood sweethearts. For all he knew Jenny was pining for him right now, back in Mortaland, wetting her pillow with her tears. He admitted it was unlikely, given that she had been stone-faced when she told him to get lost, but the hope was always there.

Once Kling was out of his straps, all four of them went down to the beck and started splashing water on themselves and each other. Rosamund, in the red velvet gown which Jack had shortened for her, soon became drenched. Her medieval turban had long since gone and her hair hung soft about her shoulders. She hummed an ancient tune and when she glanced up at Jack her eyes had a merry twinkle to them. Whenever Jack looked at her, as he was doing so now, his heart melted like butter in the sun.

Afterwards they all lay on the warm grass in the evening sun to dry. When darkness came, Spiggot lit a fire. They clustered round the flames, watching the sparks from the dry wood go skywards into the blackness above. Now that the birds had ceased their songs, and the only sound was that of one or two crickets in the grass, they could hear the defeated pixies and elves calling to one another in distressed voices. These poor creatures were hiding under stones and logs, out on the moors, hoping to find friends with whom to travel back to their homelands.

'Can we do nothing to help them?' asked Jack, after a while.

'Best not,' replied Spiggot, his squat and hairy form the darkest of those around the fire: the colour of an old conker left to weather in the sun, wind and rain. 'Best leave them be.'

'The voices are so sad,' Rosamund said. 'It is enough to make one melancholy too.'

'I know, I know. But best leave them be. Isn't that right, Kling?'

'Very right, master's son. Involvement is unwise. After all, the pixie and elf armies brought it on themselves. It was they who attacked Mallmoc. Not the other way around.'

This was true, but they had had good reason. The thrum Mallmoc was said to have released ate the roots of trees and killed them. To faerie all trees, especially the oak, are sacred. Without trees Liöfwende would become a wasteland where faerie folk would wander and go increasingly mad. A mad faerie, as Jack and Rosamund had witnessed, was a terrible thing to meet. And skaggs, well, they were giant lobster-like vermin, monstrous creatures, who could chop a faerie in two with their multiple pincers.

'I still don't understand why Mallmoc did this thing,' said Spiggot, poking the fire. 'He stands to lose as much as the rest of us. I mean, he loves iron and the cold metals of the Earth more than he does trees, but his army of ulcugga fairies will lose their reason along with the rest of us.'

'Maybe by that time he won't need them?' Jack suggested. 'Perhaps he just doesn't care?'

'Well, if we ever meet him, we'll find out,' said Spiggot, not at all looking forward to the prospect. 'I hope we never do.'

While they were talking, a figure suddenly came out of a nearby wood and stood over them. It was a mortal man in a grey cloak which shut out the stars when he stretched his arms. Spiggot gave a little cry and jumped up. The others just sat there and stared at the new-comer, wondering if this was indeed the wizard Mallmoc, come to squash these puny upstarts before they could even begin to raise an army. The sorcerer was surely now aware, through his various spies – moles, gulls, adders and coots – especially the nefarious coots – of Spiggot's intentions, since he hardly kept quiet on the matter.

'May I share your fire, friends?' the stranger asked in a low, gruff voice. 'I am always drawn to a flame.'

Jack asked, 'Who are you?'

'King of the Moths,' came the swift reply.

Spiggot let out a sigh of relief. The others, on seeing their leader was now unafraid, also relaxed. Clearly this creature was known to the boggart, who now sat down again and stirred the embers with a stick.

'Please join us,' said Spiggot, once the fire was licking the hem of the night again. 'Be our guest.'

Almost as soon as the King of the Moths sat down there was a soft fluttering from out in the darkness. Soon swarms of moths flew into the light and began dancing with their own shadows around the fire. Every so often there was a little blue or green flare as one went into the flames. The King did nothing to prevent this happening.

It appeared that this was normal and could not be helped. It was all part of what was supposed to be.

Rosamund was the first to speak to him.

'Sire,' she said, 'thou hast an air of sweet sadness about thee.'

The King of the Moths turned his mournful countenance towards the speaker and she saw how pale and dusty was his complexion.

'Moths are not happy creatures,' he told her. 'They have, by their nature, a dull and formless life. They are the shadows of butterflies, who – bright-winged and joyful – fill our blue summer skies. The wings of moths crumple to the touch like ancient garments lying forgotten in an attic. As flakes of darkness they come, from cupboards, from disused rooms, from the depths of bracken and choked briar patches. They are torn fragments of colourless dreams; the parings of cheerless thoughts; the eldritch rag-ends of pointless conversations and speeches that have lost the thread.'

There was silence for a while, then Kling blew a raspberry.

'Too rich for a water rat,' he said. 'Kling's off to bed.'

TWO

The others remained talking around the remains of the campfire. In truth, Rosamund said very little. Jack felt she was still suffering from the jump from the real world into Liöfwende. Not only was the transition physically hurtful, coming as it did as the result of some violent accident, but the mental and emotional adjustments were quite difficult too. Jack was more able to cope with the idea of a parallel Britain, a place of faerie, having read a lot of science fiction and fantasy. And Rosamund was not too thrown by the world she had landed in, coming as she did from a similar medieval society. But both of them had great trouble with having been wrenched from a fairly comfortable life and thrust into a dangerous situation.

So, Jack sympathised with this young woman, whom he found beguiling in more ways than one. He wanted to put his arm around her and tell her everything would be all right, but the gesture would most certainly be misunderstood and Jack was not a young man who took rejection on the chin. He found it better just to murmur a few words of encouragement now and then, and to do his best not to upset her too much. She was rapt now, by what the King of the Moths was saying, and Jack listened too.

'. . . so my work is to gather the dust from the wings of moths and sell it to those who need it.'

Jack stared at the King of the Moths in the glow of fire. This mortal, if mortal he was, sat straight and square. A large figure with a wide-brimmed hat, cloak and leather boots to his thighs. A Gothic figure, really, with the most frightened and frightening eyes. They locked on to Jack's when he spoke to him and sent chills down Jack's spine. In those eyes was another world, a strange place which told of flimsy, fluttering death. Death that brushed your cheek with its velvet wings in the darkness. A silent, soft messenger from that place on the other side of life. Perhaps it was unreasonable, but Jack had always associated moths and their muted, dark colours with the world of the dead. In a bad dream he had had once, Jack was put in a huge sack which was tied at the top. The sack was full of moths that bothered his skin and tried to enter his nose and mouth.

'What?' he asked now, clearing his throat with difficulty. 'What do people do with moth dust?'

Those scared eyes locked instantly on to Jack's.

'People?' said the King of the Moths. 'Why, there are no *people* involved. Only faerie. Well, now, let's see. The *thunder* moth's dust is used for faerie gunpowder. I have a purse full here.' He held up a pouch and shook it, before returning it to a pocket in his cloak. 'The green dust from the *malachite* moth is used by fairy princesses to colour their eyes. Dust from the *beaded chestnut* moth is used in brownie cooking and sometimes as flour by trolls, with which to make their bread. The *copper* moth's dust is mixed to a paste by goblins and used to paint wood to make it look like metal, which they sell to naïve boggart smiths . . .'

'This is true,' murmured Spiggot, a little too quickly, so that everyone present knew he had bought some at one time. He looked around the circle and added, 'So I have heard,' before staring intently into the fire.

'. . . the *clay* moth's wing-dust is mixed with water and used for lining terracotta pots, dust from the *smoky wain-scot* has properties which will not be spoken of here, amongst good honest folk, and the same from the *gold spot* is precious enough to be used exclusively by fairy kings. The use of dust from the *ghost* moth would be too ghastly to describe at this hour of the night, but does that answer your question, mortal youth? Or shall I continue?'

'No, that's fascinating, though. Really interesting.'

Rosamund, nodding, said, 'In my father's castle we would use the dust from a *dark arches* moth to mark a moustache and beard on a pig about to be sentenced to hang on the gallows.'

The King of the Moths nodded his approval. 'Yes, I have heard of this use. It gives the pig a more human appearance.'

Jack's head came up with a start. A shudder went

through him. This was one of those times when he and Rosamund seemed to come from different nightmares.

'Sent to the gallows? A pig?'

'Yes,' replied Rosamund, simply, 'or a donkey, or sheep, or some other domestic creature which has committed a major crime. After a proper trial, of course, and the guilty verdict has been cast. Domestic creatures like pigs are not permitted trial by fire or trial by combat, so they must submit to the judge's decision without question.'

'That's barbaric!'

'Oh no, Jack,' interrupted Spiggot. 'If an animal commits murder, or is a familiar to a witch, then it has to be punished. Capital crimes, after all. You have to agree with that. It's right and just.'

'It's *right*-wing and fascist and plain stupid,' said Jack, with great distaste.¯ 'A domestic animal doesn't know right from wrong. If a dog has bitten someone, or a donkey kicks and hurts someone, by all means take it to the vet and have it put to sleep, but to try it in a court of law, sentence it and then carry out a ritual form of punishment. Why it's . . .'

'Inhuman!' called Kling from his bed.

'Yes. Inhuman.' Jack stared around the circle of faces. 'Of course, I don't blame the Moth King, or Spiggot, because they aren't human. But you, Rosamund! I'm surprised. I really am. I can't believe things like that happened, even a thousand years ago. It's crazy.'

'Jack,' said the young maiden, 'what is a *vet*?'

'It's an animal doctor. You know, they cure sick animals.'

'And put to sleep the birds of the air and beasts of the field?'

'Sometimes, but usually pets – that is, domestic animals.'

'Witches!' muttered Rosamund, firmly. 'Dark witch-craft, Jack. I, too, am surprised. I am surprised at *thee*, permitting such vile creatures as these vets to live amongst you and practise their evil arts. Art thou not ashamed of such doings?' She frowned at him. 'There are no such things as animal physicians, Jack. Only foul witches who would link with the devil to destroy good folk such as we. Why, my father would rather lay waste to a whole village and its inhabitants than allow one sor-cerer to live. Fire-and-sword is the only method of bleaching witchcraft from the world. I would add that even an innocent, sick animal is one possessed by a demon, and therefore needs to be despatched with the utmost urgency.'

Jack once again saw the gulf between him and this otherwise sweet person who had come into his life.

'Well, there you go,' he said, weakly. 'There's another difference between us.'

Clearly he was the odd man out here, amongst this group around the fire, whose worlds were full of aerial beings, witches, long-leggedy beasties and things that went bump in the night. Both he and Rosamund went to bed upset with one another. The King of the Moths lay down at the base of a tree and moths of all sizes flew in and settled on him, covering him like a blanket. Only his pale face remained visible under the constantly fluttering layers of moths. Rosamund was on one side of the fire and Jack on the other. They turned their backs to the flames. Spiggot, never really sensitive to atmospheres such as this, bid them both a hearty 'Goodnight' before retiring himself in a hollow below an oak, where he spent an uncomfortable night being rained on by falling acorns.

The following morning the King of the Moths found a butterfly with only one wing, down by the beck. He came back to the fire with it in his hands, a sorrowful look on his face. 'This was my fault,' he said. 'I trod on it without noticing. Me, of all creatures! Apart from everything else the Queen of the Butterflies is going to be very angry with me. How the little *monarch* butterfly suffers. Can you hear her screams?'

No, they couldn't, but they all nodded in sympathy. Jack had a great idea and now saw his chance to show the medieval maid what he had been talking about the previous evening.

'Well, Rosamund, now I'll show you what a vet does to ease the suffering of poor creatures such as this one.'

He found a wild rose in a nearby hedgerow and plucked one of its petals. This he cut roughly in the shape of the monarch's good wing. Then he looked around him. Glue. He needed glue. Superglue would be good, but there would obviously be none of that in Liöfwende. Then he noticed a sycamore. Jack was ever good at improvising. He went to the sycamore and procured some amber sap. This would make excellent glue. With the others breathing over his shoulder and the King of the Moths holding the butterfly gently, Jack glued the shaped petal on to the side of the wounded creature. To

Jack's great wonder, and to the delight of the others, it flew out of the pale hands and out over the meadows.

'There,' he said, with heavy satisfaction. 'It won't last long, but then butterflies have very short lives anyway. Two weeks, I think. How old was that one, King?'

The Moth King shrugged. 'Several days.'

'There you are, then.'

While they packed up, ready to march on again, Rosamund brushed against Jack a couple of times, apologising immediately for touching him. Jack knew he had been forgiven. And he in turn of course, forgave. She was someone who did not know any better. If he had been raised in medieval times, he too would think there was good reason to hang a pig.

'I must confess something to thee, Jack,' she whispered. 'The wizard Mallmoc. I know him.'

'Well, yes, he captured you when you first arrived in Liöfwende, didn't he?'

'No, I knew him in my own land, in my father's house.'

Jack said, 'Why didn't you say so before, Rosy?'

'I was afraid Spiggot would turn me away, thinking me corrupted by association with his mortal enemy. I thought to keep it from him until he knew me well and would not think the worse of me. Whist! I will tell thee more later, Jack, when we are alone, for Spiggot glances at me . . .'

Jack nodded. He liked this idea. That he and Rosamund shared a secret. Sharing anything with Rosy was a bonus as far as Jack was concerned.

Kling was hitched up to the cart, the Moth King bid

them farewell and strode out over the lea, westward. The group was finally on its way again. Spiggot had been a little slow in striking camp that morning. The reason was they were nearly home. He had to face his father, who would be none too pleased with him, though Spiggot expected the rest of the boggart village to treat him as a homecoming hero. That much he was looking forward too. There was his old friend Boskywod, the boggart he had grown up with. And of course, Fen, his sweetheart. They would be full of wonder at his deeds and the places he had seen. He couldn't wait to see their faces.

Midmorning, in the heat of the day, Rosamund let out a cry.

'I see woodsmoke, curling like ghostly towers to the sky. There are many chimneys, from quaint little cottages with clay walls and thatched roofs. There are other chimneys *around* the village, on full-rounded mounds, letting out the thin smoke of charcoal fires. Is that thy village, Spiggot dear? Are those mounds hollow, and are they the forges of the boggart smiths with fiery furnaces as their hearts? Is that our destination?'

Spiggot shrugged. He was now feeling ghastly. Once again about to be in the bosom of his family he was appalled by what he had done. It had *seemed* right enough, out in the fields, out of sight of Gnomon, his father, and Quagmarish, his mother. Yet on seeing his home village he was horrified at his actions. To use a fairy king's armour without permission! To wander here there and everywhere in search of adventure! To accept responsibility for bringing Mallmoc to his knees! Why, it was all so absurd, all so ridiculous, all so unthinkably unboggart-like. His father was going to slaughter him and use him for fuel in the family forge.

'Maybe we should camp here for one more night?' he suggested, feebly. 'Just to gather our breath.'

Kling said, 'Master's son, you fear your father, with good justification, Kling believes. You must not put off what will come, what *must* come. Go down there and take it like a boggart. Kling too, will be chastised by the master, perhaps even put to sleep by a vet? Kling is but a beast of burden and of no consequence. Perhaps they will try me like a guilty pig.'

Rosamund put her red velveteen arm about his neck. 'We will allow no one to harm thee, friend rat. Will we, Jack? Thou hast done no wrong.'

And so they entered the village. Boggarts out and about stopped and stared. There was no cheering. They looked stern-faced. Spiggot, whose heart was beating fast, passed his friend Boskywod. Boskywod merely nodded, then turned away, as if ashamed of having acknowledged him. Fen, thankfully, was nowhere to be seen. A whispered word went out and by the time the group approached the cottage of Quagmarish and Gnomon, Spiggot's father was standing in the doorway, thick stubby arms on his thick lumpy hips. There was no thunder in his face, but no sunshine either. He simply waited for his son to approach with a non-committal expression.

THREE

Although Gnomon was not ranting, he was indeed very angry with his son. It was a quiet anger, just the kind Spiggot hated. Spiggot was allowed to enter the house, but the others remained outside. What went on behind that pinewood door, closed firmly in their faces, Jack and Rosamund never did find out. There were no raised voices, no sounds of violence. Finally the door opened again and Spiggot stepped outside. He was as pale as a stitchwort flower and trembling. Without saying anything to the mortals, nor even acknowledging their presence, he walked to the village pump. Knowing what was required of him, Kling followed. Spiggot put his head under the spout and Kling pumped the handle. Sparkling water gushed over Spiggot's head and from the way he gasped, the two mortals knew the water was icy cold, probably from some underground stream.

Jack finally went to his friend. 'Is everything all right, Spig?'

'Oh, Jack,' said Spiggot, shaking his black thatch-like hair and spraying the ground. It was as if he had just noticed his mortal companion. 'Oh, there you are.'

'I said, is everything all right?'

'Why, yes, of course.' Spiggot moved in close, dripping water on Jack's shoes. 'He was furious with me. But I told him I had been given a royal command, a commission, and he could say nothing to that, of course.'

'But I thought you boggarts obeyed your parents in all things.'

'We do, we do, but – well, I have seen the world, Jack. I expect as father says, no good will come of it, but then . . .' he shrugged his heavy-set, muscled shoulders.

Still the other boggart villagers steered very clear of Spiggot. Gnomon was known to have quite a temper on him when he was upset and no one wanted to be associated with the object of his wrath. Kling, on the other hand, was now being greeted by other giant water rats, who had emerged from forges, stables and their own private nests. They clapped him on the back with their paws, linked tails with him, and called him a fine fellow. Kling wallowed in the attention, calling each rat by his name and announcing how good it was to be back amongst his own kind.

'. . . for Kling had not only the master's son to look after, but those two hapless-looking humans over there. What a sorry pair! But, rats one and all, Kling ate like a dragon. Such feasts Kling had! Spinach and pine nut lasagne, vegetable pilaf, egg cocottes jardinière, many, many more.'

The giant rats, servants of the boggarts and fed on old cheese and turnips, let out a sigh of great envy at the sound of this menu. Jack had no idea where Kling got all this from, but they certainly hadn't eaten such fare on the road. He could only guess that Kling had at one time found a recipe book and had memorised the contents.

Jack now felt a tap on his shoulder. Spiggot had been trying to get his attention.

The boggart said, 'Never mind that boasting rat, come and meet my father.'

'Er, do you think we'd better leave this until he calms down a little?'

'My father? He's not calmed up. I mean, he's not heated.'

'Yeah, but . . .'

'No buts, Jack. And you too, Rosamund.'

'Spiggot,' said Jack, 'why are we here? Surely we should be out on the road to find the missing stone?'

'And how will we know we've found it?' Spiggot looked bemused.

This brought Jack up short. 'Um. Won't you recognise it?'

'Recognise one stone from another? Be reasonable, Jack. We're here because my father once made a quivvel . . .'

'What's a quivvel when it's up and running?'

'I'm about to tell you, if you wouldn't keep interrupting. A quivvel is an enchanted thingamajig. It's made of brass, a globe the size of a conker. It has prongs sticking from it and three metal halos, brass bands, circling it like the rings of Saturn. There's strange symbols all over it, and words you wouldn't know how to translate, even if you were Queen Mab's favourite witch. It hums most of the time, sounding like a reed caught in the wind. You can set it to find other magic objects, like lost locking stones. My father, Gnomon, has set the quivvel for us. When we're close to a magic locking-stone, the quivvel will vibrate like mad and we'll know the thing that we seek is somewhere nearby.'

'Can I see it?'

'Not yet. My father still has it. Now you have to meet him.'

Spiggot led the pair through the doorway of the cottage. The walls inside were almost as lumpy as they were outside. However, they had been freshly white-washed and the place smelled of wild flowers and herbs. There were some very odd but solid-looking chairs, a large table, and a single earthenware vase on one of the wide windowsills. This was the only ornament. No pictures adorned the walls, no rugs or carpets covered the brick floors. Something like a welsh dresser stood in the corner of the living-room, off which there was only one other room, more like a scullery than a kitchen. An uneven-looking wooden staircase led up to bedrooms above the low ceiling. A single oil lamp stood in the space beneath this staircase, looking as if it were rarely used. Boggarts (Jack knew) rose with the dawn and went to bed with the dusk.

'How come,' whispered Jack to Spiggot, 'when you think so much of trees you make furniture from 'em?'

'Not *whole* trees, Jack. Only parts of them, those boughs the trees let us have, that is.' He then pointed shyly to a slightly shorter but still hefty boggart standing in the scullery. 'There's my father, Gnomon, by the sink,' said Spiggot, shyly. 'And that's my mother, Quagmarish, next to him.'

'Hi!' squeaked Jack at the two bulky figures who simply gawked. 'How are you? Nice day, eh?'

It was still difficult for Jack to believe that these 'people' he was continually encountering were not simply malformed human beings, but races of faerie, quite different creatures from himself.

Rosamund, on the other hand, accepted them on sight. She came from a time when faerie were as real to mortals as were dormice or adders. (Just because you didn't see them, didn't mean they weren't there.) As a medieval maid she had been raised in the belief that, along with mortals, the world was inhabited by witches, fairies, sorcerers, giants, ghosts, and other such supernatural creatures. She would stare at these fabulous wonders as hard as Jack, but she was in no doubt what they were and where they came from.

Rosamund tilted her chin haughtily. She was, after all, still the offspring of a baron.

'I am Rosamund,' she announced, 'daughter of Guillaume de Arundel.'

Gnomon made a non-committal rumbling noise in his throat.

Spiggot said, 'My parents are not used to meeting mortals.'

'Never met one before now,' Quagmarish said, ignoring a glare from Gnomon.

Everyone stood there, very awkwardly, for quite a

long time. The spell was broken by the sound of rat laughter, coming from outside.

Gnomon glowered and said to his son, 'Tell that rat to get his bottom over to the forge and to let them others get back to their masters and mistresses.'

Spiggot went to the doorway and yelled the instructions, which were met by the sound of a wet raspberry. Kling was getting above himself in the excitement. On hearing this rebellion, Gnomon then left the sink and went to the doorway himself. He stood there, blocking the light, simply letting the rats know he was there. There followed the sound of scuttling claws and Jack knew that within a few seconds the village pump would be standing alone. Gnomon then came in and sat down in one of the large chairs.

'Mortals, eh?' he said, after a few more minutes of silence. 'How is it you are here?'

'Accident,' replied Jack. 'On my motorbike.'

'A frown covered the vast expanse of nut brown forehead. 'Motorbike?'

'A thing with wheels,' explained Spiggot, 'and an *engine*.'

Gnomon frowned again. 'We don't like engines here, do we Quagmarish? But what of the maid? How came you here, child?'

'I fell from the battlements of my father's castle.'

'That I understand. Castles I understand. Motorbikes, no.'

He sat there for a few minutes more, then got up and said, 'Work to do at the forge. Armour to make. Quagmarish? Will you gather mushrooms and wild

garlic for our meal, then perhaps assist me at the
furnace?'

'I shall, Gnomon.'

With that the two adult boggarts left the house,
leaving the door wide open and the breeze blowing in.
Jack heaved a sigh of relief. Gnomon, and indeed
Quagmarish, looked very powerful. Creatures of great
strength. He had no doubt they were. What if they had
taken an instant dislike to him and Rosamund? What if
there were some law or rule that mortals entering the
village should be hung, drawn and quartered? That was
the trouble with being in a strange world. Anything
could happen.

'Spiggot?'

Jack looked up to see a young female boggart filling
the doorway.

'Oh, Fen,' replied Spiggot, casually. He then turned
his back on her and pretended to be doing something
with the door jamb.

Fen came in, looked around, then saw Rosamund.
'Who are you?' she demanded. 'Are you faerie? You
don't look faerie.'

'I am mortal,' replied Rosamund, with a tilt to her
chin.

'Huh!' said Fen. She then turned her attention again
to Spiggot. 'I have missed you, Spiggot.'

Spiggot turned, all shyness fled. 'Oh, have you? That's
why you ran up and greeted me, when I entered the
village, is it? That's why you looked so pleased to see
me?' His sarcasm, learned from Jack, was lost on the
naïve Fen, who was unfamiliar with irony.

'I didn't run up to you. You must be thinking of someone else. I *was* pleased to see you, though, but how did you know it?'

'I sort of guessed, by the way you threw your arms around my neck.'

Fen was getting it now and she didn't like it.

'Who taught you to say such things? Was it this female mortal? Are you in love with her, Spiggot?'

'Not a jot,' he replied, instantly, before the indignant Rosamund could get a word in. 'But I have seen fairy princesses, who looked at me. Ah, yes. So. I have too.'

'You have been gone so long, Spiggot, that others have looked at me too.'

'Who, for example?'

'For example Boskywod, the rat-catcher, who keeps the rat stables at the end of the village. Boskywod has walked with me through the dog daisies. You were gone so long, Spiggot.'

There was a pleading in her voice as Spiggot stared at his intended aghast at what she had told him.

'Walked you through the dog daisies?'

'Yes.' She hung her head. 'You were . . .'

'I know, I know, gone so long. Yet you said you would wait for me. You didn't. You walked through the dog daisies with the first boggart who asked you, didn't you?'

'He wasn't the first,' she said, pouting. Then with a look down, she added, 'but he was the prettiest.'

'The dog daisies, after all! Where is Boskywod?'

'Right here,' came a voice. 'Outside.'

'Well come in, best friend.' Spiggot turned to Jack and

Rosamund, his hurt expression changing to one of eagerness. 'We are best friends, Boskywod and me.'

Boskywod shambled in. Jack could see immediately that Boskywod was a very handsome creature, a boggart with beautiful dark eyes, jet hair and a flawless nutmeg complexion. Clearly Boskywod had not had to work alongside his father at the forge. His skin was not burn-marked, his hair had never been singed, his hands and feet were well-balanced. Boskywod was not so well-built as Spiggot, but there was an easy faerie grace about him, and he was taller and looked lighter on his feet than Spiggot. Spiggot was a scrapper and Boskywod looked a boxer. Jack had heard his father say that in the ring, a boxer will always beat a scrapper. Jack feared for his friend Spiggot in this battle of love. Spiggot was clearly up against a formidable opponent.

Boskywod looked shamefaced. He stared at his best friend. Suddenly, Spiggot realised he should be annoyed with him. He glared. 'How could you, best friend?'

'I like her,' said Boskywod, shrugging his shoulders. 'You know that.'

'This is true. You always liked her. But what am I to do, Boskywod? You have taken away my intended.'

Jack said, 'Are you going to fight? If you are, I suggest you take it outside.'

'Fight,' murmured Rosamund, her eyes lighting up. 'Tourney? Will they battle with swords, or axes? Or mayhap with mace-and-chain? 'Twill be best on the village green, as Jack says.'

Both the boggarts blinked. 'Fight? We are best of friends.'

'But,' Jack pointed out, 'there is Fen.'

'Fen likes me,' said Spiggot.

'And she likes me,' said Boskywod. And as if this were the end of the argument, 'She has walked with me through the dog daisies.'

'If I hear any more about those blasted flowers,' Jack growled, 'I swear I'll go barmy. What does it mean?'

'It means,' said Spiggot, mournfully, 'I have lost her. She must now stay with Boskywod, who is my best friend.'

With that, Boskywod took Fen's hand and led her from the house. Spiggot stared after them, a tragic expression on his face. Rosamund moved to his side, murmured her condolences. Jack patted him on the shoulder, awkwardly, for the lumpy boggart was not the easiest creature for a mortal to touch. Kling came to the door a little while later.

'Master's son,' he said, 'you are a great faerie knight, but you have shamed your mother and father, and lost your true love. Can we have supper now? Kling is very hungry. Kling suggests wild turkey with mint gravy and walnut seasoning.'

'Cheese,' said Spiggot, absently. 'Cheese is what you'll get.'

FOUR

Spiggot took his friends on a tour of the village: the watermill, where the wild grass seeds were ground down for bread flour; the marketplace, where the goblins came to sell their wares; the spot down by the willows where the rats gathered on their occasional days off, to chatter idly; the fishing pool, where minnows were caught. Spiggot was quite proud of these simple places, which he had grown up with and which held so many memories, but his mind was strangely occupied. He spoke in a distant way to these, his erstwhile travelling companions, and when he took them up Windy Hill, to view the village from above, his voice was lost in the tangle of breezes that fought for possession of the hill's grassy crest.

Finally he turned to Jack and said, 'Should I have fought with Boskywod?'

Jack shrugged. 'I have to say I admire the way you settled it calmly between you. It was very dignified.'

'But not honourable?'

'What's honour? It's one of those things like courage – difficult to define. You have to be careful not to get pride mixed up with honour. It's easily done. I think you both came out of it very well. Why risk total humiliation? Boskywod looked fairly useful, Spiggot. He might have given you a black eye or something, and you'd have lost both your self-respect and your girlfriend.'

'You think Boskywod would have beaten me?' cried Spiggot, in a hurt voice. 'After all those battles we've been through.'

'A brawl is something different from a battle with weapons,' Jack replied wisely. 'The winner of a punch-up is usually the most useful one with his fists, unless you know karate or something.'

'Karate? Who's he?'

Rosamund had been listening in all this while and suddenly she put in her devastating two-pennuth worth.

'Methinks thee should have clobbered the upstart, Spiggot. To steal away thy lady fair! Why, 'tis a crime which thou must not let go unpunished.'

'Hang on there,' said Jack, finding himself in the unusual position of being the voice of reason, 'let's not stir things up, Rosy. These two have settled things quietly. Let's leave it at that . . .'

'I would bash him hard,' said Rosamund, using words she had heard from Jack. 'I would clobber him in a duel.' She brought her dainty little fist down into the palm of her other hand with a *smack*. Spiggot blinked several times. He was upset, Jack could see that. It would only take a little to send him over the edge. He tried to intervene once again, but Rosamund was in full flow, persuasive, and her words were having an effect on the unhappy boggart.

'Jack,' said Spiggot, turning to him, 'when we first met you said you'd kill the youth who'd stolen your Jenny Pentworth.'

'Yes, well, I didn't exactly mean *kill* him. It was just an expression. You sort of get angry for a while, but . . .'

'I shall kill Boskywod,' Spiggot said, with conviction in his voice. 'I shall brain him with axe or mace. Or use my steel sword.'

'Whoa! Whoa!' cried Jack. 'Let's not run away with things here. A fist fight is one thing. A proper duel is another.'

'Thou hast made the right decision, Spiggot. For mine own self I could never love a man who forswore fighting. A warrior for me. A great knight. If I be fair, why then, I expect a courageous lover, one who rides in valour, not with bowed head. What, Jack? Wouldst thou let thy lady be taken without argument? Wouldst thou stand aside with pallid face and trembling knees and allow some natural son of a false knight to ravish her and carry her off to some high tower, there to let her languish? For shame, sir. A scullery maid for thee, for no fine lady shall be thine.'

'Well, when you put it like that . . .'

'There,' cried Rosamund, triumphantly. 'There is your answer, Spiggot. Go forth and challenge the usurper.'

Spiggot went very red in the face. He stomped down

from Windy Hill with the other two trailing on behind him. Jack said, 'Now look what you've done,' to Rosamund. 'I hope you'll be happy after the funeral.'

'I shall shed no tears for Boskywod,' she said, and added, 'that is, I shall weep not for the other boggart.'

'No, but if he wins, what about *our* boggart. Will you weep not for him? I never thought I'd say this, but you can be a twit at times, Rosy.'

Since she had no idea whether or not Jack was paying her a compliment Rosamund made no reply to this.

Boskywod was grooming a giant rat when Spiggot found him.

'We must fight for Fen's hand,' said Spiggot. 'Boskywod, you may choose the weapons, since you're the one being challenged.'

'Eh?' said Boskywod, looking at his father, Gallibagger.

Gallibagger shrugged, looking mystified.

Spiggot cried, 'I mean it. You must meet me at the Downy Oak, at dawn. I shall bring my sword.'

Spiggot then left, fetched Kling, and both went to the village pump. Spiggot stuck his head under the spout, Kling obliged with a few pumps, and the freezing water gushed over the boggart's head. Spiggot then went home. The two mortals followed behind. One of them, at least, was appalled by what was happening. The other wore a non-committal expression. Jack wondered whether indeed Rosamund took any responsibility for being the catalyst for this affair of honour.

'What's this?' cried a thunderous Gnomon, arriving home early from work for the first time in three hundred faerie years. 'You would *fight*?'

'Yes, father.'

'Then leave my house,' said Gnomon, 'until you come to your senses. And take those fool mortals with you.'

The three companions joined Kling at his nest on the edge of the village.

'Oh, come to visit Kling at last?' said the rat, chewing on some unidentifiable piece of dry meat. 'That's nice.'

'We are not visiting,' Spiggot replied. 'We are come to stay. My father has thrown me out of my home.'

'Oh, master's son!' cried the rat, aghast. 'Have you murdered someone?'

'No,' Jack answered for him, 'but he's just about to.'

The night was a restless one for all in the forge. The rat kept remonstrating with his master's son, telling him he should know better, but Spiggot was determined to fight now. Since he had left the village he had become more than a boggart, more than the son of a metalsmith. He had become a warrior, and a warrior settles things with weapons. Jack stared into the redness of the fire, saying nothing.

Rosamund seemed to be the only one who was quite satisfied by the way things were proceeding, but then she came from a violent family in violent times. Her father had crushed more skulls and had been on more crusades than a templar knight. Guillaume de Arundel was famous for throwing people into his musty dungeons, hanging them from cell walls in fetters, lopping off limbs and heads when he was in a bad mood, riding horses into the ground, quartering kitchen lads who burned the soup. It was no wonder this gentle maid had more beating beneath her breast than a romantic heart and soul. There was a thousand years of blood and iron in there too.

The following morning was a misty one. For some reason the paths and dusty roads around villages in Liöfwende went in spirals. It took everyone twice as long as it should do to reach anywhere. But then, Spiggot explained, why hurry? Certainly the boggart was in no mood to hurry through the murk this morning. The sun was still clutching to something below the horizon, reluctant to rise above this violent Earth. Spiggot had strapped on his sword and the tip of the scabbard dragged along the spiral path to the Downy Oak where he was to meet his adversary.

When the three companions got there (Kling had refused to be stirred from his bed of straw) an amazing sight greeted them. It seemed the whole of faerieworld had risen and was there. Long-eared and short-eared pixies, elves, bogles, a few immigrant brownies, hobgoblins, leshy, one or two friendly trows, and dozens upon dozens of boggarts. They all sat around the Downy Oak, where Boskywod was waiting for Spiggot to arrive. The only ones who were missing, it seemed, were the parents of the duellists and the object of their affections. Fen was still in her parents' cottage.

'Well,' said Spiggot, walking up to face Boskywod.

'Well,' replied Boskywod.

'Where is your weapon?' asked Spiggot, seeing nothing but a sack in the hands of his enemy.

'I have none.'

'With what will you fight?'

'I will not.'

Spiggot became exasperated. 'Why are we here then?'

'A contest,' replied Boskywod. 'The winner will take Fen as his bride. I am willing to have a contest, even though I already have Fen, since I . . .'

'Walked her through the dog daisies. Yeah, yeah,' Jack finished for him, earning himself several glares from the watching faerie.

Spiggot was on top of the situation. He took off his sword and handed it to Rosamund. 'Horseshoes, is it?'

Boskywod tipped up the sack and shook it. Two large horseshoes fell out and clattered on the stony ground. The horseshoes were tied to two long lengths of rope. They each picked one up. Rosamund whispered to Jack, 'They will use them to beat each other to death.'

Kling now arrived, a little breathless. 'No, no. Kling came when he heard about the contest. They will use them to climb the oak. First to snatch the rook's nest on the very top and wear it like a hat, is the winner. There's no violence involved, bloodthirsty maid, unless of course one of them falls. Only a test of accuracy, strength and climbing skills. Watch and learn. Very exciting. That's why all the faerie folk are here.'

The two boggarts stood one either side of the tree. They began twirling their ropes (weighted by horse-shoes) around their heads. Suddenly, as if at an unheard, unseen signal, both let fly with their horseshoes over-head. Boskywod's hooked immediately around a branch, but when he tried to shin up the rope his weight broke the bough and he crashed to the ground. Spiggot failed to catch on two attempts, but on the third he managed to entangle the end of his line in some branches. He immediately shot up the rope, climbing only with his hands, his muscles bulging beneath his shirt.

When Spiggot reached his horseshoe, however, he had to untangle the bird's nest the rope had made of itself. By the time he was ready for his second throw, Boskywod was on his way up. Boskywod had reached higher with his throw and he passed Spiggot at an alarming rate. Spiggot whirled, threw again, hooked another bough above, and was himself on his way skywards.

To Jack it was an amazing sight, watching these two normally awkward creatures pulling themselves up climbing ropes with great agility. He cheered for Spiggot, of course. The rest of the crowd of spectators were partisan too and yelled for their favourite. Not the least voice to be heard was that of Rosamund.

Gradually the two combatants made their way to the top of the Downy Oak, while a rook watched over the edge of her nest with an apprehensive expression. Up and up they went, the branches becoming thinner and thinner, so that the two climbers had to be sure to secure a hold in forks where the boughs actually met the trunk. Higher and higher. Until finally they were both only one throw away from their goal. Boskywod whirled, threw. His iron shoe hooked. Spiggot threw with great accuracy and knocked his opponent's horseshoe from its hold. They both threw again, anxiously, the two horseshoes hitting each other in mid-air and clattering back down again. Spiggot's next throw was successful now, lodging itself in the crook of branch and trunk. He shot up the rope while Boskywod was aiming to dislodge his shoe. Boskywod saw he was beaten, but threw anyway. His shoe hooked over the top of Spiggot's and then he too was on his way up.

It would have been neck-and-neck if boggarts had much of neck, which they don't. Spiggot had a head start but Boskywod was stronger and the better climber. They reached the nest together. The rook gave a squawk and pecked at the two hands that shot towards her. Then she took off, her valour evaporated. One of the two pairs of hands was faster than the other.

They belonged to Boskywod. He had the nest, upturned it, almost had it on his head when it slipped from his grasp, falling to Earth. Down the pair scrambled now, leaving ropes and horseshoes behind. Branch by branch they swung themselves earthwards, as agile as apes. Spiggot hit the ground first, snatched up the nest, sat it on his head like a hat. 'Mine!' he cried. 'Mine, mine, mine.' A great cheer went up from the spectators.

FIVE

It was early morning with a pastel shade of blue creeping up through a pink-wash sky. Jack and Rosamund had fallen out once again. Neither had slept well and both were irritable. Rosamund had accused Jack of taking more straw than her, thus leaving a maid to sleep on the bare ground. Jack said he had done nothing of the sort. He had simply used what was left over once Rosamund, Spiggot and Kling had taken what they wanted.

'Jack says he is an engineer,' cried Rosamund, 'yet thou knowst nothing of siege machines. What dost thou know of the great catapult, the battering ram, the siege tower? Nought but nothing.'

Jack was about to defend himself, to talk of bridges and roads and railways, when he realised she had employed her usual trick of shifting the ground from underneath him.

'What's that got to do with it?' he said, exasperated. 'Siege engines? Who said anything about them? I don't know what you're talking about.'

'There is my meaning,' she said, nodding hard, 'thou dost not know! Thou art sadly simple, Jack. My father would have those who called themselves *engineers* thrown from the battlements for not knowing how to construct even the meanest of siege engines. Thou art a gadfly.'

Kling rolled over and opened one eye. 'Do you *mind*? Kling has not yet woken from his beautiful rat dreams.'

'Well, I woke ages ago,' Spiggot's voice came in, dreamy and full of satisfaction. 'I've been lying here thinking about yesterday. Wasn't it wonderful? Wasn't I marvellous?'

Jack said, 'Now don't get too big for your boots, Spig. Today's a good day for going to see your best friend, to shake his hand, tell him . . .'

'. . . the best boggart won?' interrupted Spiggot, rolling over.

'No – quite the opposite. Tell him you got lucky. Tell him it was a very close thing and he almost had you. Tell him he's a great opponent and you wouldn't like to have to do it over, because next time he would probably win.'

Rosamund said, 'Oh, no, Jack.'

'Oh *yes*, Jack,' said Jack, firmly. 'Spiggot can afford to be generous in victory. It's the honourable thing to do. Time to repair the damage now. Boskywod is your best friend, after all. You have been rivals in love, but that doesn't mean you can't help him get over this in the best way.'

Kling said, 'The stripling talks sense.'

'I will, then,' murmured Spiggot, getting to his feet. 'I'll go and see Boskywod, my best friend, the rat-catcher.'

There were familiar sounds coming from around the village now. The roaring of furnace fires. The clanging of heavy hammers on anvils. The clinking of smaller hammers on metal. Smoke was rising from the forges, into the clear morning air. Boggart smiths were now at work, producing their metal wares. Boskywod had somehow avoided becoming a smith, as one or two boggarts always did, and so he would amble towards the stables where he kept the giant rats he sold or hired out to any who needed beasts of burden. Not surprisingly, Boskywod was no favourite of Kling, but the water rat saw the need for his master's son to patch things up and leave no regrets behind when they went out to raise their army of faerie to fight Mallmoc.

'Off you go, then, master's son,' said the rat. 'Bring back some crusty brown bread and a few quails' eggs for Kling's breakfast.'

Before Spiggot could set off, however, they saw someone coming from the village. Spiggot recognised the shape as that of Fen, whose hand he had won the previous day from his oldest friend and newest rival, Boskywod. Fen seemed to be carrying something in both hands, out in front of her, as if the object were something she revered. Spiggot wondered if this was a gift for him, a present for winning her back. He rubbed his hands together in anticipation. Contests were wonderful things, when you came out the winner.

Fen drew nearer and nearer.

'Here's Fen,' said Jack. 'Hello, Fen.'

Fen stopped in front of Spiggot. Her face bore a mournful, nay, *tragic* expression. In her hands was a pot full of soil. Standing in the soil was a puffball. To Jack, the puffball had a rather odd but familiar look about it, though he couldn't have said why. Fen was holding the pot out to Spiggot now, who was looking horrified. Jack felt there was more going on than had filtered through to his mortal brain. He wisely remained silent.

'Boskywod,' whispered Fen, in a cracked voice. 'It is him, Spiggot.'

Spiggot let out a yell of anguish, then cried, 'How did it happen? Was it an accident?'

'No accident, Spiggot. Boskywod jumped. He climbed the Downy Oak and jumped. He killed himself.'

Spiggot let out another cry.

'Whoa!' said Jack, who knew that dead boggarts became fungi in their afterlife. 'Hold on there. How do you know he jumped? Maybe – maybe he was just running through the contest again, wondering where he went wrong, and *fell* to his death?'

'He jumped,' replied Fen, emphatically. 'I found a bunch of dog daisies on my doorstep this morning.'

'Oh, well,' replied Jack, sarcastically. 'You can't argue with dog daisies, can you? Who found him? Who found the body?'

'There was no body. Just the puffball, below the Downy Oak where no puffball was yesterday. This is Boskywod.'

'Maybe you're wrong,' said Jack, finding the logic incredible. 'I bet he'll turn up later this morning. He's

probably gone on a walk to clear his head, after yesterday. That's what's happened. He'll turn up again, you'll
see. This is probably a *real* puffball. You know, a proper
one, not a dead boggart at all.'

Fen and Spiggot were not paying any attention to
Jack. They were simply staring mournfully at the puffball.

'Will you keep him?' asked Spiggot. 'Until he dries up
and puffs into green powder, that is?'

'I shall. And Spiggot, I do not want to see you again.'

'No, that's right and proper. Poor Boskywod. My best
friend. What have we done to him, these mortals and
me?'

'They are a bad influence on you, Spiggot.'

Spiggot sighed. 'They are, but I need them, Fen. We
must fight the sorcerer, Mallmoc. If we don't the thrum
will spread further and further and eat all the roots of the
trees and we shall live mad as cuckoos in a wasteland. I
shall go and never return to the village. I have brought
shame on my father and mother, and on the village. I am
not an honest boggart, who earns my bread from good
hard labour. I seek fame and fortune, Fen, and glory and
honour, and all those things we don't hold dear.
Goodbye.'

'Goodbye, Spiggot.'

With that, the female boggart walked away. There
were tears trickling down her cheeks. Crying was not
something faerie did very often, though it was not
unknown amongst the boggarts. Boggarts, after all, had
just one or two mortal traits which horrified other faerie.

Spiggot began to pack the cart with a heavy heart, not

even looking at his companions. They assisted him, keeping their silence. In went the famous golden suit of armour. The steel sword Jack had fashioned for his friend. The magic crossbow. Jack's gift from the Northumberland fairy king, a swarm of bumblebees, hung from the corner of the cart. Food, water containers, blankets. Snacks sneaked in by Kling for the sole use of the water rat. Once the packing was done Spiggot went to say goodbye to his parents and to ask his father if he could have Kling as a parting gift. Even though Spiggot did not tell his parents that it was goodbye forever, Gnomon and Quagmarish were beside themselves with grief. Gnomon said his son had to do the fairy king's bidding, but he blamed himself, for sending Spiggot out into the wilds of Liöfwende in the first place. He said he should have kept his son at home, in the forge, and never let him go.

'You were always the dreamer, son. Always easy to impress. I should have sent someone else. Someone with less poetry in their bones.'

'Yes, father. Thank you for the quivvel. I'm afraid we have wasted a lot of time here.'

'This is Liöfwende, son. You are never *wasting* time. Especially when you are with your loved ones. Wars will wait.'

'I know, father,' whispered Spiggot, 'that was for the ears of the mortals.' Then louder, 'Goodbye, mother.'

Quagmarish's wail was heard in the next county.

First they went to the tallest tree on the highest point in the region, to see if the quivvel could give them anything.

Spiggot climbed the tree, but nothing happened, even when he put the quivvel on the end of a stick. There was no magic locking-stone here in the south of Liöfwende, he said. Ireland was a better place to look. Why? Because, he said, it stood to reason that Mallmoc wouldn't hide the stone in the heart of boggartland. He'd choose some remote place, an island, whatever, and bury it there.

'Is that so?' asked sceptical Jack, convinced that Spiggot simply wanted to go to Ireland because he'd never been there. 'I think things in faerieland are not done in any logical way. You fritter away time, you wander about the place, willy-nilly. Is there no plan? No scheme?'

'None whatsoever,' replied an unrepentant Spiggot. 'Things aren't found by plans and schemes, they're found by *chance*. That's the way things work here. Serendipity. That's the science of Liöfwende.'

'Daft.'

'But faerie.'

'Nonsense.'

'Faerie craft.'

'Absolute twaddle.'

'Rude, very rude. You always attack what you don't understand, you mortals. Now, if you can't be more polite about our ways than that, Jack, then I'm not going to speak to you. We must go to Ireland to recruit a few leprechauns. In a war, they're very good at plans and schemes.' He added this last bit with a sort of lofty air, as if throwing things back in Jack's face.

Jack gasped as the truth came to him. 'You *want* a war,

don't you, so that you can be the great leader? You don't want to find the stone, you want to march at the head of an army of fairies.'

Now it was Spiggot's turn to gasp. 'Jack, that's a *terrible* thing to say. I mean it. I won't speak to you ever again, if you say things like that. Now, everybody ready for the journey? *March*. I mean, walk then . . .'

They set out for the coast, where Spiggot hoped to find a ship to carry him to Ireland. There, the boggart knight intended to enlist the help of the wily leprechauns, who knew more tricks than any other faerie. They would surely help in the fight against Mallmoc and his ulcugga fairies. The locking-stone to the magic cairn had to be retrieved, and once the thrum had been forced back down into their underground world, replaced. Once their escape hole had been blocked, the trees of Liöfwende would be safe.

Over hill and over dale, around brake and across brook they travelled, sleeping where they could find shelter, eating as they walked. Jack found the actual journey very pleasant. Liöfwende was not a difficult land to traverse, being familiar in a sense (since it was a copy of his own world), yet with much nicer weather and unspoiled countryside. The air was clearer, cleaner and fresher. The green was greener. The rain, when it came, was light and short in duration. The sun was warm and the winds were gentle. If you had to be trapped in an alien world, why this was as good as any.

And though Jack wanted to go home *sometime*, to start his engineering degree and to see his parents (and Jenny) again, he also felt the need to see this dangerous

quest through to its end. He did not want to leave
Spiggot to go through with it alone. Well, not *alone*
because there were also Kling and Rosamund, but Jack
felt he was Spiggot's right-hand man. He was the rock on
which Spiggot relied. Rosamund was good at some
things, but a little unworldly, a little too old-fashioned. It
was Jack, who came from the modern world, who had
modern ideas. And Kling? Well, Kling was a sensible rat
in his way, but he thought too much of his stomach.
Given a choice between saving Spiggot's life and rescu-
ing a bar of chocolate, the chocolate would win every
time. He *meant* well, but he was in the end just a talking
water rat, a servant of the boggart Gnomon.

No, it was up to Jack to support Spiggot through this
time of trial. Going home would have to wait. Anyway,
Mallmoc had his motorbike and when he went back he
wanted to take that with him. Motorbikes didn't grow on
trees, after all.

'Who's that?' asked Spiggot, as they waded through
the wildflowers of a dingly dell. 'Coming towards us.'

It was a knight, by the look of him, wearing glossy
reddish-purple armour.

PART TWO

The reddish-purple knight

ONE

'Hold!' said the faerie knight as Jack walked up to him. 'Quo vadis?'

'Eh?' Jack said, stopping in his tracks.

'He asked,' explained a superior Rosamund, 'whither goest thou?'

'Well why doesn't he say so?'

Kling said, 'He did, Jack – in Latin.'

'Oh. Well, I didn't have to do Latin. Didn't see much use in it, really, being a dead language. I opted for German instead. The Germans are great engineers. So are the Scots, but they speak English. Anyway, why's he speaking a dead language? He's not a Roman, is he?'

'Can't really say what he is,' said Spiggot, 'inside that armour. Could be anybody. I don't like his red armour much, do you?'

'More like purple,' Jack argued.

'Magenta!' exclaimed Kling. 'Purple in some lights, dark red in others. Definitely magenta.'

All this while the knight had been standing there, his head going from side to side as first one, then the other of the party, spoke. Finally, he seemed to lose patience.

In the same gruff tones he used before, he said, 'Burgundy, and I asked you where you were going.'

Jack countered, 'Why do you want to know?'

'Because I wish to accompany you. I am looking for a quest. Looking for the opportunity to do great deeds. I have heard that the great knight Spiggot is one of this party. It must be the boggart – you! You are the one King Cimberlin of the Northumberland fairies charged with finding the keystone to a magic cairn and driving the thrum back down to Gilscipe. Is this correct?'

Spiggot was still savouring the 'great knight' bit and remained silent for a while. Then he came to his senses. 'Yes, I am the great knight, Spiggot . . .' Kling rolled his eyes and shook his head, sadly. '. . . but who are you?' He peered more closely at the burgundy knight. 'That's not real armour, is it? It doesn't look like metal.'

The burgundy knight said, 'Yes, it's real armour – no, it's not metal. It's the polished hide of a dragon, the toughest material in Liöfwende. Can you not see the scales? Look, closely. You can just make them out if you catch them in the right light. I killed this dragon, then skinned her. I then dried the skin in the hot sun, cut shapes, sewed them together. Finally I spent hours with a sandstone, then bark, smoothing and buffing up the breastplate and the greaves, the helmet and the other bits.'

'Wait a minute,' said the engineer amongst them. 'If it's as tough as you say it is, how come you could cut it?'

'Magic knife,' replied the other, patting the wicked-looking blade that was stuck in his belt. 'Which is how I slew the fierce beast in the first place. I tracked her for a week, through fen and brake. Took me to her lair, where she had seven eggs. Fought her from dawn to dusk. Finally leapt on her back, cut her throat from mandible to sternum, let her bleed green blood in the dying sun. The next morning she was stone-cold dead. That was when I skinned her, cured the hide, boiled up one of her eggs for my breakfast, and set about making this magnificent suit of armour.'

'Thou hast slain a mother!' cried Rosamund. 'Thou hast eaten her young!'

Jack agreed with Rosamund's tone. 'Yes, that's a bit much.'

'So, you don't eat chicken?' asked the burgundy knight. 'You don't boil chicken's eggs?'

There didn't seem to be a lot Rosamund and Jack could say to this.

'This dragon,' went on the burgundy knight, 'terrorised the whole region until I put an end to her tyranny.'

'What happened to the rest of the eggs – the other six?' asked Spiggot.

'Gave them to the ulcuggas in exchange for my freedom.'

'What?'

'Yes, they came while I was polishing my armour.

What could I do? They would have enslaved me. They asked for the eggs. I handed them over. You would have done the same.'

Kling sighed. 'So, the master's son can expect six ulcugga fairies on six purple dragons very soon. Kling believes they will hatch the eggs and raise the young. This is very bad. It's only takes a week for a purple dragon to reach maturity. Master's son, let us go home. How can we cross the Irish Sea while there are dragon-riders abroad? We will be, as the parliament of birds once said, sitting ducks.'

Spiggot realised the danger, but was determined to go ahead with his plan. He had never been to Ireland and had been looking forward to seeing it. But he did tell the burgundy knight he could not join the group. 'We don't know you,' he said. 'You could be anybody.'

'But I'm not anybody. I'm me.'

'And who's that?' enquired Jack, hands on hips.

'Can't tell you.'

'Fairy? Or some other?'

'Couldn't say.'

'Brownie, goblin, pixie, leshy, boggart?'

'Mustn't say.'

'Elf, bogle, gremlin, red cap, white cap, fachan, phooka?'

'Don't want to tell.'

'Coblynau, spriggan, tylwyth teg, gwragedd annwn, bendith y mamau?'

'That's for you to guess.'

'Seelie court, unseelie court, fenoderee?'

The group was running out of faerie races. Kling, who

had so far remained silent, now came in. 'Cloche-fee? *Ulcugga*?'

This last seemed so likely the group all took a step backwards.

'None of the above,' said the burgundy knight. 'Look, why don't you just accept me for what I am, a knight who wishes to assist you in your fight against Mallmoc and the thrum.'

'No, no,' Jack said, as he saw that Spiggot was about to relent. 'We can't have an unknown in the camp. Wouldn't work. If you can't trust us with your identity, how can we trust you to be friendly? Sorry, you'll have to find another quest. This one's full.'

Kling took this as a signal to pull the cart onwards. He did so. Jack followed, then Rosamund. Finally Spiggot tore himself away and took up the rear, leaving the burgundy knight standing forlornly by himself. Spiggot took one or two backward looks, but Jack shook his head. So the four made their way towards the coast, where they hoped to find a craft.

It became obvious, however, that the burgundy knight had not given up. He followed them.

'Let's speed up,' suggested Jack.

They speeded up. The trouble was, they could only go as fast as their feet would carry them. Not just that. They could only go as fast as the slowest of those feet, which just happened to belong to Kling, who had the cart to pull. So the burgundy knight was able to keep within hailing distance the whole time. And hail he did. He kept calling out plaintively for them reconsider, to think kindly of him, to allow themselves to trust him. He kept invoking the faerie law of hospitality (which Spiggot had never heard of) saying that when two faerie met on a road strange to both parties, the faerie of the first part (which he said was Spiggot) owed the duty of hospitality to the faerie of the second part (which of course was himself). Kling said the burgundy knight was making it all up as he went along.

When they camped on a hill in a circle of trees for the night, their pursuer camped on the adjacent hill. When darkness came he saw their fire and they his. The situation attracted some night spirits, who became confused by the strong emotions passing between the two hills. They became entangled in the branches of the trees and spent the rest of the night moaning and wailing, keeping everyone awake. An ancient stone cried out, mournfully, that there was chaos in the wind. An old log groaned and told anyone who would listen that worms were eating his heart. A stagnant pool had forgotten she was there to lure unwary travellers into her slick quickmud and related a tale of woe that had the birds weeping.

The night spirits melted with the coming of the morning sun, of course, but by that time everyone was crimp-eyed and grumpy.

A spriggan with its spiky parasite passed them on the road and said, 'Been burning the candle at both ends, have we?'

Spiggot chased the spriggan for half a mile, before returning to the others, feeling just a little better for having run off his frustration.

Still the burgundy knight tailed on behind. There didn't seem to be any way of shaking off the creature.

'Just ignore him,' Jack suggested. 'He'll soon get tired and go away.'

But that did not happen. Finally Spiggot strapped on his own armour and went out to fight the nuisance. The burgundy knight refused combat.

'I didn't come here to fight you, I came to help you.'

Spiggot pointed out that they didn't want his help.

'Well, you've got it whether you want it or not.'

There was nothing one could do about somebody so persistent. In the end, Spiggot gave in. He waved his hands in despair. The burgundy knight joined them at their next meal. The helmet remained on, however, and the knight simply opened the visor and fed himself through there. Jack tried to peek inside the helmet to find out at least what sort of creature lurked within, but the gap was not wide enough even for that.

'A knight be a knight,' said Rosamund to Jack, privately. 'It matters not who stands within the armour.'

'How about a saracen?' Jack suggested, wickedly.

Rosamund paled at the word. 'Why, 'tis certain sure no saracen would dare to step foot on England's fair soil.'

'Well, there were plenty of them around when I left the real world,' replied Jack, 'and they were English, born and bred.'

'It is not so.'

'Yep. One of my mates is a saracen. His grandpa emigrated to Britain a good while ago. Abdulla went to my school. Sat next to me in class. Abdulla's taking Science though. Leeds University. Good lad. Handy with a cricket bat. His dad works in a bank, but he does a mean

shish kebab. Went to a barbecue at their place last
summer. Like, big, big garden.'

'Sometimes, Jack, thy words are mere ripples on a
stream. I make no sense of them.'

'I find myself agreeing with the maid,' said the burgundy knight. 'The youth speaks in riddles. Pass me one
of those roasted beets?'

Not for the first time Jack felt himself to be the out-
sider. Rosamund, with her medieval background, fitted
this group far better than he did himself. He reached out
and took a roasted leg of rabbit, having killed the animal
himself with the magic crossbow. Rosamund did the
same. The pair of them sat there, hot grease running
down their chins. The faerie folk looked on in evident
distaste, remaining with vegetarian fare.

Kling tipped the balance, taking the rabbit's ribcage
and sinking his fangs into the meat.

In his eating habits Jack had accidentally turned the
situation on its head: the two would-be knights were now
the outsiders.

TWO

Jack was just beginning to think they were on a wild goose chase when they came to a forest of deciduous trees stretching for several miles. Until he actually saw the thrum – or rather, when they were pointed out to him – he didn't really believe in what they could do to a woodland. And the numbers had always seemed to him to be a bit over the top. Thousands? Well, here were several thousand of the horrible beasts. They were shovelling away the earth with their front paddle-claws to expose the roots of the trees, then chomping the roots much in the same way a machine reduces logs and bark to little bits. Instead of spewing the bits out, however, the thrum swallowed them. Every one of the outer trees of this vast wood had a group of white scorpions with red eyes the size of rugby balls razoring away beneath it.

'Good grief,' cried Jack, 'they're ghastly!'

'How ugly they are!' exclaimed Rosamund. 'Like the ghosts of lobsters. Look how their red eyes glare when they pause in their eating to regard us! Will they attack, dear Spiggot? Even with my little dagger I would feel defenceless against those vicious creatures.'

The burgundy knight said, 'They won't hurt us unless we try to stop them eating. Then they'll attempt to swarm over whoever gets between them and the trees. Their appetite is bottomless. They are eating machines. They are without lightness of being. They have no souls, no conscience, no concern for the living or the dead. Only for their own stomachs.'

'But we've got to put a stop to it,' said Spiggot.

Jack asked, 'What do you mean?'

'I mean, we've got to kill as many as we can. Look what they're doing to our oaks, our elms, our hornbeams and beeches. We must destroy them.'

The burgundy knight took several steps towards the nearest group as they gnashed at the roots of an elm, wood splinters flying like bees through the air. One of the group detached itself and rushed at the knight, its pincers clashing together, its three razor-toothed mouths snapping, spitting, snarling. The knight drew his sword and sliced the creature in two. Still it came on, the two halves scuttling separately, trying to reach their target. Two more swishes of the blade and at last the progress was stopped, though the pieces of the loathsome creature still turned on whatever leg or body part was attached. The mouth snapped. The claws scissored.

'There,' said Spiggot. 'You see how difficult it is. Get

yourselves some weapons. Staves would be best. Crack their skulls. Knock off their legs. They can't run at you with no legs.'

Jack paled at the thought of having to stir this hornets' nest. He had some idea what would happen. Just as soon as the thrum realised there was a threat which might get in the way of their eating they would attack in force. The idea of having to face hundreds of those horrible, massive scorpions was not a pleasant one. Jumping into a pit of vipers was preferable.

'Are you sure this is a good idea?' he asked.

Spiggot was putting on his armour. 'I don't know any others.'

'Nor do I,' said the burgundy knight. 'But if you get any, do let us know.'

Jack thought walking quietly the other way was a good idea and said so.

Rosamund cried, 'Jack, how can thee say thus? Art thou a cowardly dog? A craven cur? Dost thou cry *yield* before the fight has e'en begun? Nay, thou art my brave Jack, who is steadfast and ever at the side of his good friend and bold knight, Spiggot.'

'I am?' mumbled Jack, looking around for the biggest staff to cut from a willow. 'Well, that's news to me.' He knew the die was cast. They were to go into battle, all of them. 'Here, lend me your sword, Spiggot. Sorry about this, willow,' said Jack, knowing that some of them talked and hit back when hurt, 'but it's all in a good cause.' He cut a stout cudgel and several staves from the crack willow. Two of them he handed to Rosamund and Kling, keeping the third and cudgel for himself.

'Gird thy loins,' said Rosamund, turning to face the enemy. 'Cry God and Sir Spiggot for England!' With these words she ran forward, shrieking like a banshee, and began flailing at the nearest thrum.

Kling said, 'Nice girls don't talk about loins, do they?' and followed her into the fray.

They soon found they had to stand back to back, in a trio, to fight off the savage hordes of thrum, as the creatures left their feasting to rush snarling and snapping at the two humans and the rat. Jack's cudgel cracked down on the hard shells of the thrum, splitting them open. With his staff he flailed away at their legs. They came off remarkably easily. The severed limbs continued to hop around, blindly, knocking into things.

Rosamund fought like a true pikeman, jabbing at the ugly mouths that snapped and snarled before her. She would stab her staff into a thrum's mouth, lift it up and send it flying over her head into the nearest tree. Many of these tossed thrum cracked open against the bark of oaks and hornbeams, and she could almost hear the sigh of satisfaction from the trees. At last they were getting their own back. The thrum were not invincible.

The burgundy knight and Spiggot were better placed in the field, being clad in armour. They waded into the mass of white monsters, hacking this way and that amidst the scrambling creatures. For most of the next twenty minutes the group fought a desperate struggle with the nightmarish thrum, cracking carapaces, lopping limbs and hewing heads. More and more of the creatures came pouring out of the wood, until their bodies were

piled high and the exertions of the gallant knights and
their band began to tell.

'I am fatigued,' whispered Rosamund in Jack's ear. 'I
must soon lay me down to rest.'

'You do that, my girl, and you're done for,' said Jack.
'I'm getting tired too, but we've got to keep battling on.'

A fresh wave of thrum rushed at them. Kling gave out
a yell as he got his tail nipped. The two knights, on seeing
that their helpers were about to be overwhelmed, came
hurrying back. Spiggot hacked away at the edges of the
enemy attack. The burgundy knight hurled himself into
the body of the thrum and began to create great carnage
with his sword. Gradually their slaughter began to tell.
Even the idiot thrum could learn that their efforts were
being thwarted time and time again, and eventually
some of them began to desert the ranks, run off into the
wasteland north of the wood.

Finally, after only thirty minutes of fighting, it was all
over. The thrum were fleeing. Spiggot hoped that now
their numbers were down the deserters would be
attacked by other faerie groups. Jack ran after the
stragglers, laying waste to as many of their numbers as
possible as they fled the field.

Finally he returned and collapsed on the turf.

'That,' he said, gasping, 'was horrible!'

'I agree, Jack,' nodded Rosamund, 'but very necessary.'

They all went down to the stream to wash away their
sweat. They cleaned up as best as they could, before
boiling some water for nettle tea. Rosamund's dress was
now almost in ribbons. Jack asked Spiggot if they could
do something about getting her some more clothes.

'She needs something a bit more practical,' he told the boggart. 'Some shorts and a top of some kind. What do you say?'

'Can you magic her shorts and a top, Jack?'

'No, you know I only do card tricks and sleight-of-hand.'

'Then where shall we get them from?'

'A goblin market, or knock on the nearest tree house.'

'We'll see. We'll see.'

That night, they entered the wood which gratefully received its saviours to its bosom. After one or two enquiries of certain talking oaks, normally quite aggressive to parties with humans in them, Spiggot came up with an address. Follow the forest path to the seventh elm to the left of the gypsum rock. There they would find the hollow oak which was the home of the gnome Harelippen. The advice was to knock and enquire.

They reached the promised oak and found a small door on which Spiggot knocked.

'What?' came a yell from within. 'Go away!'

Spiggot explained what they wanted and said that Harelippen had every reason to be grateful to those who had stopped the invasion of the thrum. Silence followed this explanation. Then the small door creaked open and a gnome came out on his belly, being too large for his own front door. When he stood up he was about half Jack's height. He was an overweight and bleary-eyed creature, with annoyance in his features, but the eyes above the red nose were a startling green in colour.

Jack begged some clothes for the maid.

'Ain't she got none of her own, then? And if not, why not's, what I ask. What's she doin' in them there rags?'

'We've all been in a bit of a battle with the thrum and because her dress reaches the ground, they were able to bite and pincer it. We just wondered if you could help us.'

'I didn't hear no thrum.'

'That's because we stopped them,' came in the burgundy knight. 'You would have heard by tomorrow, when they reached your home.'

'What are them thrum doin' out, anyways?' asked Harelippen, his chubby hands on his hips. 'What are them thrum doin' down here?'

'Mallmoc the sorcerer,' explained Spiggot. 'He's let them loose on Liöfwende.'

'Bloody sod,' snarled the gnome, his face going very red. 'Bloody buggery wizards.'

'Quite so.'

'Who's that in them armour?' asked Harelippen, pointing.

'We don't actually know,' said Jack, 'but we call him the burgundy knight.

'More like *magenta*,' grumbled the gnome. 'Burgundy's more maroony-purple.'

'He looks different in different lights.'

'Does he, now? Well then, maid,' said the gnome, 'seems I should let you have some of them clothes I got in there. Mostly they cover me, so they's a bit small. Come on in and try some.'

With that the gnome fell on his belly and wriggled back into his house. Rosamund went down onto the ground and began to follow the creature. Jack cried, alarmed, 'Are you sure this is safe, Spiggot?'

'It'll be fine, Jack,' said Spiggot, as Rosamund's feet disappeared into the tree house. 'He won't hurt her.'

Kling muttered, 'Famous last words.'

But within a short while Rosamund reappeared. She was dressed all in green. Green shorts. Green doublet. Even a little green hat with a white owl's feather. She looked so cute she stopped Jack's heart in mid-beat. He tried not to stare at her bare legs and bare arms as she squirmed through the small doorway and stood up in the skimpy shorts. He could feel she was embarrassed by the scantiness of her garb. In the twenty-first century it would be quite acceptable, except at formal banquets and golf clubs, but a thousand years previously it would have been outrageous.

'Well,' said Jack, all hot and bothered and pretending to be dreadfully efficient, 'I suggest we head on for a while, before camping.'

'Nice outfit,' sniggered Kling, earning a fiery glare from Jack.

'Let us move on,' the burgundy knight said. 'Did you thank the gnome for his gift?'

'I did,' replied the demure Rosamund. 'And I wish Jack would cease not looking at me. I cannot help being thus attired.'

Jack shook his head. 'I can't help not looking at you. It's a bit strange having you dressed like that. You look as if you're going to an eighties' hot pants party. Once you get some decent clothes on I'll stare right enough.'

'I understand. I'm ugly.'

'No, no,' he turned and reassured her, 'quite the opposite, see. Like, you're really really beautiful and – and it bothers me. When you were in your velvet dress, it was different. You came from somewhere I didn't know. But now you're – you look like the girls I know back home. And,' he stared into her blue eyes, 'you're something else, believe me. You're a knockout.'

'Is that good?' she asked, the eyes twinkling.

'I dunno whether it's good, but it's making me dizzy,' replied Jack, turning away again. 'I'm not used to beautiful women looking at me like that. Makes my head spin.'

'Humans,' said Kling, getting into his harness again. 'Soft in the head, the lot of them.'

THREE

The burgundy knight had gone down to the river to fill his waterbag and wash. He had indicated that he would like to have privacy. 'I'll chop off the head of the first one who tries to discover who I am,' was how he put it. 'And believe me I have ways of knowing if someone is hiding in the bushes nearby.' Kling was still asleep under a tree, whistling snores through that long nose of his and blowing his whiskers back and forth. The rodent couldn't care less about the burgundy knight's identity. Rosamund was not far off, collecting mushrooms, her long slim legs still a problem to the young man whose concern over being dumped by his ex-girlfriend, Jenny, was rapidly fading.

'Listen, Spiggot,' whispered Jack, 'who do you think he is?'

Spiggot blinked in that boggart way of his. 'Who?'

'The knight in the dragon-skin armour, dope. Who do you think he is?'

'I have no idea, Jack. You see, he's encased with armour and I haven't seen his face.'

'I know that,' replied the exasperated youth, 'but can't you at least take a guess?'

Spiggot shrugged. 'It's not usual for boggarts to guess, Jack, but let me see – a wandering fairy? It won't be an ulcugga . . .'

'Of course it won't be an ulcugga, not unless it's a spy, and somehow I don't get the impression that we've got an enemy in camp.'

'. . . but it might be a Northumberland fairy. One of King Cimberlin's?'

Jack stroked his chin. 'A different kind of spy, eh? King Cimberlin checking up on us? You could be right, but I have another idea. A better one. What about Boskywod?'

At the mention of his friend's name, Spiggot's eyes immediately became moist. Boggarts did not often cry, so this was an indication of his strong feelings on the matter. He shuffled his feet and stared off into the distance.

'Are you trying to hurt me, Jack?'

'No, no. Quite the opposite. Look, Spiggot, we never actually saw Boskywod's body.'

'No, he was a puffball.'

'That's what I mean. All we saw was a puffball. What if he didn't actually kill himself? What if Fen made a mistake and that puffball was just a puffball. What if that was a trick and Boskywod's still alive, inside that suit of armour?'

Spiggot's brow furrowed. This thought was clearly

new to him. He mulled it over in his head for a few
minutes, then shook his black mane.

'But why would Boskywod . . .?'

'Well, you had won back Fen because you were a
famous faerie knight. You hid your identity for a long
time under the golden armour and then emerged a hero.
Maybe Boskywod thinks if he can get the same reputa-
tion, he'll stand another chance with Fen? I don't know,
it just makes sense to me. What we've got to do is watch
for mannerisms. You know, how the knight holds his
teacup, that sort of thing.'

Spiggot was lost. 'I don't know how Boskywod held
his teacup. Did he have a teacup? I never saw one.'

'I'm just giving examples . . . shusssshhhh, here he is.'

The burgundy, maroon, or magenta knight was back
from his ablutions, carrying his waterskin. He threw the
skin down and heaved a massive sigh, before trying to
scratch his left ear, which was buried deep inside the
helmet of course. Jack looked significantly at Spiggot,
whose return expression was one of complete bewilder-
ment.

'I give in,' muttered Jack. 'You try to help, but you
find you're surrounded by idiots.'

'Kling's sentiments, exactly,' said the rat, snorting to a
waking position. 'All his life Kling has been surrounded
by idiots. Now, what's for breakfast? Braised chicken
with sweet potato and pumpkin? Penne with peppers and
mozzarella?' The voice became gloomy when no reply
was forthcoming. 'Don't tell me, don't tell me, stinging
nettle salad and fungi, followed by berries of the forest.'

'Correct,' said Jack. 'How did you guess?'

'Kling's good at guessing,' said the dour rat.

'I'm glad someone is,' muttered Jack, with another glare at Spiggot.

They were off before the sun reached halfway over the horizon.

Down towards the Cornish coast, to a place known as Tintagel.

'How do you know we'll find a ship there?' asked Jack of Spiggot.

'I have heard.'

'What have you heard?'

'There is a wonderful ship here, made of sand.'

Jack stopped in his tracks. 'Sand?'

'Yes. It twinkles.'

Jack shook his head as if he had flies buzzing in his ears. 'Sand? But sand is – well, it's *grit*. You can't make a boat out of grit. It just falls to bits.'

Kling said, 'You can make a castle out of sand.'

'Yes, but that's different,' argued Jack. 'I mean, you need a bit of dampness to the sand . . .'

'Perhaps,' said the burgundy knight, 'the ship made of sand has a bit of dampness to it?'

'Even so,' shouted Jack, 'it wouldn't float, would it? It would dissolve in the water. You can't make a ship out of sand. Impossible. Not without magic and I don't see the point. It would sink, wouldn't it? Sand's heavier than water.'

'So is iron, but thou hast told us they have iron ships in thy time, Jack,' said Rosamund, joining the gang against him.

'If that ship is made of sand I'll eat my hat.'

'There is no hat on thy head, Jack,' said Rosamund, 'but Kling has that straw one he oftimes wears.'

'When Kling wants to looks dashing,' said the rat.

'Then I'll eat Kling's hat.'

'Rash, Jack,' replied Kling. 'Very rash. You'll have to get Kling a new one. Just as dashing.'

'That hat isn't dashing, it's a disgrace. Anyway, there won't be any eating of hats. There's no such ship as a sand ship.'

At Tintagel they found a magnificent castle below which was a bay. Anchored in the bay was the most beautiful but strangest sight Jack had ever seen.

A glass galleon!

This fairy ship sparkled from stem to stern in the morning sunlight, from mast tip to deck. Every single part of it was glass. There were fine-spun glass ropes for the rigging, stiff sheer glass sails that curved towards the bows, glass cannons, glass tiller, rudder and keel. Swathed in rainbows created by the prismatic effect of the glass, the ship rocked gently in the shallows off the Cornish beach. Its decks were swarming with pixies, who continually polished the glass with the leaves of some velvety plant. Not a speck of dust was permitted to settle on the deck. Every so often one of the glass cannons boomed out, which kept the seabirds at bay.

'There you are, Jack, a ship made of sand!' cried Spiggot, triumphantly.

'Glass,' murmured Jack, knowing what was coming next.

'Yes, but isn't glass made of sand?' Kling cried. 'Melted sand?'

Jack complained that he had been tricked. Spiggot said that was what faerie life was all about, tricking others. Jack had to eat the straw hat. To give him his due, he did try. He tried very hard and almost choked. But straw is not even hay. He might have managed a hat of hay. As it was, he failed miserably and handed the gnawed hat back to the rat, who took it and wrinkled his nose in disgust.

'Look at Kling's titfer now,' said the rat. 'You must get your rat servant a new one, Jack, as soon as you can.'

Jack whirled angrily on Spiggot and changed the subject quickly. 'Spiggot, hadn't you better go and negotiate our passage to Ireland?'

'Do what?'

'Go and speak with the owners of that vessel. Or the captain.' He looked at Spiggot with narrowed eyes. 'Do you even know how much this is going to cost?'

'No,' came the crestfallen reply.

'I can't believe this. You haven't thought about it before now, have you? Have you any money?'

'You know we don't use money very often. It doesn't mean much here in Liöfwende. The goblins with their crooked sixpences and fairy gold and all that,' said Spiggot. 'But here we bargain for something we have that someone else wants. I – I shall go and see what the pixies want.'

'Would you like me to go with you?'

'No, Cornish piskies are not fond of mortals, Jack. You stay here, all of you. I'll do the talking.'

Kling threw off the traces and took out a clay pipe. Jack stared at the rat as Spiggot walked down the cliff path, towards the faerie folk below.

'What are you going to do with that thing?'

'Smoke it?'

'I've never seen you smoke a pipe before.'

Kling put on his straw hat and stuck the pipe in his mouth.

'You haven't seen Kling smoke a cigar, either.'

'No, and I don't want to. Put that thing away. You'll frighten Rosamund. She doesn't know about setting fire to things stuck in people's – in rodent's mouths.'

Kling turned the pipe upside down and began to play a careless tune through the stem and bowl. He was never intimidated by Jack. Gnomon and even Quagmarish were figures to be feared, but Jack was just another human being. Jack shook his head and turned away, knowing he was being mocked. He watched Spiggot below as the boggart crossed the sea strand to speak with the pixies. There followed a lot of gesturing, with Spiggot pointing up at where his friends stood, and the pixies staring and laying their palms flat, as if to say, what do we get out of it? Finally, without any hands being shaken, which was a mortal thing, Spiggot left the pixies and came back up the cliff again. Jack went halfway down to meet him.

When they reached each other the boggart was a little puffed, but he looked pleased.

'Well?' asked Jack, out of earshot of the others.

'Done,' said Spiggot, returning Rosamund's wave.

'What do we give them? The burgundy knight's

armour? Kling's pipe and straw hat? My shoelaces? What?'

Spiggot replied in a nervous tone, looking away, 'The maid's eyes.'

'The *what*?' cried Jack, unable to believe his ears.

'The maid Rosamund's eyes. Not for ever and always, of course,' Spiggot hastened to add. 'Just for a borrow. When we return the pixies will give them back again.'

Jack was aghast. 'You – you can't let them have – no – no – it's unthinkable. How would it work, anyway? I mean . . .'

'I know what you mean. They will pluck them without pain and put them back in again the same way. Pixie magic. It'll be fine, Jack, you'll see. They wouldn't accept anything else. What was I to do? Now, we must tell the others. I think – I think we shan't tell Rosamund until we get on board the ship, eh? It would be better not to. Come along, Jack, don't dawdle. We must be away with the evening tide. Otherwise it'll be another twelve hours. Time and tide wait for no faerie, even in Liöfwende.'

With that the boggart began to stride upwards, towards the small group eagerly awaiting the result of his negotiations.

FOUR

'Mine eyes?' cried Rosamund, 'Thou hast pledged mine eyes?'

She turned away from a helpless-looking Spiggot in great distress. Jack went to comfort her, for once oblivious of her bare legs. He put an arm around her shoulders and felt them heave in a great sob. He was almost as upset as she was by the whole thing.

'Look, let's have no nonsense,' he said. 'Spiggot can't *make* you give up your eyes.'

'But without our ship we shall be unable to sail, first to Eri-innis to recruit the leprechauns and thence to Thristlac for the seelie and unseelie courts.' This from the boggart, who was at a great loss to understand what all the upset was about.

'We need her bonnie blue e'en,' cried Kling in a Scottish accent. 'Gie us yer bonnie blue e'en.'

Spiggot went to her and whispered in her ear, his head nodding eagerly. Her expression remained neutral, but after a while she too began nodding her head, in unison with Spiggot. Whatever he was saying to her, she was agreeing to it. Finally her mouth set itself in a firm line.

'I see,' she murmured. 'What must be, must be.'

Jack felt sure Rosamund would refuse, absolutely, to go along with the scheme. He knew she had grit and determination. Yet Jack did not know medieval maids, who were used to sacrificing – nay, *expected* to sacrifice – themselves for the common good. They had been used as ground bait for dragons, exchange goods in time of war, gifts to foreign princes and sold to old men for wives. So long as they had been maids, pure and virginal, they had been worth something, had a price, were a commodity. They were used to being used. They were used to obeying commands. Any rebellion met with imprisonment in a tall tower, even by their own fathers.

'Rosamund,' cried Jack. 'You don't need to give up your eyes for anyone or anything.'

'But Spiggot needs them and has made a great promise to me,' she replied, her head coming up. 'If needs must, then I will loan him my eyes.' It seemed to Jack she was becoming defiant with the wrong person – with him, not Spiggot! It was Spiggot she needed to take a firm hand with. He didn't understand. He really didn't.

'I will not let this happen!' cried Jack, furiously.

At that moment he felt himself being clutched from behind. The burgundy knight had pinned his arms by his side. Spiggot jumped forward and wound some cord around his wrists. Now Jack was bound and virtually

helpless. He raged, he yelled, he struggled, but he could
not loosen the cord. He called forth his tame bees, those
given him by King Cimberlin, but they misunderstood
and merely covered him like a coat. He had only two
magic commands, 'Swarm on' and 'Swarm off'. He tried
shouting 'Attack' and 'Sick 'em' but the bees did nothing
but cuddle him lovingly. In the end he yelled 'Swarm off'
and they went back to hanging on the edge of the cart. In
any case he was not sure they had stings. No one seemed
to know about bumblebees.

Some short time later three pixies appeared at the top
of the cliff. They were of the long-eared kind and rela-
tively harmless, unlike their short-eared cousins, who
were deadly. They had a jar of liquid with them.
Rosamund was taken away, out of Jack's sight, and
when she returned she had a white band around her
eyes. Kling led her, she having grasped his tail.

Rosamund was blind.

The three pixies began to leave with her bright blue
eyes in the jar of liquid.

'Wait!' cried Jack, desperately.

The West Country pixies turned and looked enquir-
ingly at Jack. They were sharp-faced, hollow-cheeked
creatures. In height they came up to his shoulders, but
they looked wiry-strong, with hard, thin fingers. There
was something strange about their physique and it took
Jack a moment or two to realise it was the position of
their knees. Their kneecaps were not situated roughly in
the middle of their legs, like those of mortals, but about
a third of the way down from the top. This gave them a
gangly sort of gait, which seemed easy and casual in one

way, but awkward in another. And their heads! Their heads were tall and narrow, with something that looked like hair on the top, but obviously was not. Jack was not sure whether they were wearing wigs of some coarse green material, some sort of *grass*.

He tried appealing to these unusual creatures, not with any sort of hope, but more out of desperation.

'Look, why not – why not take *one* of my eyes, and *one* of hers? Yes, that's it. At least she'll be able to see then. And so will I. That's the answer, isn't it? One of each.'

Spiggot shook his head slowly. 'But Jack, your eyes are *brown*.'

'So?' Jack struggled with the restraining cord.

'The pixies want blue eyes. Blue eyes see so much better in the dark. Brown ones, well, they're too muddy, if you know what I mean.'

'No, I don't know what you mean. Sounds like a myth to me. It doesn't matter what colour your eyes are, dark or no. What is this, *in the dark*. What are they going to use the eyes for, anyway?'

'They put them in and use them to go into deep caves in the cliffs, looking for spiders.'

Jack sighed. 'And what do they want spiders for?'

'To make the fine thread for the delicate muslin they weave on their looms. Have you never heard of pixie cloth? It's the finest fabric in the whole of Liöfwende. No, no, it's a noble gesture, Jack, but we can't use those muddy brown orbs of yours. They're no good in dark places. All right for the light of day, of course, or under a full moon, but as soon as the sun goes down . . .'

'Rosamund can't see in the dark any more than I can,

you fools!' gnashed Jack.

'Oh,' said Rosamund, 'I can see very well in the dark – better than most, Jack.'

Jack gave in. He couldn't fight her as well as Spiggot. The pixies left, tramping down the cliff path. Jack was finally released. He sat rubbing his wrist and nursing a terrible grievance in his breast. These idiot faerie! How were they going to take care of Rosamund now she could not see? Someone would have to be there the whole time for her. Of course she would gradually learn to cope without her sight, but not on their travels, surely. One had to be in one place most of the time, to get one's bearings by memory and feel.

Jack went to Rosamund later. 'Why?' he asked, plaintively. 'Why did you give in to him? What did he say to persuade you?'

A smile formed on those rosebud lips and her cheeks dimpled, giving Jack's heart a time of anguish.

'Why, mine eyes will see wonderful things, Jack, while they are in pixie hands. There are diamonds in those mines. Eyes have a memory of their own, Jack, for there is proof in those times when we come to a new place and feel we have seen it before. We shall be rich, for pixies spare no interest in material wealth – they care not for gold and diamonds – and will leave such treasures to us. My eyes will be returned to me, Jack, once we have been to Ireland. Then we shall collect our bounty, our fortune. I shall return to my father's castle and will use the treasure for my dowry. With such a dowry I could have any knight in the land. Even a prince. With such a dowry my father would never send me to France, to marry some old ogre with no teeth and warts on his nose, now would he, Jack?'

'Yes, Jack,' said Spiggot, full of high spirits, 'what a fuss you make! They've only *borrowed* the eyes. We'll get them back again, as soon as we return.'

'But we're sailing for Scotland from Ireland, or had you forgotten?'

'No, I hadn't forgotten. Once they've used them the pixies will pass the eyes from faerie clan to faerie clan, all the way up the coast, until they reach the spot where we will land in our beautiful glass ship. They will return Rosamund's eyes. It's all very simple. No real fuss or bother.'

'You don't think Rosamund's eyes will be somehow lost, or even spirited away if they're that valuable, as they are passed from hand to hand? That's how things become lost, Spiggot, when many hands are involved.'

'Oh, I don't think so.'

'And what about returning the ship?'

'Why, they are sending a crew with us, to sail it for us, because you know, we cannot know how to do it.'

'Oh.'

Jack said nothing more. It was clear he was getting nowhere with this sideways-thinking faerie. He had been wondering what Spiggot had said to her and now he knew. There was nothing he could do now, but he felt quite bitter towards his faerie friend. Spiggot had unashamedly used Rosamund to get what he wanted. Not for the first time, Jack felt that mortals were considered very lowly creatures in this kingdom of Liöfwende. He took Rosamund's hand and led her gently down the cliff path.

When they reached the bottom they were funnelled down two lines of hard-faced pixies, to the ship itself. There the crew were making busy to sail with the tide. The burgundy knight followed on behind, as Jack, blind Rosamund and Spiggot waded into the shallows up to the ship, where they were all hauled aboard. Had Jack been in a better frame of mind he might have appreciated the workfaerieship which had gone into the vessel. It was indeed a strange and wonderful craft. Everything could be seen, from the seabed to the tip of the mast. Down below, Jack could watch the fishes swim by just an arm's length away. Occasionally they bumped their noses on the bottom of the ship as if trying to enter. An eel was wrapping itself round the anchor chain, which was, like the rest, fashioned from glass.

Rosamund clutched his hand the whole time, quite dependent on him. Jack might have savoured her touch at another time, but he was still reeling from what had happened. Sometimes, here in the 'other England' of Liöfwende, Jack could imagine himself back in his home world, but at times like these he felt he was somewhere completely alien.

'Out of the way,' said a pixie sailor, pushing him aside. 'Work to do.'

'Hey,' muttered Jack. To Rosamund he said, 'We'd better find ourselves a corner of the deck where they're not doing things.'

'I am thy servant, Jack.'

He led her topside and they nestled at the foot of the main mast, where activity was at its least. Business went on around them, but they were not in the way. Glass ropes of various names were hauled upon – halyards, sheets, stays – and glass capstans with glass bars were turned. There was no cargo below, you could see that. And the two mortals, the two knights and the one rat were the only passengers. Every so often a gull veered too close to the vessel and the pixies ran about, yelling and screaming at the bird, anxious not to have any lime droppings on their beautifully polished craft.

The evening star came out, the only star in the sky, and the anchor was weighed. The waves lifted the vessel as the wind caught her glass sails. She surged forwards, heading for open waters. Oncoming seas climbed up the vessel's bows, only to fall back again, like half-hearted invaders of a castle with impregnable walls. Clouds scudded over the blue above, to mirror the glass ship's passage across the ocean. Wild seabirds, still anxious to leave their mark on the shining vessel, attempted to dive-bomb the decks, only to be scared off by the booming of a glass cannon. As the ship dipped up and down on the swell, the sun began to go down into a scarlet foamy bed. For some time, the lonely star and the sun shared the heavens, the light of one being almost lost in the greater light of the other.

'What an evening,' said Jack, staring at the rosy sky as the piece of the sun's disc sank below the horizon. He turned to Rosamund with wonder in his voice. 'Aren't the sunsets here in Liöfwende just fantastic?'

Then he could have kicked himself. Of course, Rosamund could not witness this beautiful sunset. All she saw was blackness. How crass of him to remind her that she was sightless.

'I'm sorry,' he said. 'I'm very sorry.'

'Why art thou sorry, Jack?' she asked, touching his cheek with her fingertips. 'Thou art not responsible. In fact I know thee did try to stop the trade, for my sake, and for that I thank thee, my dear friend.'

Jack's heart was both empty and full, all at once.

FIVE

Jack remained convinced the burgundy knight was Boskywod. As the ship rode the waves under a full moon, he studied the knight, hoping to see something which would confirm his suspicions. However, since he did not know his subject well, he could not watch for familiar mannerisms. One thing struck him: the burgundy knight's speech always sounded a little peculiar, as if the speaker were trying to alter his voice in order to disguise it. It was this particular oddity which had set Jack's mind on Boskywod's track in the first place.

'Good evening, friend,' said the knight, passing him on the deck. 'I am told we have a storm front coming. I believe I shall go below.'

'Why are you so nervous?' asked Jack, bluntly.

'Nervous?' The burgundy knight turned and Jack could feel a pair of eyes on him, from inside the helmet.

'Yes. The closer we come to the Irish shore, the more fidgety you get. I wonder why?'

'Perhaps it's the onset of a storm that's making me jumpy? Have you thought of that? See, your friend the boggart is looking very ill already. I too am feeling somewhat peculiar. We are not sea faerie, either of us. Our stomachs and our heads are turned by such unstable conditions. When we journey we like to have solid ground under our feet.'

'So,' said Jack, 'you admit that you and Spiggot are the same kind of faerie?'

'I admit that the conditions affect both of us in a similar way, that's all. What a strange mortal you are, Jack. Do you always walk in the dark halls of suspicion and mistrust? Madness lies that way. Have you heard of Hamlet, Jack? His was such a mind, and where did it lead him?'

'Into deep water,' replied Jack, just to let the burgundy knight know he was not unfamiliar with the works of Shakespeare. 'But Hamlet wasn't wrong, was he? His suspicions were right. His dad had been murdered.'

'Yes, but along with his uncle he began to suspect that Ophelia, his own mother, Polonius, Guildenstern, Rosencrantz and a host of others were in on the plot, too. Suspicion poisons the mind, Jack. It wasn't the killing of his uncle that did for Hamlet, but his mindless stabbing of Polonius and his destruction of Ophelia, both of which had incurred him the enmity and hatred of Laertes. Beware of such things as mistrust, Jack, or you will be poisoned.'

Until the last word, Jack had been admiring the burgundy knight's knowledge of mortal literature, but once
the faerie had finished speaking a chill went through
him. What was this creature saying, *really*? That if he did
not stop snooping around, he would be *poisoned*? How
easy it would be to slip a deadly substance into Jack's
drink or food. Hemlock, bella donna, something like
that. And who, here in Liöfwende, would care about the
death of a mortal? There weren't any police forces here,
no judges and juries, no law and order. In fact, when he
thought about it, Boskywod could do just about anything
to him and get away with it scot-free.

Jack swallowed, and said, 'I'll bear what you say in
mind.'

'Good, for I like you, Jack, and would not want to see
you corrupted in mind and spirit, and eventually, in
body.'

The burgundy knight then left him and went below.
Jack followed the reddish shape as it went down gangways and into a cabin. In another part of the transparent
ship Jack could see Spiggot throwing up into a bowl,
while an amused Kling shook his head. Rosamund too
was not feeling well. She was lying on a glass bunk in a
glass cabin, a metre or two below Jack's feet. In fact
Jack himself now began to feel a little queasy, as the
wind rose and the waves increased in height.

White spume was flicking from the tops of these
waves, the sea washing over the decks every time the
ship rolled to leeward. Despite the clear sky at the
moment it did indeed smell as if a storm were coming,
the air being full of salt and misty spray. What had been

rolling hills of water, now were blade-like ridges, with
deep troughs between and peaks that changed shape and
direction by the moment. There was a quickness to the
wind, a cutting curl to it. Now the ship was not just
rocking from side to side, but was shifting sharply both
fore and aft. Pixie sailors were scuttling up and down the
rigging, adjusting glass ropes and glass sails.

Jack's encounter with the burgundy knight had left
him feeling very uneasy. Could a boggart speak in such a
manner? Not actually quoting *Hamlet*, but knowing all
about it? Surely boggarts were not literary? Jack certainly wasn't, as an engineer, though he'd had to read and
analyse the necessary passages for his exams at school.
That's as far as it went, though. He wasn't in the least
conversant with Shakespeare in the way he was with the
pistons and rods of an internal combustion engine.

Jack went forward and found himself standing next to
the pixie captain of the vessel. The captain was looking
keenly at the stars and the moon, the waves on the ocean,
and occasionally he seemed to be musing over the shape
of his own feet. He did not seem to use any charts or
instruments to navigate, but did it in the way Jack
expected of faerie: by sniffing the sea and sky, noting the
shape of the heavens and the patterns of the celestial
bodies there, and by occasionally licking his finger and
holding it up to the wind. No self-respecting pixie would
navigate with anything but that which nature had pro-
vided.

'Captain,' said Jack, 'do pixies know anything about
Shakespeare – you know, the mortal playwright . . .?'

He got no further. The captain held up his finger, the

same one he used to navigate with, and said, "*Weaving spiders come not here: Hence you long-legged spinners, hence: beetles black approach not near: worm nor snail do no offence.*" *A Midsummer Night's Dream* Act two, Scene two. Lines twenty-one to twenty-four. I can see them before me, in black on white. The quill moves across the parchment. The magic blooms in ink.' The captain sighed, dreamily, as if he could actually see WS scribbling away.

Jack coughed politely and then said, 'I suppose that answers my question.'

'William,' said the pixie captain, as if he knew Shakespeare as an intimate friend, 'is the best mortal living.'

Jack had been about to reply, 'Who ever lived, you mean?' when he remembered that time in Liöfwende was not the same as in Mortaland. All time in Mortaland was available to the faerie, all periods in history, all men and women were alive *now*, just as they were all dead now. It was hard to get his head around. It was as if Mortaland were a book which a faerie could open at any page and dip into. Of course, Shakespeare was dead, but he was also alive, and at this moment writing about Oberon and Titania and all the other fairies of that marvellous play.

'So, can you quote from all the plays?'

'I could, if I hadn't got a storm on my hands and the possibility of being boarded by savage sea fairies,' snapped the captain, coming out of his reverie. 'What are you doing on the bridge, mortal? What's the secret? Tell me the secret and I'll let you stay here. Otherwise get off.'

Jack got off. He knew the pixie wanted the secret of mortal death, unknown amongst the faerie, but unfortunately unknown to all mortals as well, even though they each experienced it once in their existence on mother Earth.

The ship began to roll dangerously now, as the hills of water around it raised themselves into mountains. The wind had ceased piping and was now shrieking obscenities like a maniac. All around were broken pieces of black and white, as sea and sky began to hurl grapeshot and shrapnel at each other.

Jack was definitely feeling ill. He made his way to one of the gangways, thinking to go below and join the others in their misery, when he suddenly recalled the captain's words. '. . . being boarded by savage sea fairies.' What had he meant by that? Were there pirates out there? Or were there actually *sea* fairies, a bit like Scottish trows, who nestled amongst the seaweed and struck at passing ships?

Jack fought his way along the decks, through the howling wind, and yelled at the captain. 'Will we be attacked?'

'No doubt about it,' cried the captain, getting into his storm clothes now. 'Why do you think my crew are carrying cutlasses?'

It was true. Jack looked around him and saw that every pixie had a weapon in its belt.

'How can they attack in such conditions?' yelled Jack. 'In this storm, I mean.'

'What do you think it's for?' came the bellowed answer. 'That's why the storm's here, so they can attack.

They climb up the waves and jump from their tops on to the deck. It's the sea fairies that have created the storm. This is the first wave, so to speak.'

'Oh lord,' murmured Jack, as he hurried away again, using a safety line to reach the nearest hatch, 'we're going to be chopped to pieces now, by blasted sea fairies. And the captain doesn't even know when he's being funny.'

One hour later came the call to arms. Every being in the ship was prised from hammock and bunk, and forced to go on deck. All except Rosamund, who stumbled around below decks, calling plaintively for Jack or Spiggot. Even Kling was there, cutlass in paw, ready to repel boarders.

And they came in their dozens, riding the tops of the waves, using their large flat feet like surfboards. As the storm waves washed over the decks, so the sea fairies came with them, leaping on to the rigging or open deck space. In their hands they wielded scimitars and sickles, swishing the air with them expertly, slicing through anything in their way. In their turn the pixies, though long-eared and normally peaceful, defended themselves stoutly, giving no quarter, fighting with great ferocity.

Jack was too terrified to feel sick. The moment one of those glistening vicious sea fairies landed on the deck, all thought of illness fled him. Terror and an overwhelming desire to live to see another day replaced it. He fought with the best of them, slashing this way and that, his fear caught in his throat like a large apple, threatening to choke him sometimes. These wild terrifying creatures from the sea were silvery in appearance, with brittle faces and the eyes and teeth of sharks. When Jack's cutlass struck their bodies, they cracked, as if the had carapaces like lobsters or crabs. Even when they lost a limb, or were stabbed through some chink in their shells, they kept on fighting. Only when they lost their heads, did their bodies turn about and jump for the foaming waters below the plimsoll line.

The burgundy knight fought well, demolishing many of the enemy with the skilful strokes of his blade. On the rare occasions Jack could pause and watch he could only admire this faerie's fighting prowess. Was that really a boggart in there? Why not, for Spiggot was a boggart too, and his efforts almost equalled those of the burgundy knight. If Spiggot could secretly practise with a knight's weapons while he was growing up, then so could any other boggart.

There seemed to be a litheness, a certain agility about the burgundy knight, though, which strained Jack's theory somewhat. Spiggot was indeed good with a sword, but he was lumpy-good, like some hefty baron of old with great strength and ability, but little finesse. His burgundy comrade however, was nimble, quick on his feet, could dash and dart as quickly as the sea fairies themselves. His blade didn't swish out, it flashed, it slipped guards and feinted and zipped under. His feet were like some fancy boxer's feet – the great Muhammad Ali – dancing to a fighting rhythm. Yes, Jack could only watch and admire – then go back to desperately trying to protect himself against the hordes of sea fairies that landed on the deck like flying fish out of the monstrous waves of the storm.

Then, suddenly, it was all over. There was a grey-green light in the sky to the east. It seemed that the sea fairies, for all that they were a cruel race of faerie picaroons, could not fight in the day. It did something to them – blinded them, sent them back down to the green hell of the deep ocean. They scuttled for the gunwales, plopped down into the now calming waters, and vanished beneath the spindrift and surf. Jack was very pleased to see the last of them. He was exhausted. He went below, fell into the first free hammock he came across, and went straight to sleep.

Spiggot remained awake just long enough to find Rosamund, whom Jack had forgotten, and direct her to her bunk.

PART THREE

One-shoemaker's wedding

ONE

Jack had never seen so many shades of green. Light green, emerald green, malachite green, dark green, rich green, weak green: all these different hues, and all one island. The were at last in Ireland – or where Ireland was in Jack's world. *Eri-innis*, the native faerie called it, so that is actually what it was, for they should know the name of their own land. Jack and the others had been put ashore by the captain of the glass ship and told that he would wait ten days and three-quarters of an hour. If they were not back by that time he would sail to Thristlac without them.

It was raining in Eri-innis, of course. You could not have so much green if there were not so much rain. Mostly it kept to a misty mizzle that just soaked you through, getting into every crevice, every crease of your clothes and skin. Occasionally it increased in strength slowly and determinedly until it was battering down upon your head, flatting your hair against the crown, and splaying the end bits over your ears and eyes. Water ran in rivulets down your face, down the back of your neck, and down your legs into your shoes, filling them. Jack had never been to Ireland before and he wondered if the real one was as green and wet.

Mid-morning on the third day, when the red sandwort on the fairy clock was opening, the sun made a shy appearance. It sort of crept out from behind a cloud bank, as if expecting to be ambushed at any second, and let a few weak rays fall on the land beneath. Everywhere was still wet and dripping, but at least Jack could take off the rain-cloak he had made from chestnut leaves.

Spiggot had not had so much as a nudge from the quivvel. It would be wonderful if he locate the keystone without having to raise an army of fairies to fight the ulcugga, but there was nothing yet. He kept the quivvel in his pocket, close to his coarse skin, so that he would feel any vibration. They could not, of course, cover every inch of Eri-innis by themselves. What they would do is get to the centre of the island, send the quivvel aloft in the claws of a friendly bird, where it would have the best chance of receiving any vibrations from the missing locking-stone.

Jack had risen and was marvelling at the new day.

'How are you today, Rosamund?' he asked the maid in what he hoped was a cheery voice. 'Feeling better I hope?'

Rosamund had not been feeling worse, so she was a little puzzled by this remark. 'I thank thee for thy enquiry, Jack, but I am passing well.'

Jack had taken to leading Rosamund on a long ribbon, which was tied around her wrist and around his waist. Jack had made Rosamund some leggings out of soft bark, to cover her flesh. The poor girl had been shivering with the cold in her shorts. Now she stumbled forward as Jack pulled gently on the ribbon, lost in her own thoughts for the moment.

'Hist!' said the burgundy knight, holding up a dragonskin-armoured arm. 'Listen!'

They all listened without a sound, all except Kling who was chewing something very noisily.

'Woodpecker,' said Jack, hearing the tap-tap-tapping coming from the other side of a drystone wall. 'Greater spotted, I'll bet.'

'No,' replied Spiggot, nodding to the burgundy knight, 'it's a leprechaun, making his one shoe.'

'What are you talking about?' asked Jack.

'Leprechaun. That's what it means, Jack. One-shoe-maker. *Leithbhrogan* in their language. They're actually cobblers and you only ever see them working on a single shoe. There is a theory that while one is making the left shoe, another, somewhere quite different, is making the right shoe. Anyway, the noise has stopped now. We've been talking too loud.'

Indeed, when they went to investigate, there was no faerie there – nor was there any woodpecker, as Jack had confidently expected. There was a small pony though, a shaggy-looking beast with hairy ankles and a fringe from its mane which hung over its eyes. He was standing in a lush meadow, kicking the ground with his hind hooves. Jack was delighted. Here was just the animal to help him with Rosamund. She could sit on the pony's back and he could lead it with the ribbon. It would save her stumbling over the peaty, rocky ground, and falling on the moss every so often.

'Here, Rosy, here's one of them, what do you call your ponies – a jennet? A horse, anyway. You can ride, can't you?'

'Of course I can ride, Jack, but I don't know – this beast has a strange odour about it. Thou must be able to smell it, Jack.'

Jack sniffed the air as the two knights went to look over the wall on the far side of the meadow, to see if they could locate their leprechaun.

'Nope, can't say I can. Leastways, there's a sort of musty smell about the horse, but I expect he's drying out. His coat's been wet, obviously. Now the sun's out – or trying to come out – he's drying off. Come on, Rosy, up you go. I'll give you a bunk up. I'll cup my hands like a stirrup . . .'

'Wilt thou ride him first, dear Jack? If thou findst him gentle and worthy of a lady, then I shall indeed be happy to ride him also.'

Now, Jack had never been on a horse. He'd never been on any kind of animal, not even a donkey at the seaside. But he rode a motorbike. There didn't seem to be a lot of difference in sitting on a motorbike and climbing on this creature who was champing at the grass. The pony was taller, of course, but looked a solid and dependable creature. Surely even without experience, Jack could get on him and trot him round the paddock.

'All right,' he said, 'I'll just nip up on his back.'

Jack knew enough to mount from the left, so he gripped the pony's mane and threw himself on its back. The moment his bottom hit horse-hide however, an instant change overcame the creature. He was no longer docile. He was a furiously snorting beast, with wide red eyes, and a desire to gallop like a maniac across the field. Jack yelled in fright as the pony took off, his short strong legs going from nought to thirty miles per hour six seconds. Jack clung on to the mane, bouncing and sliding all over the pony's back, the ridged bone of the creature smashing into Jack's groin every time he came down from one of his uplifting bounces, thus giving him excruciating pain.

'Help, ho!' cried Jack, clinging onto the coarse mane with all his strength. 'Hey, there, fellah, stop, stop.'

The pony continued to charge around the field, whinnying in a high shrill voice. Each time he rushed at a gate, or a wall, Jack closed his eyes, convinced that they were going to end up a mangled heap together amongst the timbers or stones. But every time the pony managed to veer away, sending Jack sliding down one flank, or the other, depending upon which flight took the pony's fancy. Finally, he stopped in the middle of the meadow, gave an enormous kick with his hind legs, and sent Jack flying through the air. Luckily, the many kinds of rain which had made the many shades of green over the centuries had left the ground soft. Jack landed on mossy peatland and though he was buried halfway up his body, he was left merely winded, with no bones broken.

At that point the pony swerved towards him again, galloping as if to hammer him into the turf with his hooves. At the last moment he changed his form, into that of any eagle, and raked the ground by Jack's head. He would have returned for a second go, had not the burgundy knight rushed across the field waving his sword, and yelling, 'That's enough of that!'

Jack raised himself to a sitting position. He was covered in mud and grass and looked the worse for wear. He blinked, as he gathered his breath again, and looked at Spiggot, bemused.

'What happened?' he gasped.

'Phooka,' said his boggart friend, sympathetically. 'An Irish goblin of sorts. I'm sorry you fell for his oldest trick, Jack. I thought everyone knew not to get on a shaggy horse in Ireland. It nearly always turns out to be the shape-changing phooka.'

The burgundy knight added, 'He is a spirit of the most malignant disposition. There see, he circles above in his guise of eagle. There is almost as much to be feared in the phooka, as in the white lady of Eri-innis. There, he stoops, and is gone on the back of the wind, which carries him inland away from the sea which the phooka dislikes.'

'Good riddance,' said Rosamund. 'I am happy I did not ride him, Jack, or mayhap I would have taken a great tumble.'

'Mayhap you would,' murmured Jack, none too happy himself, 'instead it was me who took the tumble.'

He got to his feet and tried to brush himself down, only smearing the mud more than was necessary on his worn clothes.

'Sir,' he said to the burgundy knight, 'who is this white lady?'

It was Spiggot who replied. 'The banshee, Jack. She is the most terrifying of creatures. I hope we shall not meet her. She is said to come to some families and wail upon the death of one of them. Banshee means "woman-spirit", she being the wasted form of a mortal wench, a spirit of hideous visage and haunting nature. Her personal world is one of great sorrow and woe. Hence her horrible shrieking and wailing, when she lets forth her mournful verses. You wouldn't want to see her, Jack.'

'No, I wouldn't. That's one supernatural creature I've actually heard of before, and you can put her alongside the others, out of my sight.'

'Kling is ravenous,' cried the rat. 'Can we at least light a fire, now the rain has stopped, and cook something decent? Kling would like roasted pigwidgeons, but Kling doesn't expect to get 'em. He'll settle for Irish stew, if anyone's a mind to kill something meaty with the crossbow. There's a pheasant over there. Don't even care if it's a phooka. Kling's not that fussy.'

But Spiggot forbade the use of the crossbow, saying they might hit something they didn't understand. Instead, they collected wild berries and mushrooms, of which Kling was heartily sick, and said so. Jack had been so shaken up by his experience with the phooka, he didn't actually care what he ate. He was just glad to be alive and in one piece. He ate his vegetable stew in silence, taking time only to see that Rosamund got her share.

When the meal was over, Jack asked, 'When do we get to meet the leprechauns? Shoemakers? I thought you said you needed them to do battle with Mallmoc's ulcugga fairies? What do cobblers and cordwainers know of fighting?'

'They may not be great troops on the field, Jack, but they have a way of thinking,' said the burgundy knight. 'They're very tricky creatures and we need one or two of them as planners and tacticians. When you've got a map in front of you, and knowledge of the enemy positions, a leprechaun can show you a way to use your own forces, be they inferior in numbers and weaponry. They think sideways, Jack, instead of frontwards.'

'Really?' Jack was unimpressed. 'So, are they hiding from us in a sideways position?'

'This sarcasm does not do you justice, Jack,' reprimanded Spiggot, with a wagging finger. 'Look, I found this silver buckle behind that mulberry bush.' He held up a squarish shining object, before giving it to Rosamund as a gift. Rosamund put the buckle in the pocket of her shorts, not knowing how beautifully it sparkled in the weak Irish sunlight. Spiggot continued with, 'The leprechaun we heard must have left it behind. We'll catch one yet. In the meantime, let's huddle in the lea of that stone wall.'

This last sentence was because it had begun raining again. This time the rain was heavier, coming in slanting from the west. Jack wondered about the fact that in Liöfwende the sun almost always shone (except when the faerie wanted to go hunting; then it was winter snow for only a day or two until the hunt was over) so why couldn't the leprechauns and phookas have the same kind of pleasant weather?

'They could, if they wanted only a few shades of green,

Jack,' explained the burgundy knight, 'but they don't.
They want the whole spectrum of green, and to get it
they need constant rain. Look how it falls, in sheets from
the welkin! Such a downpour. Such torrents of water.
Will it ever stop?'

TWO

Search as they might, the band from Liöfwende could not track down a leprechaun. Tapping they heard, often. Little pieces of shoe thread, the end of a lace, part of a leather tongue, they found. But the leprechauns managed somehow to stay out of sight. It was a frustrating business. The rain kept coming, regularly, continually. It was a soggy march across the peat bogs and around the mountains of Eri-innis.

Without knowing it, one night they camped on the grave of an ancient wraith. There was a hump in the ground, it was true, but so shallow as to almost blend with the swampy ground on which it stood. Under that hump were the stick-like bones of an ancient Irish king, one who had gone into faerieland looking for his wife, abducted by phooka when she had fallen asleep under a flowering elder tree. The signs were clear to the young king that his beloved had been taken by the faerie and he determined to retrieve her. Enlisting the help of a magician, he went into the faerie world.

Now, this sort of thing had happened to chieftains before, of England, Scotland, Wales and Ireland, and in many cases the lover had found his love and had beguiled the faerie in one way or another with skill at music, or poetry or storytelling, thus winning back the lost bride. This king was a fighting king, however, and had no courtier's talents. He had a unique way with a sword and was a superb horseman, but he could not sing to save his life, or indeed his lady's life. His idea of retrieving his beloved was to slaughter those who had stolen her. The phooka were aware of his enmity and gave him a wide berth, spiriting his wife from one part of the land to another, so that the king never came within a hundred miles of her.

This kingly youth, handsome and bold but lacking in art, then simply got lost, wandered in despair for a year and a day, and finally died of a broken heart amongst the peat hags of a marsh. He was not greatly missed, except by his kin, for there were many kings in Ireland at that date, just as there were many small monarchs in most countries. In that time, people lived in parcels of land and a blacksmith's son might become a royal personage, with the right kind of friends and a determined personality.

So the young king died, still in the full blush of youth, and very resentful was his spirit of losing that comely flesh. The king's wraith lay within the cage of bones beneath the turf, glowing with anger and a fierce hatred of all things living, especially strangers. It was mindless,

of course, as all wraiths are, and only managed to feel
rather than think. Yet its aura was powerful, fuelled by
its jealousy of the living. So when a reviled English
youth, almost as pretty as he had been himself, went to
sleep on top of him, the wraith was beside himself with
malevolence and fury.

Jack woke, without knowing he had been asleep. He
yelled and ran, wide-eyed, around the camp.
  'A sword!' he shrieked. 'A sword to defend myself!'
  The dream had been terrible. Even more so because it
had not felt like a dream, but like reality itself. It had poisoned his mind just as bella donna strikes at the physical
part of a man. Hordes of dark shapes had come out of
the rocks and trees, to tear him limb from limb. They had
the claws and teeth of demons, and the ferocity of mad
wild beasts.
  Jack managed to snatch up the burgundy knight's
sword and relieve it of its scabbard before the others
were fully awake and had gathered their wits. He then
ran this way and that, slashing at shadows, kicking the
fire in his madness and sending flaming logs scattering,
the sparks raining on those half-awake bewildered souls
still in their beds.
  'You!' cried Jack, as Spiggot leapt to his feet at last,
and snatched up his own sword. 'You brought these vile
creatures to us. You are responsible for the invasion. You
must die.'
  In his madness, for the wraith had fouled his mind to
the point where every shred of reason had fled into the
darkness, Jack slashed at Spiggot. Spiggot defended

himself very well, but Jack's ferocious attack was full of high energy and it was all the boggart could do to fend off the blows.

'Somebody get him down!' cried Spiggot.

Kling obliged him by picking up a stout branch and sweeping Jack's legs from under him. The sword went skittering from the mortal's hand. The burgundy knight snatched it up and sheathed it. Jack then ran screaming out into the night and lost himself in the blackness that seems to come from the very ground in such dank Eriinnis bogs.

'What happened?' asked the wondering Spiggot, breathlessly. 'What was Jack about?'

The burgundy knight said, 'He had a fit of madness, I think.'

'Where is Jack?' cried Rosamund. 'Is he here?'

Kling took her hand with his paw. 'He's run off into the wastes,' explained the rat. 'Kling will go and look for him in the morning.'

'We'll all look for him in the morning,' said Spiggot. 'All except Rosamund that is, for she can't see.'

'I can smell well enough,' replied Rosamund. 'Thou must also take me too, for the scent of Jack is in my memory. Poor Jack. Who hath made him mad, I wonder? The bad humours of the night? He seemed in such a sweet frame of mind 'ere he went to sleep, for he made a pillow for me from the moss, and wished me pleasant dreams.'

'Who knows what?' replied the burgundy knight. 'There could have been a murder on this spot for all we ken.'

'Or a hanging,' said Spiggot. 'Shades of murders and

hangings tend to stain the air and soil long after the deed has been forgotten.'

They were speaking of the spot as it stood in Mortaland, rather than in Faerieland, and were not far wrong in their guessing. But the wraith's potency was stronger for all that he had actually died in Eri-innis, rather than in Ireland proper. He had befouled Jack's senses, both soul and mind, more thoroughly than the two faerie were aware of.

The following morning the camp rose early and went out to search for Jack, expecting to find him crouched in some hole in the turf, or asleep beneath a tree. They stayed within sight and calling of each other, not wishing to lose anyone else in a land which was alien to all of them. Rosamund kept hold of Kling's tail and did once or twice catch a whiff of Jack, but it was an old scent, left from the previous day. They found evidence of footprints too, but these petered out in the more soggy parts of the ground over which they searched. At the end of the day they returned to the camp dispirited, the burgundy knight questioning whether a second day's search was worth their while.

'Is this mortal youth necessary to our mission?' he asked Spiggot. 'He was lost before in Liöfwende. He is no worse off, lost here in Eri-innis.'

'Jack is my friend,' said Spiggot. 'I cannot leave him.'

'Friend? That is a strange thing for a boggart to say of a mortal.'

'I know, but we've been through a lot together.'

'Do not leave Jack,' cried Rosamund, overhearing their conversation. 'Thou would be blackguards, else.'

'Leave the maid too, I say,' said the burgundy knight, 'for she is an encumbrance also.'

Kling had a word to say here. 'Excuse me, master's son, but Kling would like to point out that we don't know what's inside that armour. Could be that the creature in there is trying to shatter the group, break it up, for his own purposes. Kling would be very wary of anyone who hid their face and form, then started making suggestions.'

'Kling is right,' said Spiggot. 'We don't know you. You joined us only a short while ago. All these others I trust, but not you, yet.'

'I am only stating what would be obvious to any faerie. And as for the rodent, why, he is your father's servant. Do you listen to advice from your animal servants? I do not.'

'Sometimes I do, sometimes I don't,' replied Spiggot, 'but we're not leaving Jack, and that's final.'

'As you wish. You are the leader of this expedition. But we are wasting much time over a useless boy, is all I'm saying. We could do very well without him.'

The next day they rose again and continued the search. To give him his due, the burgundy knight searched as diligently as any when it came to it. He turned over logs, kicked down patches of tall weeds and even peered up into trees, a thing faerie normally forget to do when searching for someone. At the end of the day, when dusk was flying in, they found him. He was not crouched behind a wall, or stuck in the fork of a tree, but caught on the end of a leash. Leaning on him, as one would lean on a crutch, was a giant. But this was no ordinary giant. It was one of a very ancient race of grotesque-looking ogres, having only one of everything which would normally be a pair: one arm, one leg, one very red and baleful eye, one gnarled ear.

On seeing the group, the giant hopped away from Jack, leaving him looking stunned and bewildered. Clearly, the youth's mind was still somewhere in the ether. The giant, who was actually quite agile on his one leg, shook his one fist at Spiggot and the burgundy knight. He stood, swaying a little, between his 'find' and the two faerie.

'What do you here?' he growled at them. 'Begone, ye faerie folk from another shore, for I smell ye to be foreign. Here is my land with my dirt.' The giant reached down and scooped up a handful of peat, as much as might fill the shovel of a working man, and threw it at the faerie. They dodged the clod. 'Away, ye scab-faced uglies. Back ye go to where ye came from.'

'You have our friend there,' cried Spiggot. 'We want him.'

The one eye blinked and the one hand scratched the one ear.

'Yer friend is my slave now. Came running fast in the falling hours of the night. Now he belong to us'n.'

This giant, and indeed all his race, were savage fighters. When they had been as a clan, together, they had terrorised all regions within their grasp. Now their numbers had been thinned and often they were to be found alone, like this one, surviving on old fears, old terror. Yet, the strange tall creature was not to be dismissed by any faerie. He could still tear them apart with his hand and teeth, and scatter the bits. Despite having only one leg he could hop with great agility, covering distance more quickly than a dashing hare, keeping his balance as well as any creature with two or four legs.

There was hostility in full measure in his character, too. He began to roar oaths and threats at the two faerie and their companions, telling them if they weren't careful he would as soon eat the blind maiden as not.

Spiggot began to move forward, drawing his sword. The burgundy knight did likewise. They had made only a short part of the ground between them and the giant, before the giant turned his single eye on them. Now that they were closer, both faerie suddenly recognised that deep red eye and knew with whom they were dealing. The giant's name was Balar, and there was not a faerie from here to there who did not know the power of that eye, which when fixed on an object caused it to overheat. Balar's eye had several lids and as they peeled back their balefulness increased. With all the lids removed his naked eye could boil the very Earth itself.

He opened the first lid and the grass beneath his gaze first smouldered then burst into flame.

With the second lid peeled back, the bushes and trees caught fire.

With the third lid unrolled the trunks were ablaze.

Wisely the two faerie retreated, running, taking Kling and Rosamund with them, for a fourth unveiling of that terrible eye would have melted metal armour and weapons like tallow candles before a furnace. A drawing of the fifth and last lid would have had the granite running as lava and flints exploding into fine deadly razor-sharp fragments.

'Stay away from this place,' yelled Balar after them. 'Come ye not near, or I will fry ye to a crisp and eat ye as crackling with my potatoes.'

They watched from a distance as he hopped back to Jack and held him up by the hair, his body dangling like a dead fish.

'And I'll eat him, too! I'll eat you all, ye frugamuffin scoundrels, who would steal of me my slave. Every last fatty morsel, tongue and toes included. Go far from here. Leave Balar's home and hill.'

Spiggot's heart was a lead weight in his chest, as he watched Balar drag Jack off by the hair, the youth's heels grooving the turf.

THREE

Jack was feeling very sorry for himself. Coping with the horrible madness brought on by the dream had been bad enough, with streams seeming to turn to blood and the white bones of human skeletons dancing in the trees, but now he was in the clutches of a giant ogre. This monstrous creature had tied a greasy rope around his neck and led him everywhere with it. When they were not walking, the end of the rope was tied to a stake, the line long enough so that Jack could wait on the giant's every need.

'You'll wear me out,' cried Jack, on returning from gathering wood and water, to make the fire and cook a meal for Balar. 'I'll be a frazzle before too long.'

'Weak mortal,' growled Balar, settling on his haunch and chewing on the thighbone of a bear. 'Ye shall work until ye drop.'

'How many servants have you worked to death?'

'Too many to count.'

'Wouldn't it be better to pace them, so that they last a bit longer? I just can't keep this up. You make me do everything at a run. I'm worn out.'

'Balar wear ye out more. Get me some hay to eat. Over yonder meadow, mortal boy, or I eat ye instead.'

Miserable, Jack did as he was told, wondering how he had ever got himself in this position. He fetched a bale of hay and watched as Balar ate it like a man would eat a salad. Jack wondered about this creature, tall as a house, whose strange single eye seemed to have as many folds in it as a book has pages. One arm and one leg, too, down the left side. That was stranger still, for looking at him there were no stumps: the giant was intended to have only the two limbs.

'You lot always look like that?' he asked.

Balar paused in his eating, hay hanging from his lip, for he had only the bottom one, just as he had only one nostril. One set of teeth, too – at the bottom – which crunched against the gum at the top.

'What say ye?'

'I said, do the giants around here all look like you? One of everything I mean, down the left side of their bodies? I mean, are there brothers and cousins with both right leg and arm? Or maybe some of you have a right leg and a left arm, or vice versa? Be better balanced that way, wouldn't you say? One on each comer?'

'What do it matter to ye?'

'It doesn't, just curiosity.'

'Curiosity killed the inkpot imp.'

'Cat, actually, but never mind. No, I just wondered.'

Balar grunted, picking up his bear's thighbone again. 'Giant like us, we have all down left side or all down right side – not one on each corner. Only down one side, not crossways. That's the way it be.'

'Why?'

Balar became exasperated, slamming the bone down on a log with great force. 'What questions ye ask! Make Balar's head spin. How am I supposed to know this? All creatures come different.'

'Difficult to see how Darwin's theory works in faerieland. I mean, what advantage would there be to having only half of everything? I don't get it. Maybe that's why your clan is dying out? Natural selection? Perhaps at one time you had to squeeze into a narrow opening between two rocks, but now that's no longer necessary, you're disappearing.'

'Balar not disappearing!' shouted the giant, making the distant trees shake. 'Balar still here.'

'No need to shout. I didn't mean you personally,' said Jack. 'I meant your – your people. You told me earlier there's not many of you left now. Maybe that's because you're redundant. You know. Not of any use to the world now. Once upon a time, perhaps, but no longer. All species become obsolete in the end. Remember the dinosaurs.'

'Balar do not know any dinosaurs. How can he remember them?'

'Well, anyway.'

'Listen, morsel . . .'

'You mean *mortal*.'

'I say *morsel*,' grinned Balar, baring his yellow teeth, which still had bits of hay stuck between them. 'Listen, we disappear because they kill us. That's why not many left.'

'Who kills you?'

'Other giants, other clans. Tomorrow we have one big battle again.' He looked depressed. 'Tomorrow they kill more of us. They be coming from the north to fight us. We fight hard and good, many brave giants, but we get more killed, I think.'

'Oh, shame.'

Balar stared at Jack. 'Ah, Balar know what ye think. Ye thinking Balar get killed, ye go home. Tomorrow Balar take ye into battle with him, to hold his club. Aftertime, I think ye be squashed by Balar's enemy. These other giant like to squash mortal, then after eat him.'

Jack said, 'That's disgusting. That's like eating a road kill.'

'Ye joke with Balar, but tomorrow ye be bloody mess, splashed flat by two big rocks, like fruit fell ripe from tree and squished by a big boot.'

Jack's spirits plummeted even further. Ireland. He had never been to Ireland in real life. His mother had told him they had some Irish ancestors, from way back. Some great-great-grandparents somewhere along the line, mixed in with the English and Scottish forbears (no Welsh as far as he knew, but that didn't mean he didn't have any). He had always wanted to visit this land, thinking he might have a spiritual connection with it, which would spark in his soul. Now he was here and immediately he'd become embroiled in some kind of war. What was he doing, getting mixed up in a battle between two clans of giants? That was not the way he had envisaged it. He'd seen himself walking along winding country lanes of say, County Cork, with high banks, stone walls and hawthorn hedges. He'd seen himself whistling a happy tune (something with 'Dublin' in the title) and nodding to those he passed on the road, wondering 'Is this my long-lost but distant cousin?' – that sort of scenario. Not some bloody great battle between monsters and himself as bait or cannon fodder.

'Do you lot always have to fight?' he asked Balar.

'Yes. It is proper. I be chief of my clan. I lead my giants into battle. We be the proper giants.'

'The fairies don't fight, do they? I mean, the leprechauns. They fight in England, but they seem quite peaceful here.'

'Ha!' cried Balar, wagging a coarse finger at him. 'Ye be wrong, mortal boy. Ye be very wrong.'

'The leprechauns *do* fight then?'

Balar looked disgusted. 'Not leprechauns, boy. They do nothing but make a shoe and keep them their crock o' gold. Balar talk about the *fairies*.'

Jack was suddenly very interested. 'There are other fairies here? Besides the leprechauns?'

'Leprechauns be not *fairies*, they be leprechauns. Balar talk about tuatha dé and the fomhóire. Them real fairies. They fight too – more fighting than the giants.'

'I see,' said Jack. 'The tuatha dé and the fomhóire. They battle.'

'All the time.'

'Which lot are the good fairies?'

Balar frowned, his forehead creasing like a furrowed field. 'Good?' Clearly this word did not enter into his vocabulary.

Jack put a few more sticks on the fire, so that showers of sparks were flushed up into the darkness. He was hoping to attract the attention of his friends, so they could come and rescue him. Balar was so deep in the conversation now that such tricks went over his head.

'I mean,' said Jack, 'which side is right? Who do *you* think should win?'

'Balar not care who win from fairies, but tuatha de be *proper* fairies.'

'And the fomhóire are not proper?'

'Fomhóire come from under ground, tuatha dé come from over ground.'

So, the fomhóire were the *demons*, so to speak, and the tuatha dé were the divine fairy race on this green island. Well, Jack felt quite knowledgeable all of a sudden. Not that it was going to do him any good, for it seemed tomorrow he would be squashed flat and eaten. Knowledge, however hard found and gratifying to come by, was not a lot of good to a stepped-on toad, flattened and left to dry in the sun. Knowledge sort of went somewhere else when the brain turned to crusty matter. If only he could escape this great oaf of a one-sided giant and take what he knew back to Spiggot, they would be better advanced in their cause.

'I don't suppose you'd see your way to letting me go,' he said to Balar. 'Just for the heck of it?'

Balar laughed so loud it echoed for several minutes

afterwards.

'No, I thought not,' said Jack. 'But, listen, I've got an idea which might help you win the battle tomorrow. If I tell you, will you let me go?'

'Hist!' Balar was looking out into the night. He put a stubby finger to his lip. 'Fairies,' he murmured, stamping out the remains of the fire with his one big horny foot. '*Slua si.* Trooping fairies.'

For one moment Jack thought that Spiggot and the burgundy knight had come to get him away from the giant, but when he looked out, he could see there was a horde, out under the stars. He shivered, watching them.

They seemed to be in some kind of formation. He was reminded of a battalion of shock-troops from a war film he had once seen. These were marching through the night with a sort of determined step, as if with deadly purpose and intent. Jack felt sure that anyone who got in the way of this 'regiment' of fairies would be laid low without fail.

Once they had gone by, Balar began to breathe freely again. Jack got the idea that he was greatly afraid of these fairies.

'Were they fomhóire?' asked Jack.

'No, them were proper fairies,' came the hollow reply. 'Fairy troop led by changeling general.'

Jack let this puzzling remark pass, asking again, 'If I tell you how to win tomorrow, will you let me go?'

'Ye tell me,' said Balar, his whiskers shining in the starlight, 'and I think if I let ye go.'

'No, you *promise* to release me, if you think my idea is a good one.' Balar thought about this for a very long time, then lay his head down on a log.

'We sleep first, then in morning ye tell Balar.'

Jack spent the next hour trying to undo the greasy knot in the rope, without any great success. Either there was magic involved, or Balar had tied it so tightly no one could ever undo it again. Jack tried to get a red-hot ember from the campfire, in order to burn through the rope, but Balar had stamped on the fire so effectively, there was not a piece of charcoal still glowing. Finally, he searched around for something sharp, to cut through the cord, but found nothing, not even a sharp flint. For a while he tried rubbing the rope against a stone, but it would have taken a year and a day. In the end he gave up in despair, stared out into the night, wishing for his friends.

The rest of the night passed without incident. No more fairy shock-troops passed their encampment. (Why hadn't Spiggot known about these creatures? What were they looking for one-shoemakers for when there were hardened soldiers amongst the Irish fairies?) No Spiggot emerged out of the darkness whispering, 'I'll soon get you out of that, Jack.' Morning came, damp and dreary, bringing with it not only a heavy dew, but mist that was like thick cloud on the ground. Balar rose without looking at Jack, got some firewood together, and peeling back two lids of his eyes, lit the fire with them within a few seconds. They ate breakfast. Struck the camp.

'Now we go to battle,' grunted Balar. 'Ye will fight with giants, mortal boy, and maybe live, or maybe not.'

FOUR

The giants on the slopes of the Knockmealdown Mountains all had two arms and two legs: all that is except for one, who, according to Balar, had lost the limb in a previous battle. Balar's clan, of course, each had only one arm and one leg. They were at a distinct disadvantage. Just before the battle started – a battle which to Jack looked a very rough affair in more ways that one, considering it was fought only with clubs and boulders – Balar relented and tied Jack to a tree, well out of the fighting zone.

'Ye stay. Balar come back later.'

'Listen, Balar,' said Jack. 'I'll tell you my idea. Don't go out there as you are. Strap two of your clan together, to make one whole giant. Get it? Every right handed-legged giant you have on your side should find a left handed-legged giant to tie himself to. Get some thick leather straps and bind all the halves together. Couple them. Then you can walk or run on to the battlefield, not hop as you do now. You can carry a weapon in each hand. You'll be a match for those giants who have all their limbs.'

Balar looked at Jack, his eyes narrowing. 'Strap two together.'

'Yes.'

'To make one giant with two arms and two legs.'

'You got it!'

He blinked his one eye. 'Balar think this very good idea.'

The baleful one-eyed giant went off to organise his tribe. Soon his clan were giants with two bodies, two heads, but more importantly, two arms and two legs. They strode on to the battlefield wielding their clubs and rocks with great confidence. The enemy were put at a disadvantage straight away, their confidence dented by this turn of events. After the first charge, which shook the very Irish earth, Balar's giants had their enemy on the run. They lit out after them, laying about them with great vigour. Balar's venomous eye also did its work, searing the ground around the retreating giants, burning their backsides as they thundered away into the peat bogs.

Their glorious victory over the Knockmealdown giants was so important to them, Balar's giants forgot about the mortal slave he had brought, and went back to their caves to celebrate. Jack could hear them, clashing their great goblets together, as they toasted themselves. He struggled with his bonds, worried now that he would not be able to free himself.

'Hey!' he yelled, back into the woods behind him. 'Spiggot? Kling? Rosamund? Are you there?'

He had hoped they had followed him, unable to approach when Balar was still around, but awaiting the opportunity.

No one came forth, except a large cockerel, larger even than Kling, and this fellow strutted by in the distance. Jack didn't attract this bird's attention, recalling that cockerels were quite savage when roused. He had no idea what the bird's reaction would be to finding a human tied to a tree, but Jack was not going to take the chance of getting his eyes pecked out, or his chest raked with vicious claws. A little while later a large grey wolf used the path alongside the woods, even nearer than the cockerel, but the creature passed by without noticing the youth tied to the tree. Again, Jack remained as still as death, not wishing to feel those grey jaws close around one of his limbs.

Finally, a man came by, dressed in a gay feather cloak, with deerskin boots and fresh green moss decorating his hat, which appeared to be fashioned from tree bark. There were wild flowers – white hedgerose, pink campion, yellow flags – stuck all around his belt. Even faerie did not dress like this. The fellow, quite a bit older than Jack, wore a silly smile on his face. He tipped his hat to Jack and seemed about to walk on, when Jack called him back.

'Hey! Are you mortal?'

The man laughed and looked at his own palms. 'Yes, I do believe I am.'

'So am I,' said Jack. 'How about untying me?'

A troubled look clouded the man's face.

'Oh, I couldn't do that. I don't know who left you there. Don't want to annoy anyone. No, indeed.'

'But I'm in trouble. I need help.'

'Yes, you are, and indeed, you do.'

'Please?' pleaded Jack. 'Look, have you fallen into Faerieland recently?'

'I never fell. I was brought here. Grew up here. You could say I am almost faerie.' The statement was more full of hope than truth.

Jack was puzzled. 'What, did you have a cot accident? How did you slip through?'

'No, no,' cried the man, eagerly, coming to stand by Jack now. 'You misunderstand. I was brought here. Changed, for a sickly elf.' He looked thoughtful. 'They usually die, you know. I wonder about my elf.'

Jack suddenly comprehended. He had forgotten about this aspect of faerie. 'You're a changeling!' he gasped.

The man smiled broadly. 'Wrong again. The elf that was left in my bed was the changeling. I am real. I was so beautiful as a baby the faerie could not bear to be without me. I was brought over by a bogle on an owl and the dying elf left instead. Such a beautiful baby,' he sighed, looking dreamily at the horizon. 'I was so coveted. They would pass me from one faerie to the other, just so they could hold me and look into my bonny face.'

Jack found this a bit too revolting to stomach. 'Still, being mortals, we ought to help each other, eh?'

'Colm Brody was my name, in Mortaland.'

Jack gasped. He knew a Colm Brody at school. Weird kid, whose parents had indeed originally come from Ireland. Funny accent. Colm was called Codface Brody, by the other kids, because he looked like a fish. He was more like a skate than a cod, being very thin head on, but long at the back. Teased remorselessly by the older kids and shunned by his peers, Codface once asked Jack to be his friend. Jack, like any boy of twelve who was afraid of being tarred with the same brush, refused the friendship. Codface had said he would teach Jack some really good stuff about computers, being a whizz at them himself, but Jack had stayed out of his way after that. Didn't go to his birthday parties, though he always received an invitation. Feigned sickness himself on those days, to prevent forced attendance by his parents to whom social graces were important.

Brody had always been hollow-chested, with dark rings round his eyes, a wan complexion and bent stature. He sometimes took weeks off school, ill with coughing and chest complaints, and when Jack was thirteen, Brody stopped coming to school altogether. Jack learned at school assembly that Codface Brody had died of tuberculosis. Even then Jack had not felt any guilt, about doing nothing to stop the bullying of Codface, for what can one twelve-year-old do to save another from such a fate? Only thank God that it was not he who was jeered and taunted in the playground, and followed home from school, his books grabbed and thrown in the ditch, his cap whizzed into the middle of the road to be run over by passing traffic.

Now Jack felt the guilt flooding in. An elf! Alone in the world of mortals. Reviled. Bullied. Friendless. Thoroughly unhappy, though not knowing the real source of his misery. Jack and his schoolmates had watched the funeral procession go by, seeing the two pale-faced parents in the back of the big black car, their faces marred by a long-running tragedy. Clearly, they had known their son would leave them at some time. Now the kids were silent, wondering, thinking about how they had harassed Codface. Again, not with any guilt, but simply remembering the last time they had pinched his track shoes and stuck them down a toilet pan.

'I never did anything to him,' said Jack, out loud, quickly. 'It was the others.'

The faerie-man looked at him, quizzically, his head on one side.

'What a minute,' Jack said. 'How did you know you were called Colm Brody?'

'Faerie told me,' said the man simply.

Jack felt sick. It *must* have been the same kid. What a coincidence that he should meet the *real* Colm Brody. Or was it? Maybe this was fate playing its tricks. Jack had ignored a cry for help from the changeling Colm Brody. Now the real one was ignoring his cry for help. That was only right and just, wasn't it? Perhaps Liöfwende and Eri-innis were places where justice came to roost, where you couldn't escape past sins?

'I'm sorry,' he said automatically, then remembered he wasn't talking to the right Colm Brody. 'For your changeling, I mean. I knew him, you know, in – in

Mortaland. Wasn't very nice to him. Could have been. It's possible I could have helped him at one time. He was bullied at school and I did nothing about it. I feel bad now. He died, you know.'

'As he would, being a sickly elf. Anyway, you've confessed your guilt now. That's good. You're a better person for it.'

Jack was in a truth-telling mood now, for shedding sins and feeling good afterwards can be a bit addictive.

'Look, I'll tell you the facts – it was Balar who tied me to this tree, but I'm sure he's forgotten about me now. I helped him win a fight and he's gone back to his cave to celebrate with the other one-legged giants.'

'Oh, Balar, that old fool,' cried Colm Brody, cheerfully. 'In that case, come on, quickly.'

He undid the knot without any effort whatsoever.

'How did you do that?' asked Jack, amazed. 'I've been trying all day.'

'It's easy when you know how. Something you have to learn, here in Eri-innis, otherwise you'd spend your life being tied to a tree. The fomhóire are always catching me and tying me up. Just because I'm a tuatha dé general.'

'You're the one leading the shock-troops, last night!' cried Jack, remembering what Balar had said. 'The changeling general.'

Colm frowned. 'I told you, I'm not a changeling.'

'Yes, but Balar's not very bright. He gets mixed up with words. That's what he called you.'

'I'm not a very good general, either,' said Colm, almost as an aside. 'But they won't listen.'

It was at that moment that Balar happened to return. He saw that Colm had let his prisoner go and bellowed in rage. Colm vanished, not into thin air, but almost as a wraith might disappear amongst shadows. He managed to slide away and blend in with the foliage somehow. Perhaps it was the flowers and the moss, but Jack was inclined to think that a lifetime amongst Irish fairies would not have gone past without learning something of the trade. Jack wondered about trying the same thing, but by the time he had made up his mind, Balar was standing over him on his one leg.

'How is it amongst the stork people?' asked Jack.

Balar blinked through an angry haze. 'What stork people?'

'It's a joke – I mean, you standing on one leg.'

Balar was not to be distracted. 'Who let ye free?'

'The fairy general from last night. You know, the one leading the shock-troops.'

'Him?' muttered Balar, a certain amount of uncertainty entering his tone. 'Well, then.'

At that moment water bubbled out of the ground. A thousand springs burst forth amongst clusters of rocks, at the base hills, in amongst the reed beds. The waters rose quickly, until both giant and youth were surrounded by a wide shining lake. The ground on which they were standing became a small island with a single tree. Balar sat down and leaned his back against the trunk of this tree with a resigned look on his face.

'Fairies!' he muttered.

Jack wondered, then asked, 'Is this Colm's work? The changeling general?'

'Not him, but his fairies.'

'Why have they trapped us?' asked Jack. 'I mean, do they intend coming here?'

'No – it's because Balar shouted. Ye can't yell at fairies or their generals. They get annoyed. Now, us will wait till morning.'

'Not another night away from my friends?' cried Jack. 'They'll leave me behind. I don't trust that burgundy knight. He'll tell them to go on without me, I'll bet.'

'All my friends wassail,' grumbled Balar, not listening to Jack and certainly not caring about his woes. 'Tonight they hunt the grey-cowled wolf and the bristled boar, and Balar must stay here with stupid mortal.'

'I'm not stupid. You're the idiot.'

'Be careful, or I squash ye.'

'Oh, go to buggery.'

'Not nice.'

They put their backs to the tree, so that they faced away from each other, and stared out into the descending darkness.

FIVE

Jack dreamed that a light came out of the darkness. It was several minutes before he realised that it was not a dream at all. He was staring out over the black-slate surface of the lake. There *was* a light out there, bobbing around on a mast. The mast was attached to the deck of a raft, and yes! There on the raft were Jack's friends, including the sightless Rosamund. He hailed them in great joy. 'Here, here! Over here!' Wonderful faerie, marvellous rat, splendid girl. They had found him. He had doubted them and their perseverance, but he would beg their pardon for that. There had been no desertion. They had obviously been looking for him the whole time.

'Spiggot!' cried Jack, as the raft gently bumped against the beach of the island. 'You searched for me and found me!'

'Who's that?' asked the boggart, peering into the darkness. 'Is that you, Jack?'

'Yes, of course.'

'Well, you're the last person we expected to see. We were trying to escape some one-sided giants who hopped after us all the way up a hill. Then we decided to use the quivvel . . .'

'Did you find anything?'

'No,' replied the boggart, sadly. 'Being more or less close to the centre of Eri-innis, I asked a hawk to hover with the quivvel high up in the sky, over a friendly mountain. The hawk reported tremblings all right, but when we tracked down the keystones they were still on their own cairns. None of them was the missing keystone. You see, the quivvel can't pick and choose. It trembles a bit when it feels the presence of any magic locking-stone.'

'So *then* you came to look for me?'

'No, the giants arrived and we ran off over the next hill, only to find a great lake on the other side where there had been none previously. Luckily, this raft was there, moored to the bank, or we never would have escaped from those roaring ogres.'

'You mean,' said Jack, flatly, 'that you did not come looking for me?'

'Good grief, no. We'd given you up long ago,' said Kling. 'We thought you were dead.'

'Thou art not dead, are thee, Jack?' asked Rosamund, who could not see him. 'Is this a ghost before me, or live flesh and blood?'

'Of course I'm not dead.'

She came forward, out of the darkness, and felt the

lines of his face, just to make sure he was warm and a true likeness of the youth she knew as Jack. When her fingers answered the description in her mind's eye, Rosamund was at last joyful, and threw her arms around his neck and kissed his cheek with her rosy lips. Jack could smell the perfume of her warm sweet breath, like honey and flowers, and he was mollified.

'Stop that, Rosamund,' said a disgusted Kling. 'Leave that boy alone.'

'But he is our own dear Jack.'

'So he might be,' replied the rat, 'but we must retain a little decorum.'

The group included the burgundy knight, who greeted Jack rather less effusively than Rosamund. Jack then went on to explain that there was a giant on the island, named Balar, asleep under the tree. Now, when they listened, they could hear the snores. Spiggot started to run back down to the raft, but Kling held him by the collar.

'No, master's son, we must stay here until morning. A storm is brewing. If the giant hasn't killed Jack, who is a most irritating mortal boy, then he won't bother with us either. That stands to reason.'

Jack resented this remark, but did not say so. Instead, he allocated sleeping places, saving the softest for Rosamund, whom he allowed the mossy bank on which he had been resting himself. They had only just bedded when the storm swept over the lake like a dark phantom, and raged for several hours, spraying this way and that, the wind high and shrieking in a horrible way, and thunder crashing and lightning bolting. Certainly, the raft would not have survived out on those monstrous waves. It was miracle enough that they had found a land-fall before that storm broke.

The following morning Jack woke to find the water gone. So too had his erstwhile captor, the formidable Balar. Most of the others were already awake and had broken their fast. Jack went down to a stream to wash, wondering where all that water had gone in such a short space of time. Clearly it had drained away, possibly to some underground caverns somewhere. When he got back to the campsite, they were anxious for him to hurry.

'The burgundy knight has seen a leprechaun,' cried Spiggot. 'Quickly, quickly, Jack. We must follow the creature to its lair.'

'I don't think leprechauns have *lairs*, do they?' he asked the burgundy knight, but the knight scurried away to track the faerie he had seen.

Jack and the others followed the wake of the burgundy knight. Once or twice, ahead of them, Jack caught a glimpse of a creature not unlike an elderly man, with white whiskers, beard and hair. It was wearing clothes of a rather dull shade of green and a leather apron. On its head was a shapeless hat which held the white curls in place. They could see it held a parcel in its hands, which it seemed to regard as rather precious. Very soon the creature came to a place, a clearing in the woods where several animal-shaped rocks formed a ring. There, Jack and the others stumbled into a whole nest of one-shoemakers, for the clearing was covered in leprechauns.

'What do ye here?' cried a leprechaun rather larger

than most of his fellows. 'What seek ye in this sacred glade?'

The leprechauns surrounded them, threatening them with cobblers' hammers which they waved like weapons.

Jack said hastily, 'Why are *you* here? As you so rightly say, this glade is sacred.'

This remark, flung back at them, rather threw the leprechauns, who looked at each other quizzically. The one with the parcel, the creature they had been following, then stepped forward. He laid his parcel on the ground and unwrapped it carefully. Inside was single shoe, but it was an exquisite piece of footwear, being made of silver and the softest leather, with fine patterns wrought into the sides. On the top of the beautiful shoe was a silver buckle decorated with tiny diamonds, which flashed in the woodland light. The heel of the shoe, clearly made for the delicate foot of some female, was of stained glass. This glass threw colours on the ground as might the windows of a church within whose nave a trapped sun rose.

'What is it? What is it?' cried Rosamund. 'I cannot see, but I hear thy gasps of astonishment.'

'A silver shoe. A wondrous shoe,' answered Spiggot. 'With a silver buckle encrusted with diamonds.'

Rosamund was about to say, 'Like the buckle Jack gave me,' but her words were drowned in the general gabble from the leprechauns.

'It is a wedding,' one managed to shout, above the clamour of the rest. 'The wedding of a fairy princess to her king. We are the hosts, the givers of the ceremony. Ye steal our glory, boggart, mortals, rat and whatever. Ye must leave this place or suffer the consequences.'

'What is the bridegroom's clan?' asked Spiggot.

'Tuatha dé,' came the answer.

Jack whispered to Spiggot, 'I've been told about these fairies. They're very fierce fighters, according to Balar, my giant. They are constantly at war with another clan of fairies called the fomhóire. We ought to be recruiting them instead of these cobblers. Cobblers can't fight, or plan battles, Spiggot. They're not the right sort. Anyway, who ever heard of leprechauns crossing the sea to England and Scotland. I'm fairly sure they wouldn't do it. We should wait for these tuatha dé and recruit them instead.'

'What about if they're so fierce, they slaughter us?' replied Spiggot with wise insight. 'What if they're in a rage about us invading the wedding of their king? Perhaps we ought to go?'

But the group did not have time to go, for into the clearing came a fairy king, riding a rather stately-looking giant hare. The hare's ears were pricked tall, with their black tips gleaming. It picked its way with high-stepping feet, the way a horse would do at dressage. Clearly the fairy king was showing off. Someone had taught his mount equestrian discipline, probably the king himself, for it was put through its paces there on the green grass of the clearing, the practised manoeuvres perfectly in sequence.

Following the king were his retinue, his court. After these came an army of fairy warriors, themselves led by someone Jack recognised. At the head of the forces, resplendent in fairy armour and bristling with fairy weapons, was Colm Brody. Having lost his flowers and moss he looked a formidable general to Jack, who was very impressed. Mortals weren't all lost souls then. Some could rise in rank within the fairies, to become respected among the magical folk. Colm had obviously done this.

'Hi, Colm,' called Jack. 'How are you?'

Colm started at the sound of his name, then grinned under his helmet.

'You! You escaped the giant Balar, then?'

'The name's Jack. Yes, I saw him off, all right. And you got back to your troops in one piece.'

Spiggot and the others were quite impressed by the fact that Jack had a friend amongst these tuatha dé. So were the leprechauns, who nodded amongst themselves. The fairy king however was suddenly aware that everyone had stopped looking at him and were interested in a scruffy mortal with some equally scruffy companions. His brow darkened. He was about to do something nasty to the intruders when he heard the sound of fairy trumpets, fairy drums, fairy fifes and flutes. His princess was coming! Hastily he turned his hare to face the opening to the glade, so that his beloved bride would see him first, and be struck with awe at his beauty, dressed as he was in nothing but shining cobwebs still glistening with morning dewdrops, a crown of petals on his head and a belt of bergamot about his waist.

She came, tripping light of foot, her bare toes dancing. Her hair powdered with pollen, her cheeks rouged with briar rose, she wore a crown of emerald dragonflies and a damselfly dress of azure blue. Spiggot gasped. Jack gulped. Whoever was inside the burgundy armour made a noise which was of equal worth. The princess was dazzling. There is nothing so lovely as an Irish colleen, except her fairy counterpart. This slim beauty, whose complexion was beyond compare, drifted past Jack in a haze of happiness. Her musicians came after, filling the glade with the light airs of romantic sound, sweeter than birds, a lilt, a tune to beguile the angriest of kings who might have been kept waiting by his fairy bride.

'The shoes! The shoes!' cried the king of the tuatha dé. 'Bring her the shoes!'

She stood there in the glade, the sunlight falling soft on her bare shoulders, her feet awaiting the enchanted footwear.

The leprechaun who had already shown Jack and the others his precious shoe came forward and presented his gift to the princess. Then another came forward, with a similar parcel to the first, and before the enthralled throng, unwrapped the brown paper. When he opened it up to waiting eyes, there was at first the breath of expectancy, then a gradual fading of brightness. The leprechaun jumped back with a startled cry. The fairy king croaked like a frog. The princess burst into tears.

The second shoe was identical to the first, except that there was no silver and diamond buckle on the bridge.

'Is this a trick?' cried the fairy king, turning his hare so that its hind legs were ready to kick the responsible leprechaun. 'Do you dare to joke with the king of the tuatha dé?'

'No, sire,' cried the leprechaun. 'The buckle was there, I swear it was. I can't think what happened.'

The crowd were horrified. Lord knows what would have happened next if Jack had not stepped forward, bold as brass. He held up his hand for silence, even though no one was speaking, and made a statement.

'We found your buckle on the way here,' he said. 'Rosamund?'

Under the round-eyed gaze of the fairy king Rosamund reached into her pocket and withdrew the buckle. She held it out towards the sound of Jack's voice. Jack took the object and handed it to the leprechaun. The faerie cobbler quickly found some silver thread in his pocket, a needle came from his hat, and swiftly he sewed the buckle to the shoe. When it was done, he stepped back, placed the second shoe next to the first. Everyone heaved a great sigh of relief. The fairy king nodded. The princess's eyes shone.

'It is well,' said the king. 'The buckle has been returned. How came it to be in your possession, mortals? Did you steal it?'

'No,' replied Jack, firmly, 'it's as I said. We found it in the grass. It must have fallen from the shoe when the leprechaun was hurrying along, like Alice's white rabbit. I'm only glad we could do this favour for you. It's not often a mortal can do a favour for a fairy king.'

'I know this mortal,' said Colm Brody, stepping forth, 'and I know him to be an honest youth.'

'In that case,' said the king, 'he shall go unpunished.'

Jack thought about retorting, 'How about "he shall not go unrewarded"?' but thought better of it.

It was then that the princess let out a wail. The leprechauns, on realising why she was suddenly so upset, scattered, leaving the glade in their dozens. The fairy soldiers of the tuatha dé unsheathed their weapons and looked about them, ready to slaughter some unseen foe. The king's mount reared and made a squealing sound: the sort of noise a rabbit might make when caught in a snare. The king himself looked bewildered and demanded to know why his beloved was shrieking like a banshee.

'My beautiful shoes,' she screamed, her face twisted into a knot, 'they're exactly the same. They are both *left* shoes. Oh, one-shoemakers, do you not speak to one another, agree on which shoe you will make for which foot? You foolish faerie cobblers have ruined my wedding day.'

And she stamped on the ground with her little left foot, shattering the glass heel and causing the Earth to monstrously quake.

PART FOUR

The faded fairy

ONE

The princess went home in tears of hot rage. The wedding was off. Naturally, the fairy king was rather upset. He'd been looking forward to feasting and having a good time. Now (according to him) there was nothing to look forward to. Jack thought that weddings were about two people (or in this case, fairies) who loved each other so much they wanted to be together all the time and for the rest of their lives. Colm Brody told him this wasn't exactly the case with faerie, nor indeed with humans. Certainly not the Irish, and he didn't think the English were that much different.

'It's an excuse for a really good bash,' he told Jack. 'You know, they get drunk on honey-ale and eat far too many fairy cakes and pigeons' eggs. They dance, they sing, they listen to fairy music. The have wrestling matches in the peat bogs. There's magic contests. They have side activities like throwing the welly, and bungee jumping. Some of the wellies end up in the next county and you should see them jump and bounce on the end of a spider's thread. It's fun to watch, fun to take part.'

'But the princess. Doesn't she feel robbed of her day in the limelight?'

'Not really. It's not as if she hasn't had a dozen others before. Fairies don't stay married very long, you know, most of 'em. Those English fairies, what were their names? Oberon and Titania, that's it. They were sort of hitched for life, but they didn't see a lot of each other really.'

'So, what's going to happen now?'

'There could be a hunt,' said Colm Brody. 'They often go out after the boar or the deer if they're feeling fed up. But I can't see any signs of them turning the land to winter, so perhaps not. My guess is they'll settle for a game of hurling. Eri-innis faerie folk love a game of hurling.'

Jack asked, 'What's hurling?'

Colm looked at Jack as if he had come from another world (which, of course, he had) and then shook his head, sadly. 'You've never heard of hurling?'

'No. Do they chuck round stones down the ice?'

'I think that's *curling*. The seelie and the unseelie court do that. No, I suppose the nearest English game is hockey.'

Jack snorted. 'Hockey's a girls' game, isn't it?'

'Right,' nodded Colm Brody, then he yelled out to the tuatha dé, 'One hurler for the opposing team here. Says it's a game mortal girls play.'

Irish fairies grinned from pointed ear to pointed ear.

Rosamund cried out, 'If 'tis truly a game for maids, I should be permitted to play.'

'You can't see,' Jack pointed out. Then to Colm Brody, 'She's loaned her eyes to Cornish pixies in exchange for our voyage to Ireland.'

Colm Brody said, 'Fearghus could give her shadow-sight. She won't be able to see as clearly as she could with her own eyes, but there's nothing wrong with her mind, is there? Fearghus could enhance that part of her brain which *senses* the shapes and shadows of things around her. It's not like real sight, but it might do until she gets her eyes back.'

'Who's Fearghus?'

'Why, our king, of course.'

And so King Fearghus was persuaded to *enhance* Rosamund's mind's eye, so that she was aware of dark and light. Now at least she had a monochrome world within her vision. Shadowy shapes were there, or moved across her path. The shadow-sight, as Colm Brody had called it, was a dreary way of viewing the world, but until now Rosamund had been trapped in a world of blackness. Her release from that dark kingdom of the blind was a great relief to her. She was ready to play any-thing. Jack could see she would have taken on the All Blacks or the Springboks single-handed at rugby. She was in a fighting mood.

A stick with a broad, flat, curled blade was thrust into Jack's hands by a fairy with an evil smile on his face.

'What's this?' he asked.

'Hurley.'

'My hockey stick?'

The grin became more than evil.

'Right. And who's on my team?' He looked round to see a miserable-looking trio consisting of the burgundy knight (still in his dragon-skin armour of course), Spiggot and Kling. Rosamund was there, bouncing a leather-covered ball on her hurley. 'It's called a *slitter*,' she said, indicating the ball. 'These Irish names are passing strange, Jack. Thee can only pick up the slitter with the hurley and carry it along to hurl it into that thing called a *goal*.'

'I know what a goal is,' grumbled Jack, seeing the posts and the net. The goal posts extended above the net, a bit like rugby posts, and he wondered about that. Did you put the slitter in the net, or over it? He asked Colm Brody.

'Both. Better to hit the net, for three points, but you can score one if it goes over the top and between the posts.'

'Right,' said Jack. 'I'm getting the hang of it. Can I pick up the slitter at all?'

'You can grab the slitter once you've picked it off the ground with the hurley, but you can't pick it up directly from the floor, nor run with it, nor throw it with your hand. You can only hit it with the hurley. Now, I'm on your team, Jack, so don't let me down.'

'Are you a good player?'

'I'm terrible. So are the rest of the fairies on our team. Fearghus wants to win, of course.'

Jack cried, 'Well, that's not fair.'

'Fair doesn't come into it. Death and injury, but not

fairness. Watch your head. A slitter hit by a tuatha dé can take your head right off its shoulders, Jack. Just do the best you can.'

Jack was shaking at the knees. He had been long enough in Liöfwende to know that faerie had boundless energy. This hurling looked a dangerous game.

The game began. Before Jack knew it, the slitter whizzed past him at a frightening speed, close enough to clip his ear. He yelled involuntarily. Then it was mayhem, with fairies and humans running this way and that. He tried using his hurley to pick up the slitter but found himself being tripped every five seconds by the hurleys of his opponents.

'Foul!' he shouted. 'Dirty foul!'

'Cock-a-doodle-doo!' screeched a fairy in his ear. 'That's the only foul you're going to get.'

The king rushed past Jack and swiped at the slitter, which as usual was flying near Jack's head. The slitter missed him, but the king's hurley gave him a haircut. Then there was just a forest of clashing sticks as Rosamund rushed into the fray. Jack saw her grit her teeth, flick the slitter up into the air with her hurley, and then swipe it towards the goal. She hit it a fair lick and it went through the legs of one fairy, struck a root or stone, flew up over the shoulder of another, and smacked into the back of the net.

'*Yes!*' cried Jack, excited. 'Brilliant goal, Rosy. Brilliant!'

'Foul!' cried the king.

'Cock-a-doodle-doo,' cried Kling.

The battle raged for over an hour. Jack really got into

it. He and Rosy were both natural sportspersons and they played to and off one another. The fairies were good, of course. In fact, they were very good. But the two humans, along with the rat and the boggart, gave them a hard game. The burgundy knight was no slouch, either. He was in there with the rest of them, hurley sticks bouncing off his dragon's hide. Rules seemed to go by the board for most of the time. It was simply a matter of getting that slitter and putting it into the back of the net. So long as none of the major rules were broken – like carrying the ball in the hand – no one seemed to care much. Surely the clashing of the hurleys, the yells and the smacking of the slitter into fairy or human flesh, could be heard as far away as Liöfwende?

When it was all over they were thoroughly exhausted, covered in mud, but happy. The king's fairies won – there was no question they wouldn't – but they had had to fight for it. The king was most pleased with it. His princess bride had been forgotten for the moment. To his great pleasure, Jack was made player-of-the-match and awarded the slitter. Afterwards, when it had all quietened down, he gave this prize to Rosamund.

'Here, Rosy, you keep this – just in case something happens to me.'

'Why, Jack,' replied Rosamund, surprised, 'whatever will happen to thee?'

He shrugged. 'I dunno. I've had a funny feeling of late. Anyway, I want you to have it. You played as well as I did. Better. The king just doesn't think much of girls at the moment.'

'I shall take this and keep it for thee,' Rosamund

replied, gravely, accepting the slitter. 'This is thine, but in my safe-keeping.'

At that moment King Fearghus ordered the feast to be served to the players and spectators, some of whom were wedding guests anyway. They all tucked in with great gusto, Rosamund included, the hot fat of roasted boar running down their chins, the lumps of boiled pheasants' eggs bumping their cheeks, and the smell of ripe fruit in their nostrils. It was a glorious repast and everything tasted delicious. The fairies had the secret of herbs: chives, marjoram, sage, parsley, rosemary, thyme, et al. They used them deftly, and with great finesse, to produce a taste which lingered long after the food had been devoured. Jack was probably the only one there who had not been to a banquet before and he was amazed at the amount of food that was put away, especially by the demure maid at his side.

While the feast was in progress, the burgundy knight spoke quietly with the fairy king. After which he came to Jack and Spiggot and said that he had procured the king's promise to provide an army. It would be sent across the sea to Liöfwende when it was called for. It would be an army of tuatha dé, of course, for the king was an enemy of the fomhóire and would not allow his fairies to fight alongside such creatures. He said he would not have the same reservations about the giants, but thought that those large clumsy creatures would have trouble crossing the ocean.

'So far as I am aware,' he said, 'giants do not travel well.'

Spiggot was a little put out that the burgundy knight

had wrapped all this up so neatly. It was a mission which
had been given to him, Spiggot, to undertake. But when
Jack pointed out, 'You're a boggart. You're a *terrific* one,
but still – I don't think a fairy king, over here in Eri-innis
would let his fairy troops go under your command. The
burgundy knight looks the business, Spiggot. You've got
to give it to him. And if he wants to do you a favour by
speaking to the king on your behalf, well let him – and
take the credit for being the overall commander of the
operation.'

Spiggot was persuaded by Jack's words. He did not in
the end cause a fuss. But he told himself he would not let
it happen again. He was the boss. It was Spiggot who
was captain, Spiggot who was second-in-command and
Spiggot who was third-in-command so far as he was concerned. The burgundy knight might think he was taking
over, but he wasn't. Maybe Jack was right, thought the
boggart, maybe the faerie in that armour was his best
friend and rival. Well, if Boskywod thought he could
trick Spiggot into believing he was dead, just so that he
could turn this quest into a farce, he was much mistaken!
Boskywod would get a shock.

Spiggot went to bed that night on an old giant rook's
nest of twigs and grass, vowing to unmask the burgundy
knight very soon.

TWO

Jack stayed up later than the rest of his party. He felt a need to talk to Colm Brody. He could not get over the fact that here was a youth, a man, who had experienced only a supernatural upbringing. Colm Brody knew nothing of school, of parents, of all the technological and electronic wonders of the modern age. He had no idea what a computer was, or a cellphone, or even television and radio. A CD meant nothing to him. Photography would be regarded by him as magic. Not to mention all the big things, like high-powered jet aircraft, racing cars and ocean liners.

It was difficult for Jack to decide whether Colm Brody had *missed* a childhood, or whether he had enjoyed nothing else *but* childhood, and would have it with him for the rest of his days. Was Colm Brody a man who had been expected to fend for himself from a very early age, or was he still a boy in a man's body?

Colm was sitting, staring into the flames of a campfire, occasionally stirring the ashes with a twig. Jack sat down beside him.

'Hi,' said Jack, quietly, so as not to wake anyone. 'How are you?'

Colm Brody blinked. 'How am I? I am as you see me.'

'Can I ask you a question?'

'You can ask me many questions, Jack.'

'Do you miss your mum and dad? Your *real* mum and dad, that is? I mean, you're a bit of a Peter Pan, aren't you? A waif and stray, so to speak.'

Colm Brody smiled. 'I cannot miss what I never had. What is it like to have parents? What do they do?'

'Do? Well, they love you for a start, or should do. They look after you, protect you until you reach an age when you can protect yourself. They feed you, clothe you, make sure you get an education. Stuff like that. They try to help you grow into a good adult. A balanced human being, I suppose. It doesn't always work. Sometimes it goes wrong. Sometimes the parents aren't all that they're supposed to be, and then you turn out confused and sometimes do antisocial things which get you in trouble. Of course, lots of kids only have one parent, who have to do the job of two, but still manage to do all right. Then there are orphans, who have no parents, but grow up with a lot to offer the world.' Jack paused, realising he was getting into subjects deeper than he could cope with. 'No one really understands it all.'

'I don't know what a lot of that means, but I know the fairies love me. That's why they stole me,' said Colm.

'Yes, but in a different way. I mean, they took you

because you were an object of beauty, like, say, a diamond. Precious to them, but still just an object. Once you had lost that bloom of babyhood, why, I bet they just pushed you aside.'

Colm shook his head. 'No, no. I was the king's hench-man from a very early age. I was loved by the king and his queens. They took me everywhere with them. They fed me, clothed me, educated me in the wiles and ways of the natural world. Now I am a general in the king's army. I lead fairies who are powerful creatures. I have great responsibility. But tell me, how would my parents have loved me?'

'They would have loved you for what you are, their own flesh and blood, their – their kin. You are part of them and they are part of you. There's nothing closer in the world than parents and their child, even when that child has grown to a man. It's hard to explain family love. But you missed other things too. You missed the company of friends like yourself, boys like me, and girls. Oh, yes, you missed the girls.'

'Would you have been my friend, Jack?'

Jack thought about this. In truth, Colm might not have been one of his close friends, but it was hard to say. Certainly he hadn't taken to Colm's changeling, but that wasn't Colm. The Colm who had been raised in Faerieland was a likeable and adventurous creature – interested and interesting – but who would Colm have been in real life? He might have been a spoiled brat, a thug, a spiteful creature. It was hard to tell. The nurtur-ing he got from his parents might have produced someone Jack did not take to at all. Yet, also in truth,

Jack liked most people until they did him wrong, or they
proved to be unlikeable because of their morals.

'I think we would have been friends,' he said, honestly.
'You seem a genuine bloke.'

'Genuine? That means *real* doesn't it? I like that,
Jack, thank you. Sometimes I don't feel real to myself.
Here in Eri-innis, I'm not very real and nor are you. We
don't come from around here. We don't have the powers
of normal creatures. It's the faerie who are *normal* here.
It's we who are not normal, and we who are inadequate,
not quite up to scratch. We can't do magic. You have to
be able to do *some* magic in Faerieland, or you're not a
normal creature. Even the animals are magical. They can
change their size and shape. The trees can talk. The
rocks can move. We're very dull beings in this world,
Jack. We just *are* and not much else.'

Jack thought about this and disagreed.

'No. If we're out of the ordinary here, then we're
special. One faerie is ordinary to another faerie, but
we're different so we're extraordinary. There's only a
very few of us, so we're rare creatures and therefore precious to the normal, ordinary beings in this world.'

Colm smiled and stirred the fire again with his twig,
sending sparks up into the air.

'When you put it like that, Jack, I have to agree with
you.'

Jack knew what Colm meant, though. He meant they
were vulnerable in this world. Almost like fish out of water,
but not quite as bad as that. They could move around,
breathe, eat, drink and sleep. But their talents and skills for
survival, alongside those of a faerie, were very limited.

And Colm was much better informed and able to cope with Faerieland than Jack, for he had been raised amongst a glittering folk, had seen ten thousand wonders, had been taught the secrets of the forest, field and brake from an early age. He could *speak* faerie, was privy to their strange way of thinking (and probably thought that way himself now). Colm was inside the cryptic world of insects, birds and mammals, and knew their ways as well as any faerie. He could tell which way a startled spider was going to run and on which branch of a tree a mistlethrush would settle. Colm Brody could never leave Eri-innis now and would probably end up marrying a fairy – Jack remembered from stories that fairies often married humans, both in this world and in his own – and Colm would never know the love of a human girl, unless he met someone like Rosamund, that is.

This brought Jack up short. Rosamund! Surely Colm would not get sweet on a medieval maid? Would he? How would Jack feel about that? Pretty hacked off, that's how he would feel. Did that mean he was in love with Rosamund himself? Not necessarily. You didn't have to love someone to not want someone else to get them. People were more selfish than that. Still, Colm hadn't shown any inclination to get moony over Rosamund, so Jack didn't really have to torture himself with all these questions. But he would keep an eye on the pair, just in case. Even if Colm wasn't attracted to Rosamund, who's to say she wouldn't get a crush on him? Colm was good-looking, presentable, and much better suited to be Rosamund's boyfriend than a boy from a world of high technology. Colm had been raised in faerieland, not as a real boy. Faerieland was medieval.

Jack went to bed on a bank of moss with thoughts racing around in his brain.

THREE

Spiggot told the Irish fairies he would send birds forth and call them to arms when the time came. The fairies bid farewell to him and his crew. The five set out once again to find their transport home.

The ship was not there to meet them in its assigned place. Spiggot was very upset, but not as upset as Rosamund.

'Even should we discover a way to reach the distant shore, my lovely eyes be still in the hands of pixies.'

Spiggot was vexed with this added problem. One problem was enough for any boggart to handle. As soon as they started to multiply he became confused and worried. Spiggot didn't like being confused and worried. He wanted to stay focused on the missing ship, which should have been standing off in Galway Bay, waiting to take them on board. It wasn't there and that was his concern. He couldn't deal with this girl fussing over a pair of missing blue eyes. And anyway, surely it should be up to someone else to say whether they were *lovely* eyes or not? The maid was vain.

'You should never have traded them,' he grumbled. 'I wouldn't have let my own eyes go out of my head for anything.'

Now Jack was incensed. 'But you *asked* her to. You said it was the only way of obtaining a ship!'

'Well,' he said, unreasonably, 'you don't have to do everything I tell you, do you?'

Kling said, 'I do.'

'Yes, and would you have let your eyes go?'

Kling replied, 'A rat's eyes are very precious to him.'

'I can't believe this,' cried Jack, his hands on his hips. 'Spiggot, you promised Rosamund she would get her eyes back. You can't make promises and just go back on them.'

Here the burgundy knight came in. 'The mortals are right, Spiggot. Promises are very special to folk like them.'

'Oh, you know as well as I do,' said the unrepentant boggart, 'that faerie are notoriously unreliable. We hardly *ever* keep our promises. Look at those pixies. They didn't keep their promise to be here with the glass ship, did they? Even Puck forgets to keep appointments and fails to do things he promised to do. Especially promises to *mortals*. Why, in the general scheme of things, mortals don't count. They're worth less than dried figs on a goblin market stall.'

The burgundy knight disagreed. 'When Puck makes a

promise, he makes it *knowing* he's not going to keep it. You, on the other hand, really meant to keep it, didn't you?'

'Well . . . yes.'

'There you are, then.'

Spiggot suddenly got testy with the burgundy knight.

'Who are you, anyway? I bet you're some boggart like me, copying my fashion! It was me who invented wearing armour to hide myself. Is that Boskywod in there? Is that Fen? Come out, I say. Show yourself.'

The burgundy knight stepped forward. 'I am no boggart. I am fairy. Beware, blacksmith's son. You overstep your mark.'

The words were spoken so coldly, so assuredly, Spiggot knew they could not have been spoken by a boggart. Indeed, only a fairy could have filled his voice with such confidence. He fell back on a defensive footing, switching the subject quickly to hide his fear and embarrassment.

'If you're fairy, tell us how to cross the sea without a ship.'

'We use swans, like the mamau.'

'I could have thought of that.'

'But,' said Jack, 'you didn't. The burgundy knight thought of it. Where can we get these swans? I thought the mamau were Welsh fairies. We're in Ireland – or rather, Eri-innis.'

The burgundy knight said, 'There are swans here too, Jack. In fact if these swans had been on the other side of the water we wouldn't have needed to sail across the sea. We could have flown.'

'Yes, but don't we need mamau to fly them?'

'I am a swan rider too . . .'

So, thought Spiggot, he's probably a mamau!

'. . . even though I am not mamau myself.'

'Ha!' cried Spiggot. Then seeing the burgundy knight was about to take him to task again, added, 'Come on, what are we waiting for? Let's find some swans.'

'There are some wild swans at a place mortals call Coole,' said the burgundy knight, leading the way over the green landscape with light feet. 'Nine and fifty of them. Poets have written poems to them. They have carried folk here and there, when the occasion has arisen. We shall request their aid. I have a way with such swans and I see no real difficulty in the scheme.'

They found the fifty-nine swans sleeping, their wings fluffed and arched in that beautiful way. These white birds were floating on the brimming waters of an amazing lake that mirrored the sky. They were larger than swans in Jack's world: giant swans, just as Kling was a giant rat, though most Faerieland animals and birds remained true to their Mortaland sizes. Woken, they first became aggressive, but the burgundy knight's boast was true. He did have a way with them. Soon they became submissive and agreed which among them would carry the rat, the faerie, the mortals and the cart.

'I don't know about this,' said Jack, voicing his unease. 'I went on the big wheel at the fair, once.'

The others stared at him, expecting him to expand on his statement. He did not. He felt his meaning was obvious. Going aloft, on something which was not secure, was a terrifying experience. He felt sick to his stomach and knew he was not going to enjoy the ride.

'Are you going to be all right?' Jack asked Rosamund, transferring his concern from himself to the weaker sex. 'I mean, you fell from the battlements of your dad's castle, didn't you? You're probably frightened of heights, a bit like me.'

'Jack, I have flown without wings and found myself in this strange land, without harm to my person.'

Now it was Rosamund who felt she had explained everything in a simple sentence. How could she ever fear heights again, when no harm had come to her after leaping from high parapets to the stone floor of a bailey?

The two faerie, ignoring these exchanges between the mortals, started to organise the flight.

The first swan had Kling's cart containing the suit of armour lashed to its back. It looked very unsteady but the burgundy knight assured everyone that this swan, larger and stronger even than the other giant swans, would be able to carry the load easily. Next, Jack and Rosamund mounted, each sitting at the base of a swan's neck, while keeping their legs clear of the leading edges of the great wings. Rosamund was very excited about riding a swan. It was something, she said, which had filled her dreams since childhood. She had always wished for such an experience, and now it was actually happening. The burgundy knight and Spiggot climbed on to their creatures without any fuss. Kling, the last to mount, seemed reluctant. He was a rat, he said, and rats did not fly. Rats liked to keep their feet on the ground, where they could dig in their claws to keep a purchase on the Earth. Flying for rats, much the same as pigs, was not a natural occupation. However, this one time he would make an exception, for the sake of the master's son.

They were airborne with a creaking of wings.

Jack clung on to the neck of the swan. To say that he was not good with heights was an understatement. When he looked down butterflies in the stomach were not in it. He actually felt a sensation not unlike a thousand spiders running berserk within his loins. It was difficult for him to keep his head. As it was he yelled in fear, a shout which Rosamund took to be one of exhilaration. She cried out too. 'Isn't it wonderful, Jack?'

'It – it's all right for you – you can't see properly.'

'Tell me what it is like, Jack. Describe it to me. I cannot see properly with this shadow-vision. We are too far from the ground.'

Jack forced his eyes open. They were a long way up all right. A very long way. Jack gripped the soft feathers of his swan with white-knuckled fingers. There, a long way below, were the tree tops. They were skimming over forests, heading towards the coast. Green fields, boglands, lakes, rivers, hills, valley – all were spread out beneath like a giant's attempt at fretwork. Jack tried to describe the scene to Rosamund, but was not quite up to the task in his present state of mind.

The wings of the swan rose and fell. They still made that peculiar creaking sound. Now they were above the ocean. Jack relaxed a little. There was a false impression that falling into water, even so far below, would be less damaging than hitting bare stone. Jack could see the wave tops furling, curling, running over the green-blue surface of the water. Here and there were sailing vessels, some so strange in shape and form that Jack could not see how they managed to stay afloat. Surely that craft shaped like a vizier's shoe could not remain upright in such choppy waters? And that elegant barge was an artistic piece of floating flummery, but where did its buoyancy come from? And that glass ship . . .

'Our glass ship!' cried Jack, pointing down at the vessel. 'There it is, on its way over to Scotland!'

'Hourglass ship?'

Spiggot, as usual, got things the wrong way up at first and started looking overhead, but finally, following the direction of Jack's finger, soon saw the craft in which he should be crossing the Irish Sea. He was indignant.

'They're going to the right place,' he said, 'but without us!'

'We should have been on board two days ago,' remarked Kling. 'They must have given up waiting for us.'

'Two days ago?' Spiggot blinked. He looked at his stubby fingers. It was true! He had wondered why he'd used the same two fingers twice. They must have been in Eri-innis for twelve days, not ten. 'Why didn't you say something, you silly rat?'

'Not up to Kling to say something. Up to the master's son to know what's what.'

At this moment, Rosamund happened to look up at the sun. To her it was just a brightish light: the sort of light the moon gives out. In fact, she thought it was the moon. This surprised her because she knew it was daytime, even though under her shadow-sight it was always night.

'Oh, how beautiful the moon is,' she whispered to
Jack. 'Look how it hangs like a lamp in the sky!'

Jack instinctively swung his head to stare – directly
into the sun.

It blinded him, of course, and he let go of the swan's
neck to cover his eyes with his hands.

'I can't see . . .' he began to say, but on releasing his
grip he lost his balance. He slid sideways and felt himself
falling. The others gave various shouts as they saw him
plummet towards the sea. Jack's swan dived, swept
under him, trying to catch him on its back again, but by
this time he was going too fast. He dropped quickly, his
arms and legs flailing, as the terror in his breast made
him grasp irrationally for holds that were not there.

'I made a mistake, you can understand that, can't you?'

The voice was soft, female and sweet. Jack opened his
eyes. He was standing in a street in his home town.
There before him stood an anxious-looking Jenny
Pentworth, his ex-girlfriend. She was wringing her
hands and looking at him as if he were expected to give
her an answer to a question.

'Jack, don't be like this. Answer me. Why do you keep
closing your eyes as if you can't stand the sight of me? I
said I'm sorry. I made a mistake. How many more
times? Everyone makes mistakes. Can't you forgive and
forget? Please. Don't make me beg any more. It's so
humiliating.'

'What?' he blinked, trying to get a hold on what was
happening. Where were the shores of Liöfwende?
Where were Spiggot and Kling? And, more importantly,

where was Rosamund? Surely he should be wet? Did he not plunge into the sea? He could remember the salty cold water closing over him as he had hurtled into the waves. That had been real. This was not real. This was a shadow-world of what was true and substantial.

Traffic roared by. People jostled them in the street. Jack could smell familiar scents, of tarmac, of perspiring shoppers, of fast food restaurants. That one was curry. That one was beefburgers. That doner kebab. Was he going mad? Was he *already* mad?

'Jenny?' he said, turning to the girl staring into his face. 'Is it really you?'

'What's the matter, Jack? Look, aren't you supposed to be going to an interview this afternoon? I thought you were meant to be up north? Where's your motorbike? Have you decided to stay here after all and not go to college? Oh, I've just thought of something.' She put her hand over her mouth. 'You haven't given up on university because of me, have you? Were you depressed, Jack? I've been pretty down, too. I thought – I thought we were meant to split up, but I've been quite miserable.'

The pavement was hot beneath his feet. Jack could see the cracks in the paving stones. Heels were clacking back and forth. A toddler with chocolate all over his mouth was screaming at his mother as she dragged him along by its arm. A dog was sniffing along the gutter. Someone threw a newspaper into a bin in disgust. This was the real world. Over there was a graveyard with some dusty, mouldy old gravestones around a dusty mouldy old building with a down-and-out sitting on its steps. A bus stopped nearby and its doors swung open without assistance. Magic! There was magic here. The bus doors hissed shut. A man lit a cigarette and threw away the match. It was all a whirl, a blizzard of sound and movements.

'There was a ship!' Jack was aware he sounded like the Ancient Mariner, but couldn't help himself. 'There was a ship and some other people. Not people, really. One of them was. Rosamund was a person.' He narrowed his eyes. 'You left me for another bloke, Jenny.' Jack was latching on fast to what she was saying now, even though he was still a bit bewildered by the speed at which everything was happening.

'Oh – him.' Jenny's face screwed up into that ugly-doll expression Jack hated so much. 'He wasn't worth it.'

'He dumped you, didn't he?'

'No – no, it wasn't like that.' Her tone was defensive.

'He dumped you, just like you dumped me.'

'And so now I know how it feels, Jack, and how I've hurt you. I'm sorry. I didn't realise how awful it was to be rejected. Now I do, and running into you in the street like this has made me see sense. You're the perfect person for me, Jack.'

'Why, because I do everything you tell me?'

'No – no, because you're kind and sweet, and you – you love me, Jack. You do love me. I know you do. You said so, even when . . .' she stopped abruptly.

He said, 'Even when you told me to sling my hook. "Get lost!" you said. "I'm bored with your company," you said. Well, boring old Jack hasn't changed in the last few weeks . . .'

'Days, Jack. Hours even. It's not been that long.'

'Whatever. Look, Jenny, you must give me some time to think. You said some pretty nasty things to me when we split up. I can't just forget them, just like that. I have to mull this over for a while.' Something occurred to him. 'Then there's Rosamund to consider.'

Jenny said with a little of her old fire, 'Well don't take too long *mulling*, Jack. You're not the only . . .' Then comprehension flew into her eyes like brown sparrows. 'Rosamund? Who the hell is Rosamund?'

Jack was well used to her venom and had formed a protective shield against it.

'Rosy is a girl I know. We've just met.'

'And I suppose she adores you?' spat Jenny. 'She would, wouldn't she, after a few hours? Wait until she gets to know how dull you are, you jerk.' She stopped and her eyes started swimming again. 'Oh, oh, Jack, I didn't mean that. It's just that it sounds so sudden. Where did you meet, you and this Rosamund? She sounds a bit old-fashioned to me, with a name like that. What's she got to do with us, Jack? You and me? We have a history. You and this girl don't even know each other. You can't do.'

Jack thought about that. 'Not – no, we probably don't – but I do want to get to know her, Jenny. Wish me luck!'

'Wish you . . .?' Jenny's mouth twisted. 'You can go to hell, Jack. You can certainly go to hell. I'll wish you something. I wish you . . .' With that, she came out with a string of insults, abuse and words, like the murder in *Hamlet*, most foul. People stopped to stare at her in the street. And at Jack. They pursed their lips and tutted.

Jenny then turned on the pursers and the tutters and
gave *them* a piece of her mind. Finally she stormed off,
yelling that if ever Jack tried to get in touch with her,
she'd brain him.

'I wouldn't bother if I was you, love,' said a woman.
'I'd let her go stew.'

'I think I will,' replied Jack.

Feeling hungry now that the smells of cafés and
restaurants were nearby, Jack crossed the road and went
into a burger place. He ordered a burger and fries, and a
diet Coke. Reaching into his pocket he pulled out a
handful of crooked sixpences which had been given to
him by Spiggot. Staring at them for a moment or two, he
returned them to his pocket and found a five-pound note
in a zipped back pocket. Paying for the food he went to
an alcove and ate steadily, looking out at the people and
traffic in the street, wondering if he had been dreaming.
Yet, there were those bent tanners in his pocket. They
were proof that something unusual had happened. It
surely wasn't a dream. It was all too vivid. It felt real.

He suddenly put his head in his hands. 'Oh, heck,' he
groaned, 'how am I going to get back to Rosamund? I
don't want to stay here. I belong *there*. At least until I
know whether I stand a chance with her. And Spiggot
needs me at this time. He's trying to get an army of fairies
together. He needs me to help him.'

'Of course he does – you great berk!'

Jack looked up to see one of his friends, Alex
Minehead, looking down at him.

'What are you going on about, mate?' cried Alex, grin-
ning. 'You gone bonkers or what? Like, you've been

sitting there this last five minutes chuntering away to yourself. An army of fairies? Get a grip, pal. Hey, can you lend me some dosh? I'm hungry as a horse.'

Jack stood up, reached into his pocket, and absently gave Alex a handful of crooked sixpences.

'Don't let the goblins cheat you,' Jack said earnestly to his gobsmacked friend. 'I'm off to find an orchard.'

FOUR

Jack knew he should contact his parents, tell his mum and dad that he wasn't going to be able to attend the interview. Yet, since time had not passed the same here in Mortaland as it had in Liöfwende and Eri-innis, then they would not be worried. They wouldn't even know he had failed to attend at the college. So, his first priority now was to get back to Liöfwende before any more time passed by in the real world. Yet how was he to do that? He (and millions like him) had not known that Liöfwende existed. One or two people, like him were shocked into going there. But Jack could hardly get on another motorbike and hurl himself at a wall. Or climb a building and jump four storeys to the ground. He would most likely kill himself if he did. Faerieland had happened once, but it might not happen again.

He knew from his experiences with Spiggot that

orchards were sacred places to faerie. If they visited Mortaland at all, it was to walk through an orchard – or something like it: an olive grove in Greece; a thicket of mango trees in Fiji – and gather what thoughts they may. Over the course of history, people went missing in orchards, stolen by the faerie. Jack had been told of Sir Orfeo's wife, queen of somewhere or other, who had been taken by a fairy hunting party, back with them to Liöfwende. Sir Orfeo had gone after her, played a lute or some such instrument thereby beguiling the fairy king, and returned with his beautiful wife to the real world.

Jack felt if he were to walk in an orchard, he might be given a chance to go back with some faerie to Liöfwende.

Too late he remembered that Sir Orfeo's wife had been stunningly lovely and therefore desirable to the faerie.

Jack was not stunningly anything and desirable only to one or two females of his own age whose natural good taste had been overwhelmed by emotions and hormones after having only recently emerged from puberty.

'This is not going to work,' he told himself, standing amongst some greengage trees in a back-of-the-flats allotment. Jack stared at an elderly man tending his cabbages. 'This is not a place where faerie gather.'

'This ain't usually a place where sods like you stand and gawp, neither, but it's happenin',' muttered the pensioner, under Jack's gaze.

Jack wandered off, leaving the senior citizen to de-blackfly his greens. He did not want to go home. He knew if he went back to his parents' house, that would be the end of it. No more adventures. He would settle back into his old life and soon Liöfwende would be a distant memory. So, having decided not to go home, there was nothing for it but to wander the streets and try to think of a way to get back to Faerieland. Jack sighed heavily. It was going to be a long day and night. He was not good at thinking. Not in this way. Give him an invention to consider and Jack would win cups at thinking. But with such a flimsy, intangible goal? Difficult.

However, Jack surprised himself. After stamping around town covering several acres of streets, in an alley at the back of a disco, he remembered something. *Cloche-fée*. The cloche-fée lived in Mortaland. They hid in the bells of churches and cathedrals. They were a vicious breed of faerie, banned from Liöfwende by the fairies, who accused them of stealing human babies without leaving behind a changeling. Road kills, Jack remembered Spiggot telling him, were often the result of a killing by the cloche-fée.

Jack set out for the church. As luck would have it, the door was open for worshippers to enter. Jack entered. The vicar or his curate was in there, doing something with candles, along with some visitors. Jack crept past them, heading towards the bell tower.

'Excuse me!' the voice was imperative. 'Just a moment.'

'What?' asked Jack, aggressively.

The vicar or his curate was not intimidated. 'Where do you think you're going? There's no visits at this time of day. I'm just about to lock up, I'm sorry. You'll have to come back tomorrow, or another time.'

'Who are those people, then?'

'They're waiting for me. We're about to discuss a christening. Now, if you'll just . . .'

'Can't I just go up the bell tower, while you're talking to them?'

'No, you can't. I'm not holding discussions here. We're going back to the vicarage.'

Jack said, 'I could bring the key afterwards.'

'No, I'm sorry. We'd be responsible, you see. If you did something silly – or hurt yourself – we'd be responsible.'

'It's only for a minute. I want to look inside the bells.'

The vicar or his curate blinked. 'What for?'

'Owls,' said Jack, quickly. 'I'm a bird watcher, you see. A – whatsitcalled, a twitcher. Ornithology's my game. You have a rare owl up there. Several. I saw 'em go in through the shutters. Scops owls. Yes, that's what they are. Can I go up now and look for them?'

'Scops owls? I never heard of such a thing. Scops owls live in pine forests, don't they? Are you sure . . .'

'Definitely saw them go in.'

The vicar – definitely the vicar – glanced at his parishioners, who stood meekly waiting for him to finish his argument with the mad young man.

'Well, look. Only for a minute. All right? I'll wait by the door. Once you've confirmed what you suspect, come down. You can return to see them tomorrow. Do you have a torch? There's no light up there.'

'I don't . . .'

'Borrow this one,' said the vicar, reaching behind a curtain where a table was stacked with bibles. 'Don't forget to put it back.'

'All right. Thanks. You won't regret this.'

'No jumping.' joked the vicar. 'The church doesn't approve of suicide.'

'I promise,' grinned Jack.

Jack climbed the bell tower not without a touch of apprehension. The cloche-fée, if they were there, would take some persuading. But Jack was desperate. And he felt he could promise to speak with the fairies on behalf of the cloche-fée. If they would truly agree to change their ways he was going to try to get them readmitted to Faerieland. These were the vague plans which Jack carried with him into the belfry.

However, once he had inspected the bells, all he found were bat droppings. There were no cloche-fée. Disappointed, he descended the spiral staircase, only to find that the vicar had gone. Jack replaced the torch where the vicar had told him to. Then he left the church and went out into the graveyard. Since he had been inside the church, nightfall had occurred. It was dark amongst the gravestones. Jack did not like spooky atmospheres so he left the vicinity quickly, wondering what to do next.

All was not yet lost. He remembered that bogles, too, visited Mortaland quite often. These cousins of the goblins, he recalled, lived in junk shops and attics, inside old furniture. Jack had seen a bogle shaped like a portmanteau and another like an umbrella stand. There was a junk shop in the middle of the High Street, a musty, dusty sort of a place, called simply Polkinghorne's Antiques. Jack had never been in there since he had no interest in antiques. Anyway, old furniture and ornaments were expensive and Jack did not have that kind of money to throw away. Nevertheless, he knew there was a back alley which led to the rear of the shop. What was more he did not believe there was a flat over the premises. Once he got inside he could search for bogles to his heart's content and would probably remain undisturbed.

First Jack went to an all-night garage and bought a spray can of rubberised foam – the sort of stuff that people use to fill cavities in houses and in cars they wish to repair. He then found the alley and eventually the back gate to the yard behind the antique shop.

'Here goes,' he muttered to himself, looking around at the houses that backed on to the alley. 'I hope no one's watching.'

He vaulted over the gate and went to the back door of the shop. There was no doubt in his mind that the place was alarmed, but Jack's interest in engineering had meant he had spent time with a security alarm firm for his work experience from school. He knew how to disable one. The alarm bell housing was high up on the wall of the shop, but Jack could see that if he climbed up on to the ground floor windowsill, then leapt for the drain pipe, he could shin up and be within reach of the alarm housing.

This he did. Once he could reach the housing he put the nozzle of the spray can to a grille in the alarm bell housing and squirted foam rubber inside the casing. Jack knew that within a few minutes the foam would have set. When he entered the shop and set off the alarm, the bell would not ring because the foam rubber would stop the clapper from moving. It was all very simple.

Jack then had to hope and pray that there was no direct
connection from the alarm to the police station. He knew
this was an expensive option, but the antique dealer
might think it worth it. If such a connection existed, the
police would be round as fast as their car could carry
them.

Jack waited for the rubber to set, then with his heart
beating fast, for he knew he was breaking the law, he
forced open a window. Climbing through, he found
himself in some kind of small kitchen which the antique
dealer no doubt used to make his cups of tea. From there
he made his way through some musty curtains into the
back of the shop. Jack began to search through the most
likely sized furniture for signs of bogles, at the same time
calling on them or any other faerie to expose themselves
to him. 'It might be to your advantage!' he called softly.

To his great despair he found nothing. No bogles. No
other faerie. He could have wept.

'I have to get back to Rosamund,' he said, his soul now
very bleak. 'I've only just met her. I can't never see her
again. It's not fair.'

He sat on a piano, wondering what to do next. It
didn't seem possible that he had run out of ideas. There
had to be some way of getting back to Liöfwende.

It was at that moment that he saw the ghost.

A creature slid through the wall right in front of him.
The hairs on Jack's neck bristled as he witnessed a grey-
green shape drifting past him. It seemed to ignore his
presence completely. A low moan came from the mouth
of the ghost. It seemed confused by the litter of antiques.
Many was the chair or lamp that it brushed against,

without knocking it over or causing anything to topple. It was as if the ghostly form were lightness itself and had no power to move solid objects. Truly it was a phantom which appeared to be made of mist and its presence frightened the human.

'Who are you?' cried Jack, jumping from the piano and cowering against a nest of tables. 'Where do you come from?'

The ghost wailed in a tinny voice.

'Don't do that!' yelled Jack. 'It makes my head ring.'

The spectre stared at him with hollow eyes, then darted from the room, only to return a split second later. It went back to where Jack stood and seemed to sniff the air around him. Something about Jack's aroma seemed to interest the supernatural being. It hovered around the trembling human, filling its nostrils with his scent. Then it wailed again. This time it was not just a cry of despair, but a word which Jack recognised.

'Liöfwende!' cried the spirit. 'Home! Home! You smell of the land which was mine before I lost myself in this world of mortals.'

Jack was shocked. Now that the ghost was still and he could study it he felt he recognised its features in a general sort of way. That he had not met this particular creature before he was certain, but there were familiar aspects of its visage, its lines. He had seen this shape before, or something very like it. It took him just a little while to sort out his thoughts, before he shouted out loud in great excitement. 'Ulcugga! You're the ghost of an ulcugga fairy!'

'Not a ghost. No phantom, I,' replied the spectre in the

hooting tones of a tawny owl. 'I am still ulcugga, but faded. A faded fairy. Many centuries have I been here, in this place, and my form has gradually grown dimmer and greyer with the passing years. Now I am but a wisp of morning mist, a breath of smoke. Nothing left but the shape of a fairy, with no flesh, no bones for my spirit to cling to. O woe is me! O woe, I say. Youth, who are you, that smells so strongly of my homeland? Take me back. I will give you anything, everything. Just get me back to Liöfwende.'

FIVE

The faded fairy had forgotten her name, it had been so long since it had been used. She knew she was female and that was all. Once, she had been a dancer, for she knew the steps of the woodland pavane, but what other skills she had possessed had long since vanished from her memory. She no longer skipped lightly through the hours and days, but wandered back and forth in a melancholy state, dripping with unhappiness.

'Mine is a world of deep shade,' she told Jack. 'The shadows are eternal. They do not run with the setting sun, nor disappear when the thing that casts them is gone. If a house falls, the shadow remains. If a lamp is sold from the shop, the cast of the shadow lives on. If a tree is felled outside, the pattern of its branches tangle with the shadows in the shop. They lay thickly about my feet and form a black swamp. It is a miserable world, this place of half- and no-light, for shadow is overlayed with shadow and the gloom thickens and grows more dense with every passing day.'

'So ghosts are not ghosts, but faded fairies?'

'There are ghosts too, but it would be difficult for mortals to tell us apart.'

Jack was amazed that the fairy had managed to stay sane for so long.

'Have you tried to get back?'

'Have I tried?' cried the faded fairy. 'Have I not searched everywhere for an entrance, an exit? I have looked under the eyelids of cats. I have listened to the secret whispering of mice. I have studied the tongues of insects, learned their several complex languages, to enquire whether or not they knew the way to my homeland. Only to meet with failure at every stage. Now I drift on a sea of hopelessness and despair.'

Jack agreed this sounded very unpleasant, but he was astounded to learn that the fairy had lived so long in Mortaland without finding a way to return to her own world.

'How did you get here in the first place?' asked Jack.

She replied, 'I came to help a sorcerer to get into Liöfwende, but I was left behind. No one returned for me. I was a new fairy at the time and did not have the skills to get back on my own. So here I stayed.'

'The sorcerer's name wouldn't be Mallmoc, would it?' asked Jack.

The ulcugga fairy stared at him with the deep dark pits that had once been her eyes. 'How did you know that?'

'Oh, just a lucky guess. But how did you come to be trapped in this antique shop?'

'This was Mallmoc's house, when he lived here. This is where his den was, where he studied magic and learned the dark arts. It was not a shop in those days, of course. Over there were shelves where he had gathered his collections of unique and rare books on magic. Those he took with him,' muttered the bitter fairy, 'leaving me behind.'

Jack remembered that the shop looked very Tudor from the outside. Now that he studied it from within he could see that the walls, ceiling and floor were not even. He switched on the light, risking being seen from outside. There was evidence of woodworm in the beams above his head. It was indeed a very ancient house. It even smelled old. He turned off the light again because it was evidently painful to the fairy.

'You don't like light, then?'

'I am happy only with natural light. Artificial light hurts my head.'

'That's understandable, I suppose.' Jack's thoughts turned crafty. He had always been taught by his games master to know his opponent, on the running track, on the football field, in the boxing ring. *Know your enemy,* was the way Mr Toop had put it. Well, here he was in the place that Mallmoc had lived when in Mortaland. Mallmoc was his enemy. There might be some papers or something here, which would help Spiggot in the fight against the sorcerer. 'Mallmoc's house, eh? Well, we'll just have a look round while we're here. Is there anything of his still in the house? You must know. You've been here since he left, haven't you?'

'There is a bottle . . .' began the fairy, hesitantly.

'Yes,' encouraged Jack.

'I don't know. I was told never to reveal where the bottle lay.'

'By Mallmoc? But he *left* you here, to fester for centuries. He could have sent someone back to fetch you, but he didn't bother, did he? What do you owe Mallmoc? Not much, by my reckoning.'

'You're right,' said the faded fairy, with some anger in her voice at last. 'The bottle is in the chimney. It's up on a ledge.'

Jack looked around the room, saw an inglenook fireplace, one large enough to stand in and put your head up inside. There were fireplace tools displayed: polished brass coal scuttles, pokers, tongs, brushes. He removed these and then began feeling around up inside the large chimney. The first thing that came down was a wad of soot. It hit the bottom with a *plud* and immediately broke into a cloud of choking dust. Jack was not deterred. He continued to feel around on the ledge above and finally was rewarded. There, right at the back, his fingers closed round something. He took it out, carried it to the kitchen, and there washed the soot from it.

While the faded fairy stayed in the front room, Jack again switched on a light and studied his find. It was indeed a bottle: a very strange-looking bulbous green bottle with lots of weird letters and shapes etched or embossed on the outside. Disappointingly, it seemed to be empty, but what with the mottled greenness and the density and the distortion of the glass, it was difficult to tell for certain. There were no cracks in it, but it had melted just a little – probably from the heat of the fire when it had been in use – and was slightly twisted. A belt of serpents decorated the outer middle of the bottle and there were winged demon-like figures around the base and neck: these had the faces and claws of lizards but the bodies of men. Words in a strange language were scattered willy-nilly *within* the glass, trapped there. On closer inspection they seemed to be floating in the wall of solid glass in the way that jellyfish swim through green sea-water, the ends of the alien letters trailing like tentacles, retracting instantly when they touched another letter. There were hundreds of these seemingly live words.

The stopper was a wax plug, but the wax had gone so hard it was like stone.

Suddenly Jack yelled and dropped the object. It fell on hard tiles but the glass was so thick it merely bounced across the floor.

'What is it?' cried the faded fairy from the other room. 'Are you hurt?'

Jack sucked his hand. The bottle had suddenly grown so hot it had burned his palm. When he inspected it, there were red marks – letters from a bizarre alphabet – seared into his hand. Jack looked around the kitchen, found a first aid kit in one of the cupboards, and smeared some cool ointment on the burn. The intensity of the pain left him and he relaxed a little.

'It's nothing,' he said to the fairy. 'Just – nothing.'

He bent down and gingerly touched the bottle. It was cool. He picked it up and felt the heat surge through it again. He dropped it again, quickly.

'All right,' said Jack, 'booby trap, eh? To stop people

from stealing it.' He stared at the red sore patch on his hand. 'Probably works on the principle of live cells touching it, because it doesn't grow hot when it's touching inanimate objects. Fine, we know what to do then . . .'

He went back out into the front of the shop and told the faded fairy to cover her eyes. Switching on the light he searched the room until he found a large enough box. It happened to be an antique writing case. With some tongs from the fireplace he picked up the bottle and put it in the box. Closing the lid he now had the bottle enclosed and could carry it where he wished. Jack didn't know what was inside the glass container, if anything at all, but the vessel must have been important to the sorcerer for him to leave it booby-trapped. The only puzzling thing about it was why leave it behind at all, if it was that important? It was a question Jack would keep asking himself, but he couldn't come up with a sensible answer.

Switching off all the lights again, Jack and the faded fairy were once again without artificial light. However, the moon had now risen up behind the houses opposite and its beams lit the interior of the shop. The faded fairy quite liked the light of the moon. She said the beams bathed her spirit and gave it the strength to carry on.

Once more, Jack sat down and tried to apply himself to the main problem: getting back to Faerieland.

'There's got to be a way of getting back,' he said. 'I don't believe it can be that difficult.'

'Oh, there is one way,' interrupted the fairy.

'Yes?' Jack's head came up, hopefully.

'Walk through a field of hay when the maybugs are rising. You will be instantly transported, if the birds haven't pecked you to death of course. I couldn't do it, you see. I can't leave the house.'

'Maybugs?'

'Beetles. Cockchafers are their real name. Country folk call them maybugs. Every year around mating time, just before nightfall, they rise up out of certain fields in their tens of thousands and the birds descend to feed on them. It's a sight not to be missed. Birds of all kinds swoop down and feast on the flying beetles. The loud buzzing, the unusual penetrating noise of their flight, creates cracks in the fabric between worlds, just as thin glass sometimes shatters with a high note. You can slip from Mortaland to Liöfwende just like that – when you walk through a field of maybugs rising.'

'And when does this great event occur?'

'Once a year around the middle of July.'

'Terrific,' muttered Jack, aware that he did not stand a chance of finding a field of cockchafers, let alone catch them rising. 'Any other bright ideas?'

'No – that is . . .'

'Yes?'

'You could try dropping through the bottom of a well, but it's dangerous for you. The wells in Liöfwende are the other ends of the wells in Mortaland, like two ends of a long tunnel. Many a mortal has found him or herself in Liöfwende because they fell down a well.'

'Can't you just sort of *crawl* through?'

'No, you have to be dropping like a stone.'

Jack shook his head. It sounded almost as bad as
driving full pelt at a tree on his motorbike. Still, he might
not know a field where the cockchafers were rising, but
he did know where there was an old well. It was actually
inside the guildhall yard in the middle of the cobble
market square (which was now a car park). It shouldn't
be too difficult to break into the guildhall, he thought.
The windows had rotten frames. He knew because he'd
tried to carve his and Jenny's initials in one, as he'd
waited for the last bus home one night. In fact, if he took
a poker with him, one of those with the flat bladed ends,
he could force open a window in no time.

'It's not as if I'm going to steal anything,' he said out
loud, to convince himself he was not a criminal. 'I'll bring
the poker and the writing case back to the shop owner,
when I come home.'

He was aware of the faded fairy, looking at him with a
bleak expression.

'And I'll send someone back for you,' he promised.
'I'm not sure they'll be ulcuggas because we're not on
speaking terms at the moment – the ulcuggas and me. A
fierce lot, eh?

'Very fierce, though you would not think so to see one
such as me, left here to fade away. Had there been a
candle flame these last few years, instead of that infernal
electric bulb, I would have drifted into it like a flimsy-
winged moth and ended my waiting. But now you will
help me?'

'I'll make sure you don't get left here to fade away to
nothing.'

'You promise this?'

'Cross my heart and hope to die.'

'I too hope you won't die, when you fall down the well,' said the fairy. 'It does sometimes happen.'

'Thanks for that,' muttered Jack, 'it fills me with great confidence.'

PART FIVE

There may be giants

ONE

Rosamund gasped in dismay when Jack fell from the swan. She saw him drop through the shadowy space into a much darker shadow below, never to rise from its depths again. Until that point her feelings for Jack were mixed. She liked him but she thought him strange enough to have some of the wizard in him. Now he was gone, dead without a doubt, she did not care about the wizard bit. She wanted him back. He made her laugh, he made her sad, he made her *think*. She had not understood half of what he said, nor why his mind whirled off in certain directions, but she thought him a handsome creature. She knew he was fond of her and it is always difficult to resist someone who thinks you're special. Now she was alone, the only mortal in this motley group of errant souls.

And she was still trapped in a perpetual early dawn, a

world of grey shades and dark shadows that flitted across her line of sight. That in itself would have damped the soul of a lesser maid, but Rosamund was formed from stern material.

'I have my father's iron in my blood,' she said to herself, with a defiant thrust of the chin. 'I can be strong.'

The swans landed on a large stretch of water, ploughing furrows across the surface. They then ferried the rat, faeries and the maid to the nearest bank and there they left them. Unfortunately, the swans had not carried them up into Scotland – or Thristlac as the faerie call it – but had landed on Lake Windermere in Cumbria. This was a long way to the west of the Northumberland fairies and outside the protection of King Cimberlin. As such they were now the possible prey of Mallmoc's ulcugga fairies, who were scouring the countryside for them.

'We need to go north, over the hills,' said the burgundy knight, 'where we will best avoid the ulcugga hunting parties.'

'Kling must eat before he drags a heavy cart up such steep inclines,' said the water rat. 'Kling would like some potted shrimp, or nice thick duck pâté with crispbread. Perhaps a Caesar salad to start? Then something substantial to follow, like roast pork or beef steak? What does the master's son say to that?'

'The master's son says you'll get dry bread and dripping, and like it,' growled Spiggot, who did not like being usurped by the burgundy knight. Spiggot was the one who was supposed to be making the decisions as to where they should go and what they should do next. The trouble was, the burgundy knight kept jumping in just before Spiggot was about to speak, and saying exactly what Spiggot was about to say. It would be churlish and foolish, the boggart realised, to change those plans just for the sake of getting one over on the burgundy knight. Over the hills was the only way to go, but he felt he had to assert himself in some way.

He said, 'There may be giants in those hills.'

The burgundy knight said, 'There are *certainly* giants in those hills. Hilly regions are where giants live best. But I'd rather face giants than the ulcugga, wouldn't you?'

Spiggot weighed these two choices in his head and definitely came down on the side of facing giants. 'There's nothing else for it then, is there?' he said with a sigh. 'Kling, get that bread and dripping down you. We need to be on our way.'

'Shall we not wait for a time, to see if Jack returns?' asked Rosamund, ever hopeful. 'Perhaps he managed to swim to the shore? I think we should stay awhile, for dear Jack's sake.'

'We all saw him drown,' Spiggot said, hanging his head. 'I want him back too, but he is only mortal, and mortals die. He has at long last uncovered the secret we faerie all wish to learn, but he can't tell us what it is. This is what makes the secret so terrible. You have to go away forever to find the answer to it, so the faerie will never ever find out. Oh, Jack, wherever you are, please tell me the secret in a dream or I will go mad.' This was followed by a sudden outburst. 'Jack, I shall *hate* you if you don't!'

'Why dost thou go on so?' Rosamund said, angrily. 'Living mortals too can only guess about what happens after their death. Good souls believe in a paradise, in the afterlife, but no one can know for certain. Surely this is the great mystery and if we knew for certain it would be a lesser thing?'

'You don't understand us faerie. We *hate* secrets. If there's a secret around, we *have* to know what it is. It wounds us, it tears at our insides,' explained the burgundy knight, his gloved fingers curling into his palms, revealing the strength of his frustration at being reminded of the deep secret of the mortals. 'It is a like a worm eating at our hearts. Not to know such a huge secret, the biggest secret of all time. Even little secrets gnaw away at us, but this secret mocks us to our very faces. It makes us feel small and contemptible, and faerie *cannot* feel such indignities.'

'Then it is too bad,' said Rosamund, 'but we must hope for Jack's sake that paradise has taken him to its bosom.'

'The *ocean* has taken him to its bosom,' observed Kling, matter-of-factly.

'The rat is right,' agreed the burgundy knight. 'The boy has gone to a watery grave.'

'The little fishes will be eating him,' continued Kling, a sort of dreamy, far-away look on his pointed face. 'Poor, poor Jack, food for the saltwater swimmers and afterwards, the wading birds. Now the hermit crabs will be feasting on his toes, the mudskippers on his fingers, the lobsters on his nose and lips and rosy cheeks.' He made the mistake of licking his whiskers after he said this, which gave away his true feelings on the matter.

'Oh!' cried Rosamund. She turned away from the insensitive rat.

'Well,' Spiggot said, uncomfortable with the naked sorrow of a mortal maid, 'we'd better be on our way.'

They set off into the purple hills, following a rushing beck to its source, a place high up on the hillside where the water came thrusting, gushing from a crack on the rockface. Spiggot passed this place warily. He had no wish to run into any monsters from the undergound, such as skaggs. Galscipe, the subterranean city of the fairies below the surface of the Earth, was full of such creatures. Sometimes they forced themselves through exits like this. Of course, since the locking-stone to the cairn had been missing, skaggs and their cousins had been wandering out all the time, creating havoc over the countryside of both Thristlac and Liöfwende.

As they crested a hill they came upon their first giant.

He seemed to be one of those who have been banished from his tribe, for he sat alone in the mouth of a cave and stared moodily over the hilltops. There were such giants, whose usefulness had gone, and who were more a nuisance than an asset in giant communities. Creatures who ate more than their worth and did none of the essential work.

When the party approached him, in order to pass his home, the giant turned his head to stare. They saw immediately that he was a very short-sighted giant, for he had fashioned himself a pair of spectacles out of clear quartz, fitting the lenses into crude frames made of iron wire. The wire had rusted, staining the ears and cheeks of the giant, who peered at them closely as they attempted to walk on by without even a 'how-d'ye-do'.

'Where are you bound?' asked the giant. 'Do you not know this is border country?'

'Your presence would confirm it,' said the burgundy knight, 'for giants are always to be found along the borders of our realms.'

'This is true.' The giant was sitting cross-legged and he plucked at one of his toes, and sighed. 'Will you not stop and pass the time of day? I have not spoken to a soul in years. Unlike most giants I have a lively mind. It's true I have the opportunity to think a lot, while sitting here outside my cave and looking down on the world, but I do crave conversation.'

An intelligent giant! A rare thing, but not unique. Spiggot was anxious to be on his way, but Rosamund said they should give the giant some attention.

'Yes,' said Kling, 'we have to stop for lunch. Ask the big fellow if he has any spare food.'

'I can make you some dampers and twist,' said the giant. 'I have flour. I have water. I can make a fire.'

Kling screwed up his face. 'Dampers and twist? Kling's eaten better down a sewer. Still, beggars can't be choosers.' He unhitched himself from his cart and began gathering dried grass and wood for the fire, which the giant said he would light using his spectacles. 'I shall direct the sunlight through one of the lenses and so ignite the grass. It will save you using your tinderbox, boggart.'

Rosamund sat down opposite the giant. There was nothing for it but for Spiggot and the burgundy knight to join her, and Spiggot admitted to himself he was glad of the rest.

'Those are a fine set of spectacles,' said Spiggot. 'I would like to own such a pair.'

'Faerie don't need glasses,' Kling said, as a knot of dried grass burst into flame. 'Faerie eyes are perfect.'

'Still, they would give me a grand air. They make him,' he pointed at the giant, 'very distinguished-looking. Giants are not usually known for that. They're usually big, clumsy idiots who have runny noses and dribble a lot. You're different. Is that why they banished you?'

'I kept correcting their grammar,' said the moody creature, looking up from his fire-making. 'And a few other things.'

The burgundy knight said, 'No, they wouldn't like that. Taking a lot on yourself, weren't you? Giants don't need perfect grammar to get by in life. Their strength is their strength, so to speak. Any weakness in intellect tends not to be noticed, usually.'

'This is true, but I can't seem to keep my big mouth shut. It pains me to hear a misused gerund or the subjunctive tortured to death. It's just the way I am. However, I have the creatures of the wild for my companions: wolves and bears drop in occasionally. And for intellectual stimulation, I read the heavens at night, which to me are the open pages of a vast book.

'The comets and meteors trace the brilliant words of twice-told tales, the planets of the solar system serve as punctuation marks. Each star, each set of stars, every red dwarf, white giant, every cloud of astrodust tells its own tale. Such stories are there. Histories. Biographies.

Quirky novels and quick, darting poems. The whole, illustrated with astrological figures.'

Kling tucked into a damper which was only just about baked, the core being still tongue-burningly soft and runny. 'He really is a bright spark, isn't he?' murmured the rat. 'Could you pass that piece of twist? That one there, by your hand. It'll burn to crisp if someone doesn't eat it.'

'If thou art indeed a sage, mayhap even a philosopher, with a deep knowledge of gramarye,' Rosamund said eagerly to the thoughtful giant, 'could thee not turn thy mind to my friend, Jack? He fell into the sea from a great height and is feared dead. Art thou not, with thy certain knowledge of alchemy, sorcery and magic lore, versed in ways to raise the dead?'

TWO

The giant adjusted his glasses. He told them his name was Jobwot and that he was not at all well versed in magic. 'I would like to help the maid,' he said, 'but I do not know how. My learning amounts to nothing but pure knowledge. I have never applied it. It is true that a witch once passed by here, some hundred years or so ago, and she did leave me with the ways and means of raising the dead. But I am not a practical giant. I have never used knowledge for any useful purpose. Except of course, for cross- stitching, which I use when making my shirts and kilts.'

'You could try,' Spiggot suggested. 'We would, like to have Jack back with us. Do you need a body? We have no body – Jack was lost in the waves, leaving nothing behind.'

'No corpse is needed – they are messy things anyway –

but we need a personal item.' Jobwot heaved a great sigh. 'This magic stuff is somewhat baffling, but I could attempt it, I suppose, so long as you don't blame me if anything goes wrong. I'm no expert. I'm book-learned only.'

'We will not blame thee, giant,' said Rosamund, excitedly. 'What dost thou require to assist thee in this art?'

'Anything that was this Jack's.'

Rosamund triumphantly produced the slitter which Jack had been awarded by the Irish fairies. She placed it reverently on the ground before her. Jobwot peered at it, picked it up, examined it.

'A ball,' he said.

'A slitter, from a game of hurling which we played with the fairies of Eri-innis,' explained Rosamund. 'Jack was given this because he was considered to be a fine player.' She said the last with some pride in her voice.

The giant stood up for the first time and Rosamund gasped at how large he was on his feet. He stood some seven metres high, but it was not just his height, but the girth of his arms and legs, his thighs, his torso, that impressed the young maid. And also his hands and feet were even larger, and out of proportion with the rest of his body. He looked as if he might be the clumsiest creature on the Earth, yet he held the slitter between thumb and forefinger with the utmost delicacy, and she could see the tiny stitches in his rough-weave kilt were neat and tight; excellent sewing for a creature with fingers like tree stumps and the eyes of a mole.

'Yes, we could try,' he said, 'but I cannot guarantee the outcome.'

'Never mind, we want Jack back,' said Spiggot.

'Right, then,' said Jobwot. 'Some gathering to be done. Please go out and look for the following herbs, plants and seeds. Acorns, costmary, mandrake – mandrake is essential – vervain, aloe . . .' The list of nature's bounty went on. Then another started, of semi-precious stones. Then a further list of living and dead creatures, such as toads with warts on their bellies and a weasel's nape hair. Finally, the lists were drawn up in full and faerie, rat and mortal went forth, to search for the items. These, despite their variety and number, were not difficult to find. Liöfwende is not like Mortaland's England. Its natural resources are plentiful, since it has never been plundered by greedy men. There were rough diamonds lying around waiting to be picked up and gold nuggets ready to be kicked aside by uninterested faerie. Diamonds and gold were not on Jobwot's lists, so they were ignored by the searchers. Long purples were the only plant that gave them any trouble and that was because goblins eat them faster than they can grow. Rosamund found some in a hidden shady spot and the lists were finally completed.

With a charcoal stick and a white marble slab, Jobwot had ticked off the items as they were brought in. He looked at the rows of plants, minerals, stones and dead creatures with great satisfaction. 'Well done,' he said, 'and you didn't have to kill anything to get a dead one?'

'Only the crested newt,' said Kling, 'and it didn't scream much.'

Jobwot stared at the water rat in horror, until Kling said, 'Just kidding. I found it already dead of old age.'

'I should hope so. I should hope so,' muttered the giant. 'Now, we must get started. I know the chants, but we have to boil things, strike precious stones together, and cut up the dead creatures for their spleens and such. I shall allocate tasks. I want no fuss and bother. Just get on with the work I give you. Where's the slitter thing? Ah, there it is. Thank you, maid. That is of course, essential to the whole operation, for it bears the odour stamp of the dead youth.'

They all did as they were told, even the burgundy knight, who couldn't have cared less about raising Jack from the dead. Finally, at midnight, all was ready. Jobwot had made a crude figure of a man, out of sticks, stones and mud. A sort of covering cloak had been fashioned from various plants, giving the effigy a coat-of-many-herbs. Hair from a weasel covered the turnip skull. Skin, for the face, hands and feet – the essential areas – and had been taken from the bellies of toads. Two rather ugly wild boar's warts made the eyes. Figs were put in place of the ears. A lizard's head, the nose.

It was a ghastly-looking image, but Jobwot assured them all that Jack would not look like that when he returned from the dead.

Fires were burning in several spots around the cave. The smell of singed hair and flesh was in the air. Then the chanting began. The words were terrible and not fit for the lugs of a faerie, let alone a mortal maid, so Rosamund was told to put her hands over her ears and hum. At first she was a little curious and let two or three words slip past her guard, but the sound of them chilled her to the bone. They were horrible words, which made her feel physically sick to her stomach, even though she understood not a syllable. Soon she was pressing hard against her ears and humming loudly.

Thus Rosamund could not hear, though she could see, what was going on around her. After what seemed to her to be a very long time the stick-and-clay effigy began to jump and twitch and jerk. The mouth gaped. The stick-arms flailed. The stick-legs kicked. These movements became smoother, sinuous, as the scarecrowy-figure started to dance. Its turnip mouth formed a ghastly grin and its seedy eyes opened wider. The steps of the dance were so odd, so peculiar, they frightened the young maid with their serpentine movements. As the effigy danced the leaves, thatch and other materials of which it was formed began to change to flesh and bone.

A transfiguration was taking place before the eyes of the medieval maid: the shaping of a living creature from inanimate materials. In the end Rosamund had to look away, unable to bear the sight of the strange transformation a moment longer. Even so she could feel the thump of its boots on the hard hollow ground.

A while later, Spiggot gently peeled her hands away and told her to look at the figure on the other side of the fire. There was her dear Jack, standing there, smiling. Joy rushed into her heart like a flood. Sweet Jack. He was back from the dead and they could now talk and laugh together, as of old.

'What are you all looking at?' snarled Jack. 'What am I, an object of interest? I think not. Stare at something else, if you please.'

The smile, which had been a rather peculiar smile in any case, was now gone from the youth's face. It had been replaced by a sneer so very nasty in its lack of warmth, in its absence of any majesty. Jack's real smile had been something of great worth to Rosamund, a thing to be valued. His new smile was something to be thrown away, which now it had been, and something worse was in its place.

'Jack, why dost thou look at me so?' asked Rosamund. 'We have brought thee back from the unknown. Art thou not pleased? Art thou so lacking in gratitude? Why dost thy eyes start from thy head? Why dost thy lip have such a malignant curl? Art thou indeed Jack?'

'Of course I'm Jack.'

Spiggot said, eagerly, '*Now* you can tell us the secret – you've been there – you *know*.'

Jack's eyes flashed in contempt. 'The boggart speaks! Well, well. But let him speak to someone else. I've no time for such lowly creatures. They are all hair and mouth. Boggarts smell of *work*. Talk to that creature next to you. Yes, the rat. You're two of a kind.'

'Jack?' cried Spiggot. 'Is this a mortal joke?'

'Oh dear,' Jobwot said, 'has your friend changed?'

Kling said, 'This one *looks* like the serf who once polished my boots, but he doesn't *sound* like him.'

'Ha!' cried Jack, grimacing, 'the rodent speaks now! What next? That oaf in the red armour?'

The burgundy knight growled and his hand went to his sword hilt.

'Oh dear, oh dear, oh dear,' muttered the giant, taking

off his glasses to polish them on his kilt. 'Perhaps it would have been better to leave him in the land of the dead. Things *do* happen to them, you know. I'm sure you can't mix with dead people and come back untainted.'

'What a lot of rot you talk, giant. It must be that your brain is too small for that dome-sized head. Or the worms have got to it. And what about this popinjay here,' said Jack, indicating the burgundy knight. 'How he struts! A maggot in dragonskin, I should say.'

Spiggot shook his own head at this display of bad manners.

'I think I have an answer to this little problem,' replied the burgundy knight with some asperity. He drew his sword. 'Let's send him back to where he came from.' He made a swipe at Jack with the sharp edge of his blade. Jack leapt backwards with remarkable agility. In fact he did a double somersault. It was a breathtaking piece of athleticism.

'You'll have to be faster than that,' said Jack. 'Much faster. I move with the speed of a snake.'

'You *are* a snake,' said Spiggot.

'Now that's not a nice thing to say, even if you are a common boggart.'

'Let me at him again,' said the burgundy knight, annoyed by his miss. 'I'll cut the fiend down to size.'

Jack folded his arms and looked petulant. 'I don't know what I've done to deserve this. I go away for a little while and when I return, what happens? I'm shunned and attacked, that's what happens. Well, I hope you'll all be sorry when you learn your mistake. I shan't shame you with it, saying I told you so, but you'll be sorry, anyway.'

Now this was so much like the old Jack (even, sad to say, the petulance) that Rosamund was having second thoughts. Was it possible the giant was right? Perhaps Jack *had* been badly affected by his experience in the afterlife and was indeed being treated harshly? But Jack had never shown any skill at tumbling, while this Jack was most acrobatic in his movements. It was all very confusing. Rosamund so wanted Jack back, she was ready to give second chances.

'Mayhap,' she said, 'Jack's time in the world of the dead has addled his brain like a duck's egg left in the sun? I say we leave him be and give him time to become the Jack we all know and love. Let us stand away from him and presently direct our attentions elsewhere.'

'I don't know what to say,' said Spiggot.

'Yes, you do,' said the Jack. 'You just said it!'

'I mean, I don't know what's happened to you. You don't seem the same at all. Should we send you back from whence you came?'

Jobwot coughed into his massive fist, standing high above the group and making them crane their necks to look up at him. 'Um, I'm not sure we *can* send him back. Now that he is here, he must stay.'

Now Jobwot lay down on the ground in front of his cave. He was tired, as they all were, it being well past midnight. Everyone but Jack found him or herself a space by the fire, there to lay a blanket and sink down upon it. The travelling group had walked many a mile that day, climbed many a hill. The spring had gone out of them. Jack, however, was obviously still nervously lively. Too lively. He did not go to bed, but stayed pacing around, walking off and talking to himself in a low voice, returning to poke the fire or stand with his hands on his hips to stare around at the resting forms. Then he would make some remark designed to irritate the hearer, except that by now everyone was fast asleep.

All night long Jack wandered up and down, sometimes going as much as a mile away from the cave, but always with his nose to the breeze in case the travellers woke and moved on without him. He could scent any movements in the distant camp. They would not get away from him in a hurry. In the meantime, he attempted to explore as much of the surrounding countryside as he could, seeing things, touching things, smelling things. There was a great deal to learn when one's environment had consisted entirely of fire and brimstone and very little else. There was nothing of the smell of sulphur in *this* world, nor anything of fierce heat.

Things like grass, flowers and trees; beasts, birds and butterflies; even wind and rain. All these were new experiences. Many of them turned out to be quite unpleasant. The fragrance of a wild flower for example was a disgusting stench to someone who had never before drawn a sweet scent into his nostrils. The feel of a struggling rabbit's fur sent shivers down Jack's spine. Even after he had huffed in its face and killed it with his foul breath, still it remained horribly soft and fluffy. He did not like the touch of green leaves, nor did he favour the sight of a blossom. Things were most unsavoury here, for a creature such as he.

And worse was to come.

The sun came out and covered him with a loathsome

yellowy-warm intangible substance, filling him with revulsion.

Incredibly sharp daylight arrived, piercing his sensitive eyeballs.

There came with the dawn a sudden yelling of songbirds from every bush and tree.

Insects began shrieking through the air.

There was that huge draught they called the wind.

Chaos and confusion.

THREE

When the others awoke Jack was nowhere to be seen. Spiggot felt somewhat relieved. This relief was accompanied by guilt, but he decided he could handle that better than he could the returned Jack. Something really bad had happened to Jack in the nether world of the dead. Perhaps he had seen such horrors as would send a creature mad, for mad he certainly appeared. His eyes were not like the eyes of the old Jack. They darted here and there. They had a flinty glint to them which spoke of a stone heart. His words were not only harsh in meaning, but harsh in tone. It was as if his voice came from two grating sandstones, rather than from a human throat. Jack looked thinner and wretched. His flesh hung on his bones. Clearly he was not the Jack who had left them such a short time ago.

'I must help him recover,' said Spiggot to himself. 'He

has been a good friend to me. I must help him reach inside himself and find his old soul – the soft one with the good manners and honourable thoughts. He's in there, somewhere. He has to be. We must bring him out.'

'What? Boggart? Talking to yourself? Demons talk to themselves, you know. Perhaps you're a demon in a boggart body?'

Jack had reappeared, strutting around, hands on hips. His face wore that horrible sneer he seemed to have brought back with him from the world of the dead. Spiggot sighed, hoping he would be able to keep his patience until the old modest Jack emerged from within this arrogant Jack. Modesty was not a virtue amongst faerie, in fact it was almost non-existent, but it suited mortals and was a strength in them. An arrogant mortal was somehow worse than an arrogant faerie. Overweening pride did not sit well on the shoulders of a mortal, whereas a faerie could get away with a little loftiness. This swaggering Jack was like bile in the throat.

'Please, Jack. Try to be more polite,' said Spiggot. 'You're turning even Rosamund against you.'

'The maid?' Jack frowned, as if he had just this moment thought of the female member of the party in terms of friendship. 'She likes me, then?'

'She *did* like you. Before.'

'Then she will like me again, when she sees how clever I am. I shall do tricks for her. Tricks I learned elsewhere.'

'I'm not sure that'll do it, Jack. I think she wants you to be yourself.'

'I can be myself. Yes. I can do that.'

Rosamund came back from fetching water from the

giant's well. Jack went to her and bowed low. 'Fair wench, let me carry that waterskin for you?'

'Why, I thank thee, dear Jack,' said Rosamund, delighted.

'And I accept thy thanks, for I am enthralled by thee, fair Rosamund. Thou hast bewitched me with thy beauty. Shall I compare thee to a summer's sky? Thou art more lovely and more temperate. Rough winds do shake the darling buds of May and summer's lease hath far too short a flight. I made that up. Clever, eh? I'm very clever like that. A genius with words, in fact.'

''Twas indeed clever, Jack.'

'Oh, you don't know the half of it,' he said, swinging the waterskin on to his back and striding by her side. 'I'm a superb horseman. I can fence with the best swordsman in the land. I wrestle, I pen poetry, I write songs and sing them beautifully. I am, in short, the perfect courtier. Ladies swoon at my feet. Kings would have me at their elbow. You're very lucky I count you among my friends, Rosamund.'

Rosamund frowned. 'Thou are becoming a braggart, Jack. I like thee not for such a turn. A courtier shows modesty in all things.'

'Modesty, yes, modesty. I'm good at that, too.'

Jack strode ahead and plonked the waterskin down beside the burgundy knight, who was running a rag over his armour, polishing the bits that had received grazes.

'Here, robin redbreast, you can carry the water now.'

'I shall carry your head if you're not careful,' growled the knight. 'And drop it in the nearest bog.'

❖

Jobwot was now up and treading carefully around, making sure he didn't squash any of his guests. He and Kling were talking about food. It seemed the giant was of the same opinion as the rat, that food was one of the most important subjects under the sun. Quality, not quantity, Kling was telling Jobwot. Faeries stuffed their faces with any old muck, but a gourmet such as himself saw that as crass. The trouble with Liöfwende was the lack of chefs, Kling said. There were plenty of cooks, but very few . . .

He never finished his sentence. At that moment, there came a yell from behind the hill. Something rose in the air above the well, then fell down again in some thorn bushes. This *something* thrashed around for a few minutes, making a terrible noise, then it seemed to extricate itself from the briars. It came tramping over the hill. It was . . . Jack. A soaking wet Jack who looked as if he been shot from a water-cannon.

'Jack?' cried Spiggot, looking first at the Jack beside him, then at the Jack who had suddenly appeared from the well. 'Is that you?'

Jack, the most recent one, was picking bits of vegetation out of his shirt and complaining. 'Every time I come to Faerieland I find myself in a thorn bush. Why does it always have to be so violent? Couldn't I sort of just walk in, like Alice through the looking-glass? Why do I have to be catapulted into briar patches every time? It's not *dignified*. Oh, hello, Rosy. Spiggot? Kling. Whoops, that's some giant you've got there. How are you, big fellah? And the burgundy knight — and who's this — a newcomer?'

Jack obviously did not recognise himself. He stared at the other Jack, knowing there was something familiar about him, but unable to pin it down.

'Did we go to school together?' he queried.

'We shall fight to the death,' cried the other Jack. 'One of us has to go back to the land of the dead.'

'Eh?' said Jack. 'What's he on about, Rosy?'

Rosamund was pale and fearful. 'I know not what is and what is not,' she said, confusing the situation even more. 'I am in great doubt.'

Jobwot coughed into his fist. 'I think I can explain,' he said. 'This one,' he pointed to the Jack who had been raised from the dead, 'is a cipher. It looks like the original, and to a certain degree, sounds like it – but is not. There are wraiths in hell who can see into the world of the living, who latch on to some innocent creature there, following it as if on the other side of smoked glass, copying its walk, its speech, its habits. Gradually the wraith grows into a likeness of the mortal with whom it is obsessed. This is a shadow of the living Jack. The spell will throw up such creatures if the original is not there, in the land of the dead, to be removed. We have reached inside and, finding no *real* Jack, have pulled out something which resembles him. This is very bad. I have no idea how to send it back again.'

'Send me back?' cried the cipher, hands on hips. 'You've got a hope!'

'The other one,' said the giant, ignoring this last remark, 'is of course the real Jack, who has been attracted to this point like an iron filing to a magnet by the very presence of his cipher in the world.'

'You mean,' the real Jack said, 'if he *hadn't* been called here from the land of the dead, I would have missed this lot?' He indicated Spiggot and his friends. 'And would have landed up in any old well?'

'I believe so.'

'Then I have this copy of me to thank.'

'Don't bother,' sneered the cipher, contemptuously.

'Indeed,' explained Jobwot, with some regret, 'the reason that the two of you are now together, is because there must be a contest, between the two Jacks. Single combat. The winner remains in the world of the living, the loser goes to the world of the dead.'

Silence greeted this awful pronouncement. The real Jack had gone a ghastly grey colour. 'You mean I've got to fight myself, and win, in order to stay here?'

'I'm afraid so,' replied the giant.

'But this is a demon or something, isn't it? Can't we just send him back where he came from? Spiggot, don't you have spells for this sort of situation? Or you, burgundy knight? What about the big fellah, here? He seems to know a lot about it.'

Jobwot said, 'I can do nothing.'

Spiggot argued. 'Surely our Jack has more claim than the false one?'

'Not to my knowledge, which is vast, but not infallible,' replied Jobwot.

'You could be wrong?'

'Of course.'

The cipher said, 'Why doesn't someone ask me? I know everything. I'm also an expert at single combat, as all courtiers should be. Call me a shadow, call me a shade, I shall put Jack into his grave. I choose the axe for my weapon of war and will send this boy Jack to the land of hot tar.'

Jobwot nodded. 'This is certainly a cipher from the world of the dead. They have no ability to rhyme. It is beyond their ken. They get it almost right, but always fail in the end. The poets call it *bastard rhyme*. You will remember he tried to recite a Shakespeare sonnet earlier and somehow the ends of the lines came out wrongly. That's because he finds it impossible to rhyme with accuracy. The words twist in his throat, for poetry is too beautiful for the mouths of demons. Their tongues knot.'

'I can rhyme,' flashed the creature from hell. 'Listen to this! Jack be nimble, Jack be quick, Jack jump over the candle stock. No, wait. Wait. Listen. Jack Spit would eat no fat, his wife would eat no . . . Arrghh. I can, I can. Ding-dong-bell, pussy's in the wool. Never mind. I shall fight this usurper from the well. See, see, I *can* say *well*. You thought I couldn't. I can say *Sprat* and *stick* too.'

'But not to make them rhyme,' said Jobwot, 'no matter how hard you try.'

'Get him a weapon,' screeched the cipher. 'Arm him!'

A flint battleaxe had suddenly appeared in the cipher's hands. A second later he was suited in stone armour. No one had seen from whence these trappings had come. The weapon and the armour had formed from the air. The breastplate and helmet were of a slate mined from the very hillsides of Cumbria. The rest of the armour had the consistency and hue of wet granite, hacked from quarries north of the border. He had been armed by the very rock and dirt from which he came. The cipher peered through a slit in the stone helmet, his hard fiery eyes glaring at our Jack, promising no quarter, promising no mercy, promising naught but death.

'I don't want to fight,' said Jack, quietly.

'You don't have to do battle with yourself,' Jobwot told him. 'You can avoid the struggle by simply going home. You came through the wells, did you not? Return the same way you came. There's still time. No one will think badly of you. It is a terrible thing to fight with oneself.'

Jack looked at Rosamund. She stared back at him, plainly. There were no demands on her face. The decision was his.

'But what will happen to him – this creature who is me?'

'He will stay and continue to plague your friends.'

'They won't be able to get rid of him?'

'No, he is a pestilence.'

Jack turned to his stocky brown boggart friend and said quietly, 'May I borrow your armour, Spiggot?'

'Oh, Jack, as to that . . .' Spiggot began to protest, caught Kling's censuring eye, looked down, then said, 'Yes, of course, Jack.'

'Thank you.'

Jack went to the cart and took out the precious golden suit of armour. Spiggot helped him put it on. The armour, being magical, adjusted itself to Jack's size, fitting him comfortably. Spiggot then handed Jack the sword that Jack himself had helped to make: the sword with the deadly steel edge. Finally, Jack was ready for combat. His legs were shaking. In fact his whole body was shaking as the realisation hit him: he was about to fight himself to the death. There was no telling, of course, that he would not end up in some other weird place. (After all, he had been killed thrice now and each time had found himself either in the real world, or in Liöfwende). There must surely come a time though when he would truly be dead.

The cipher was swinging the battleaxe back and forth, making it swish through the air.

'Come on, come on,' growled the cipher. 'Let's get on with it.'

'What about crossbows?' cried our Jack, remembering that he had a magic crossbow. 'How about we settle it with crossbows?'

'Are you afraid of single combat with me?' cried the cipher, his eyes sending glints of light through the slit in the stone helmet. 'You can run away, you know. I shan't chase you. But you'll be despised and shunned – an outcast for the rest of your days.'

Jack glanced at Rosamund. 'Let's get to it,' he said, through gritted teeth.

'Wait!' cried Rosamund, and our Jack's heart lifted. Rosamund was going to object to the battle. She was going to save him from certain humiliation and defeat, and more likely, a horrible death.

'What is it, Rosy?'

The maiden stepped forward, removed a piece of green gauze from her pocket, and proceeded to tie it to her Jack's armoured wrist.

'A favour,' she said, 'for my champion.'

'Oh,' said her Jack, disappointed. 'Oh – thanks – thanks, Rosy.'

Jobwot then came across to him. The clouds had
lowered on the hilltops and Jobwot's head was above
them, out of sight. However, the giant bent very low
(which was difficult for such a huge creature), said
loudly, 'Good fortune be with you, Jack,' and then
whispered, 'Remember, attack his weakness, strike at his
soft spot. It's the only way you can win.' Then he
straightened up, his head and shoulders vanishing into
the clouds again, before Jack could ask, '*What weakness?
What soft spot?*'

Jack studied his adversary, clad from head to foot in
thick slate and granite. He could see no soft spot. All he
could see was a demon, ready to chop his head off at the
first opportunity, hidden behind a wall. How could you
fight a moving wall? It was more formidable than metal
armour. At the first stroke his sword would probably
shatter.

The cipher stepped forward, wielding his weapon.

'Prepare to die, mortal, for I shall crush you with the
first blow.'

FOUR

Jack skirted the cipher warily. He was not so intimidated now that the creature had his face hidden. It had all been a bit disconcerting when the cipher had been another Jack. Now he was just the enemy. Nevertheless, Jack had a tight lump in his throat. He had never, in his wildest nightmares, ever imagined he would be fighting himself at single combat to the death. It was difficult for him to believe he was doing it now.

'Come on, our side,' cried Kling. 'Stick him, Jack.'

Trust Kling to sit on the fence, Spiggot thought. Which Jack did he mean?

'Have at ye!' cried the cipher, stepping forward and swinging the mighty stone axe.

It missed Jack by a whisker. The granite blade smashed into an elm close to Jack's shoulder. A huge

white splintered gash appeared in the trunk. The whole
tree shuddered with the blow. A horrible thin scream
rent the air. It took Jack a moment to understand
where this came from. It was in fact the elm that had
screamed, having been sorely wounded. Jack had forgotten he was in a land where trees had feelings and
could give voice.

'Missed!' growled the cipher. 'Never mind, take this,
and this, and this.'

Jack had winced at the scream which the elm had let
out. He felt for the tree which had been an innocent
bystander. Diliberately he leapt between the stone knight
and the damaged trunk, determined to protect the vulnerable tree from further wounds. It was a brave thing to
do, for the cipher now had Jack's back against the wall
and could hammer away at him with the battle-axe,
knowing his victim could not retreat.

Jack's adversary began swinging wildly, right and left,
the battle axe crashing into stone and earth, as he came
on. Jack was nimble, Jack was quick. Jack jumped over
a deadwood stick. He could hear the others shouting
encouragement, but a realisation was coming over him.
The cipher might come out with bold talk and indeed
brag about his prowess, but the creature was not as
skilful as he pretended. Jack found himself able to
dodge the blows quite easily. He even tried a couple of
slashes himself, with the sword, but found as he sus-
pected that the blade clashed violently with the stone
armour and did no damage whatsoever.

The cipher was so well-protected Jack could not see
how he was ever going to wound the creature.

'I can't get in!' cried Jack to his well-wishers. 'There's no way – Ow!'

At last the cipher had struck him, just above the knee. The armour prevented any serious wound, but the force of the blow knocked Jack off his feet. He fell in the dust with a cry of dismay. He heard a groan of despair from his friends as the cipher stamped forward. Now he was really in trouble. He was no cat with nine lives. He had to die sometime.

Jack looked up, into the blinding sun, seeing the stone axe raised above him.

'Die, mortal!'

The shout was triumphant.

The battle axe began to descend. Jack remembered Jobwot's words.

Find his weak spot.

What was his weak spot? Jack would never know. The axe would fall and that would be that.

Just then Jack had some help from an unexpected quarter. The elm tree, incensed at being a victim of the axe, let fall a rotten old bough. It struck the stone knight, knocking him off balance. The axe glanced off Jack's helmet, sounding like a gong. Jack's head rung with the blow. He shook himself sensible then saw that the cipher had been knocked sideways and lay beside him in the dust. Jack climbed to his feet.

'How about we call it a draw?' he suggested. 'You go back to the land of the dead and I stay here with my friends?'

The stone knight's eyes glared from behind the slit in his helmet.

'Never! You die, or I die.'

'Fair enough,' Jack replied, at last recognising the cipher's weak spot. 'If that's the way you want it.'

With deadly accuracy, Jack thrust at the slit in the stone knight's helmet. The point slipped through the crack with a steely ringing note. There came the ghastly sound of metal piercing flesh and gristle. Then Jack withdrew the sword. There was blood on the blade. The stone knight got to his feet. Jack could no longer see the eyes behind the slit in the granite. Only a kind of inner darkness. In truth he felt rather sick. He could hear Rosamund, yelling herself hoarse in the background, but it was as if he were stumbling around in a dream. Someone, it sounded like Kling, was telling him to go in and finish it, but his stomach churned at the thought.

'You – you – bumbling oaf!' groaned the cipher, staggering back and forth. 'You've killed me. You've killed yourself.'

The creature tried swinging the axe at Jack's head, but it was a blind attempt. It spun the cipher slowly round and off his feet. He crashed to ground, face first. The stone axe shot out of his grip. The creature lay there, unmoving, while Jobwot reached down and picked up the axe. The giant threw the weapon, far away; an impressive throw. Then everyone surged forward, offering Jack congratulations. They stood over the stone knight and crowed.

Spiggot said, 'Jack, I'm so proud of you.'

'I gave him a chance to surrender,' Jack said, still feeling awful. 'I didn't want to hurt him.'

Jobwot sat down and picked Jack up in one hand,

peering at him through his quartz spectacles. He was a very wise giant and he knew how momentous this short combat had been. It was a battle which normally took place within men, but this being Liöfwende, alter egos and other such inner adversaries were manifest. Jack might well have been struggling with some part of his soul which was leading him to destruction. The combat might have been between him and an addiction to something unsavoury, something which would in the end destroy him. Or between himself and a decision which would lead to dishonour. Or between himself and something rotten within the state of Jack which had to be overcome.

'Jack, you have achieved one of the most difficult tasks that can ever face a living creature. You have defeated the enemy in you and have come out the victor. It could so easily have been different. Your inner enemy might have defeated you, leaving you wretched and ashamed. That must sound like gobbledegook, but it is perfect sense, believe me. I know it must feel like a sour success, for a man who had struggled with himself and won has to wonder if there is anything good to come of such a victory. However, it is a great thing you have done, though it might take some time for it to sink in. I am quite jealous of your talent to overcome such odds.'

Jack felt very humble. There was no pride in him at the moment, which was a good thing. There was only a kind of relief.

'Oh, Jack,' said Rosamund, when Jobwot put him down. 'How I feared for thee! Yet thou art a most magnificent knight. Did my favour help thee to thy victory?'

'This?' Jack touched the floating piece of gauze attached to his wrist. 'This was my soul's armour, Rosy.'

Now where had those fine words come from?

'Oh, Jack,' Rosamund blushed, looking away.

Kling stuck two claws down his throat and made retching noises to illustrate his disgust with the two mortals.

When the burgundy knight turned over the cipher, the stone suit of armour fell apart. The helmet, empty, rolled away down an incline. The legs, arms and torso simply fell away from each other. There was nothing in there. They left the pieces where they lay, amongst yellow ragwort and purple willow herb, to weather into ancient stone. The hollow granite would soon become a home for a swarm of insect-sized fairies known as drots, who every faerie decade went off with the wind and found a new hive for themselves, their old one being cluttered with echoes.

A fire had been lit. They all sat round it, staring into the flames as darkness fell. No one said anything for awhile. All that could be heard was the distant howling of grey wolves out in the night, the snuffle of stiff-haired wild boar in the thickets, the yelling of disgruntled goblins down in the valleys below, arguing about whose turn it was for the chores. In a forest not far away there were ominous munching sounds, and Spiggot wondered how many more oak and hornbeam roots were being eaten.

Various thoughts were going through the heads of those around the flames. Spiggot was admitting to himself that he felt a little envious of Jack: of his victory and the accolades he was receiving. Then he remembered he had a higher calling: to eradicate the land of the thrum and their underground kin. It made the boggart feel better.

Kling was thinking of his stomach and wondering if his tail was going to grow any longer.

The burgundy knight was lost in his own cryptic thoughts.

Rosamund was glowing with pride, knowing that her suitor had performed with great honour.

Finally Jobwot, whose head was once more above the clouds, bent down and spoke.

'In order to celebrate this most momentous day,' he said, 'I shall play you a tune on my magic flute and you must watch what develops from the music.'

'Ahhhh, magic,' murmured Kling. 'Good, Kling thinks. Cream puffs out of nothing? Bakewell tarts? Hot cross buns?'

While the giant was tuning his instrument, getting the pitch just right, Jack spoke to Spiggot.

'What I can't understand,' he said, 'is why the ulcugga fairies are supporting Mallmoc in this thing. Surely they're fairies too and as such love the oaks as much as any of you?

'That is indeed a mystery, Jack, but I have heard that Mallmoc is denying he has stolen the locking-stone to the cairn. He tells his fairies it is a plot to turn them against him. Mallmoc is a very persuasive creature, an ancient mortal with great powers, and it seems the ulcugga believe him. They believe their master and are convinced that others have stolen the stone to bring about his downfall.'

'He would,' snorted Jack. 'Devious.'

'Devious is the word.'

'Speaking of the ulcugga,' said Jack, 'there's one who helped me get back here, trapped in an antique shop back in Mortaland. She's been there for centuries and has almost faded away to nothing, but I said I'd try and rescue her. I think all this with Mallmoc happened after she left Liöfwende, so I don't consider her an enemy. Can we help her, Spiggot?'

At that moment, Jobwot began playing his tune: a haunting melody in a minor key. As he played the first of his floating notes turned to pure white feathers and the feathers gathered together in the air. The lament, for such it was, gradually formed into a beautiful white bird with trailing scarlet tail feathers. The lovely creature hovered above them in the firelight. Jack was completely enthralled, as was Rosamund, by this special talent of Jobwot, the best of giants. They watched as the bird, once completed, began an aerial dance. Such elegant celestial movements, bewitching in their sweeps and swoops, their twists and turns. Once the lament was over and the bird took flight, out into the darkness, there was a lump in every throat. No one quite knew why, but within each breast was a feeling of great sadness, of loss, of someone or something missed. An unquenchable yearning.

FIVE

The next day, they said farewell to Jobwot, that gentle and most intelligent giant. Jack started to tell him he was the most fascinating giant he had ever met, then realised he had met but a very few and that the compliment would be a bit lost. So in the end he stumbled through by saying that of all the *creatures* that Jack had met in Faerieland, Jobwot was the best. This of course upset his very good friend and companion Spiggot, who wanted to know why *he* was not the best. Jack tried to explain that present company didn't count. Of course, Spiggot was the very best, but he was not a stranger, he was almost family.

'You mean that, Jack?' asked Spiggot, as they wandered down the hillside towards the border. 'Like your own family?'

'Spiggot, you're a brother to me. You're a funny

fellow, all lumps and muscles, and hairy arms and legs, and don't look like me at all. But underneath, inside, we're almost identical twins. We're what they would call *soulmates* back home, except you haven't got a soul . . .'

'I haven't?' exclaimed the boggart, surprised.

'Well, I don't suppose so. I mean, you're faerie. Faerie are pagan creatures. They worship nature – rocks, trees, flowers, streams – all that sort of thing. Personally, I think paganism's got a lot going for it. One of your midnight revels, with birch-bark masks, reed flutes and log drums, and bonfires on which strange effigies are burned can be pretty exciting, and I don't think terrible things happen at them, do they? No one gets hurt, do they? No, I didn't think so. If you've got a soul, it's a green one, I bet.'

'So you think I might have?' asked the worried boggart.

'Well, I sort of think you've got *something* in there, somewhere. Not sure what it is, but I'll bet it's as good as what I've got,' replied Jack, generously.

Jack left Spiggot and dropped back to speak to Rosamund. She was wandering by herself, idly picking pink campion and herb robert, along with the occasional white bunch of pretty stitchwort, humming a tune which Jack might vaguely recognise as a medieval song of chivalry, if he had ever had cause to listen to such music, which he hadn't. Jack thought she looked just as cute as anything in her goblin's hose, but he kept his tongue in his head and carefully avoided looking at Rosamund's knees. She could be astonishingly shy about ankles, let alone anything above them.

'What's that you're humming, Rosy?'

She blushed, furiously, and said, ''Tis called, *Now I can delight in love*, or *Ar Mi Posi*. 'Twas writ by Peire Cardenal, who some say is the last of the great troubadours. I myself have heard him sing this song while accompanying himself on the dulcimer.'

'Do you know any more?'

'Yes – one of my favourites is *The Song of Nothing*. 'Tis the story of chivalry's quest for joy. Dost thou know of it, dear Jack?'

'Nope, too far back for me, Rosy. The oldest song in my book is *Peggy Sue* by Buddy Holly. I only know that 'cause my dad's a fifties fanatic. He used to play that over and over because of Mum. Her name's Peggy, too, but her middle name's Joan. Doesn't really go, does it . . .' He began singing, 'Peggy Joan, Peggy Joan, pretty, pretty, pretty, pretty Peggy Joan, oh Peggy, my Peggy Jo-oooan!'

Rosamund put her hands over her ears.

'Well, it's not that bad,' grumbled Jack.

''Tis much like a watermill with the stone worn out of shape, dear Jack. It grates. 'Tis like a rusty iron gate that has never seen the like of olive oil. 'Tis like the creaking of a winded horse after a gallop . . .'

'All right, all right, I get the picture. Look, Rosy, there's a nice flower over there. You know all the wild flowers, don't you? What's that one? The pale white thing by that rotten log?'

'Wood anemone,' she said, promptly. 'I shall not pluck it, for it is one alone and 'twould be a great shame.'

'Better not, either,' said the log, 'or you'll get an earful from me.'

Rosamund went pale. 'Did it speak, Jack?'

'Yep, I've had this before,' said Jack. 'Rocks and bits of wood making remarks. You have to watch yourself in this place. There's no telling what's alive and what's not. Hey, log! What's up?'

'The sky for a start.'

'Ha. You haven't seen any ulcugga fairies around, have you?'

'Not for a long time. We had a hunting party through here, several years ago. I remember it was a winter's day, with the snow thick on the boughs, falling with a soft *plop* every so often. They came riding through here with blood in their eyes, chasing a red deer. That was some time ago, though. One of them jumped me, I remember, and his horse's hind hooves caught me a whack as he went over. They don't care, the ulcugga.'

They passed through that mossy place, with its stagnant pools overhung by twisted elder, and out into a wide meadow. On the far side of the meadow was a brook. There was no bridge, only stepping stones, so there was no need to fear trolls. The party reached the brook and began to cross, when suddenly a group of faerie came out of some gorse bushes on the far side. They were brownies, led by a killmoulis, a queer-looking brownie who normally resides in human mills. The ordinary brownies were armed with sickles and scythes and seemed hostile. Spiggot immediately donned his armour and told Kling to keep to the rear with the cart. The burgundy knight went first, then Spiggot, and Jack and Rosamund took up the rear.

'That's as far as ye go,' said the killmoulis, who so far as Jack could see had a huge nose for a face, but no mouth. Its voice came out of the hanging hair of its cavernous nostrils and when it spoke its curled ears twitched violently. 'That, and nay further, ye ken. This here's the border, which we guard wi' our weapons o' war.'

The burgundy knight ignored this warning and hopped from the last stepping stone on to the bank.

'I warned ye!' shrieked the killmoulis, the brownies crowding round him. 'Another step and ye'll be screechin' fer yer mither.'

'Ah havenae got a mither,' snapped the burgundy knight, in perfect imitation of the killmoulis's accent. 'So dinna fash yersel. Ah havenae got a fether, else. Away an' blaw yer face, ye silly scunner. Yer all snot and snuffle, so ye are. Bogeys fer brains, that's whut ye have.'

The killmoulis's head came up with a jerk. He looked as infuriated as any nose could look at being told to blow itself. Yet he was unsure of himself now. The burgundy knight sounded as if he came from north of the border. It could be that he was a good mimic, but there was a confidence to him that worried the brownie chief. There was no telling who was behind that reddish-purply armour. Could be that a great laird or Highland fairy chieftain was inside the dragon skin.

Spiggot, in turn, confronted one of the brownies. 'Stand aside, mountain faerie.'

'Woodland folk,' hissed the brownie. 'We want nay woodland folk up here.'

'Heather folk,' snapped Spiggot. 'Stand aside and let me pass.'

'Will not.'

'Will and will again, unless you want your nose tweaked and your eyes to water.'

At this point, the burgundy knight thought it advisable to remove his helmet for the first time. He now revealed his identity. Lank red locks fell about the creature's shoulders. They were tied with strips of rag torn from tartan cloth. He had high cheekbones that were so sharp at the points they looked about to pierce the skin of his face. His eyes were hard and sharp as quartz chippings. Staring at the killmoulis, who had backed away quickly, he said, 'Now ye see who it is that yer dealing with, Borderer.'

'Aye,' replied the killmoulis in a low reverent voice, 'an unseelie court, so ye are.' The great nose looked round for his brownie friends, only to find they had vanished into the mist. 'Ye'll be wantin' to cross the burn, I'm thinkin',' said the nose, 'so I'll just be stepping out of yer path. Ah've just recalled that ah've some messages to run.'

The killmoulis now left them, humming a deep vibrating note through the nasal passages in his face. He walked away, trying to appear casually uninterested in life in general, while clearly terrified out of his skin.

Jack said to the burgundy knight, 'I've seen you before, haven't I? In Standing Stone City, King Cimberlin's place.'

'Ye have indeed, mortal.'

'You certainly managed to disguise your accent.'

'It wisna easy. Mah throat feels aye tangled. Now, ye'll be wondering why ah'm here with ye. It was King

Cimberlin who asked me tae watch out for ye, till ye crossed the border. Ah've done mah best, but yer on yer own now. Ah'm away back, to Northumberland.'

'But,' said Jack, 'if you're a friend, why hide your identity from us?'

'It wisna you, it was them in Eri-innis. There's nay love lost between leprechauns and the seelie and unseelie courts. It's a sair job ye have, boggart,' he said, addressing Spiggot, 'tae unite the two fairy nations against Mallmoc. Gude luck tae ye, and may ye fare well.'

All the while he had been speaking he had been divesting himself of his armour. When he had finished, he gathered the armour up in his thin arms. Then he unfolded those dragonfly wings and took to the air, leaving Jack and Spiggot staring after him in awe. There was a flash of colours as the sun caught his wings, then he was gone amongst the clouds.

PART SIX

The eyes of an eagle

ONE

'Well, I think he might have told us who he was before that,' grumbled Spiggot. 'These fairies think they're just the bee's knees, don't they?'

The boggart was slashing with his sword at some delicate clary flower that sprouted from the foot of a drystone wall as he spoke. The group were walking past a loch, the sun shining on it as on a silver disc. In the background were the dark-purple mountains, louring as it were, down upon them. Spiggot felt very insecure in such a place, used as he was to the gentle rolling downs of his native southern Liöfwende. There was too much drama here in the north, both in the scenery and in its folk. He was, at heart, a gentle creature who got rid of all his isms by bashing at iron with a heavy hammer. All this tension and tautness of the northern fairies, all these eagles flying around, all these thunderstorms and stuff, all these dark mountains, why, they made a boggart feel very vulnerable.

And every so often the quivvel trembled gently, for there were many cairns in Thristlac, with many locking-stones.

'D'ye mind?' cried a shrill metallic voice, as Spiggot ran his sword point over the surface of a pool they were passing. 'Are ye quite finished?'

Kling shook his head, asking, 'Who said that? It made Kling's head ring. Kling thought someone had twanged his brain stem.'

'Don't know,' replied Spiggot, jumping back.

Rosamund said, ''Twas a voice from the pool.'

'A really *irritating* voice,' added Jack.

Suddenly, a physically horrible creature broke the surface of the pond. It was not easy to describe, being of a greenish hue, but Jack thought it looked goatish, sort of, but at the same time, stoatish and a touch wolfish. Certainly, it had arms and legs, a thin gruesome torso, and a large elongated head from which sprouted clumps of coarse hair. There were eyes in there, somewhere, buried beneath folds of greasy skin above the stubbled cheeks, and a long thin nose that curved downwards towards its own navel. The joints of its fingers and toes were large and knobbly, and wicked-looking nails kept springing into view.

'Can a body no enjoy the pleasures of his ain pool, wi'out disturbance frae the likes o' you?' enquired this strange, ugly creature.

Spiggot, who had been searching his mind for the name of the being, suddenly found it in a dusty corner of his brain marked 'solitary creatures'.

'You're an urisk,' he said.

'So whut?'

'No, nothing. Just wanted to classify you, that's all,' replied Spiggot, sounding the knowledgeable scholar to his friends. 'You might have been kelpie, shellycoat or selkie. This is your pool? You live here alone?'

'Aye.' The urisk folded its thin arms, as if expecting an argument. Then he seemed to notice Rosamund and Jack for the first time. 'Aaaahhh, mortals,' he said, turning shy.

'Don't you like mortals?' asked Jack.

'They're mah favourites,' replied the urisk, with a gruesome smile.

Rosamund let out a sharp exhalation of breath, thinking as she was that the urisk meant as a food. It did not. It simply liked the company of humans and in the real world it sought them out, followed them home, made itself very unwelcome by its constant presence, its desire to be friendly. It was worse than a spaniel when it came to fawning. It was a closer companion and less desirable than a louse.

Thus when the group continued on its way, the urisk trailed along after them. It kept touching Jack's heels as he walked, plucking at his socks and trouser bottoms with its toes. When Jack turned round and glared, the urisk gave him one of its horrible curving smiles. Pretty soon Jack's temper frayed. Apart from anything else the urisk smelled of rotting pond weed and its presence was offensive to the mortal youth.

'Look, what do you want? Go away, will you? We're looking for the seelie and unseelie courts and they won't want to see you with us.'

The last was a sort of threat, to banish the urisk. However, the obsequious creature simply stared at Jack with a hurt look on its face.

'What have ah done tae fash ye?' asked the urisk in a whine. 'D'ye no have feelings, man?'

'Yes, I have feelings – right now, I feel annoyed with you.'

'Annoyed, but no angry?'

'Angry as well.'

'Och, that's no fair. Ah've done nothing tae upset ye.'

'Except follow me all over the place and keep tugging at my shoelaces.'

Spiggot cried, 'Come on, Jack. Stop messing around with that urisk. Catch up, will you?'

Jack ran and caught up with the others. He took Rosamund's hand because she was stumbling amongst the rocks, still hindered by having only shadow-sight. The urisk now turned his attentions to the maiden, pulling at her hair which hung long down her back. She found this just as irritating as Jack had done, but she was more used to being treated as an object of affection, and so was able to stand it without retaliating. The group continued walking through the mountains, the glens, crossing burns, skirting lochs, until they reached a place where it was suitable to camp.

Jack and Rosamund, like the others, were tired. Both found a mossy place and lay down to sleep for a hour. Kling shed his harness and enquired whether there was any 'raspberry coulis' to go on the bread that Spiggot was handing out. Spiggot himself sought the shade, for like Liöfwende, Thristlac's weather was governed by the fairies. They liked spring weather, neither too hot nor too cold, with the occasional brief blast of winter to make a change. Thus, the cool breezes that blew across the heather-covered mountains, bringing soft scents of wild flowers and the murmuring of ptarmigan in the heights, soon served to lull Jack to sleep.

Jack woke with a start to find he was being cuddled, but not by Rosamund or anyone who looked remotely like a human. The odour of mud and pond weed was unbearable. As was the touch of a squamas creature which might have crawled out of a black lagoon.

'What are you doing?' cried Jack, jumping up and shedding the urisk with a shudder. 'Get off, get off!'

The urisk looked sulky. 'I like ye, Jack.'

'Well, I don't like you. Frankly I find you a bit creepy, if you don't mind me saying so.'

'Is that an insult or a compliment?'

'Neither, it's just a statement of fact. Now, will you stop following me, or do I have do something drastic?'

'Like whut?'

Jack called his bumble bees. They left their position on the cart and came swarming to him, covering him like a shirt. Jack actually hated the feel of them, crawling all over him, but he warned the urisk that they stung and that the creature would suffer if it touched him any further.

'That's no fair,' cried the urisk. 'Ah've done nothin' to deserve this, have ah?'

'Yes, you have. You've bothered me. And if you don't leave now, I'll order my bees to sting you. As you can see, there's thousands of them, so it could be pretty nasty.'

'Huh!' The urisk said, eyeing the bees with great suspicion. 'Bumble bees dinna sting.'

'They sting like fury,' said Spiggot, having woken up himself. 'They'll sting someone with a soft skin like you, easily enough.'

'Huh!'

Clearly the urisk was not very sure of himself and eventually he wandered away, looking back over his shoulder every few paces in case Jack changed his mind. Once the urisk was out of sight, Jack sent his bees back to the cart.

'I wish you'd warn me about all these faerie we keep coming into contact with,' he complained to Spiggot. 'You're supposed to be my guide in this weird and wonderful land of yours. Listen, I need to know how to get my faded fairy back into Liöfwende. I promised her. Can you put your mind to it? You, too, Kling. Sometimes you're good at these things.'

'Kling is good at most things.'

'All right, what do we do?'

'Magic,' replied Kling. 'Magic is what you need. If you know the name of the fairy, it would be easier to call her back.'

'She didn't tell me her name. She couldn't. She'd been there so long she'd forgotten it.'

'Not good,' said Kling. 'A rat would never forget its name.'

'That isn't helping,' said Jack through gritted teeth. 'A rat is neither here nor there.'

'A rat is here, not there. All right, all right, Kling is thinking. You could *give* the fairy a name. Be its mother, so to speak. Once you do that, though, the name would have to stick. Better be clear and sure that she'll like what you give her, or the whole thing could become a nightmare for you, Jack.'

'Why don't you name her? Or Spiggot?'

The boggart shook his head. 'I'm not naming any fairy. You don't know what you're asking, Jack. You don't seem to realise we have a strict hierarchy here in Faerieland. It would be like – like you naming one of your Queen Elizabeth's babies. I mean, she would chop off your head if she didn't like it, wouldn't she?'

'Queen Elizabeth is not allowed to chop off heads.'

Spiggot protested. 'Oh, come on, Jack, that's a bit rich. She's already lopped off quite a few. Her half-sister Mary's for one. Several of her courtiers. That's what she's good at, hacking off heads.'

Jack said, 'You're talking about Queen Elizabeth the First!'

'Is there another one?' Spiggot said, his face frowning in puzzlement. 'We are speaking of the Virgin Queen, Gloriana.'

'No, we're not. I live in the twenty-first century, Spiggot, not the sixteenth.'

'Well, anyway, you understand what I'm saying. It would be a terrible thing if I gave a fairy the wrong name. A terrible thing.'

'What about if I did it?'

'Even worse.'

'Well, I'm going to. And the first creature we meet

with any magical powers, I'm going to recall her to Liöfwende. She's fading fast, back there. She needs to be here, to restore herself.'

'What shall Jack call her?' asked Kling. 'Give us a name.'

'What about Titania?'

Spiggot scoffed. 'That's not an ulcugga name.'

'Well, what is, then?'

'Something like, Raminago'bris.'

'Right, then.'

Spiggot gave his mortal friend a crafty look and laughed again. 'Ha! Fooled you, Jack. That's the name of a cat who used to live in Liöfwende. A talking cat who was a vile poet, but thrust its evil rhymes into the hands of wayfarers. Travellers used to dread being accosted by Raminago'bris, and having to read her poems out loud to the birds and trees, before the cat would let them go.'

'Too bad, Spiggot,' said Jack, his eyes narrowing. 'You've already gone and named my fairy.'

Spiggot swallowed hard. Jack had tricked him.

'I – I didn't. You can't do this to me, Jack.'

'I already have,' said Jack, airily. 'My faded fairy has been given the name of Raminago'bris, by the boggart Spiggot. It's over and done with. Now all that remains is to find a magician.'

TWO

'Fairies are the most numerous, with pixies and elves close behind,' Kling was explaining to Jack and Rosamund. 'Fairies swarm over Liöfwende, Thristlac and Eri-innis. Pixies are found mostly to the south-west, while elves are mostly midland and southern. As for the rest: goblins and their cousins, like the master's son; brownies; trolls; gnomes; dwarves and all those others, they're not found in any great numbers. They live scattered amongst the vast fairy tribes. The vastest of which . . .' He paused to regather his thoughts, realising that 'vastest' did not sound right. 'The biggest of which are the ulcugga hordes.'

'That's why the fairies control these islands?' Jack said.

'No,' replied Kling. 'They hold the power because they are powerful. There is nothing to withstand a fairy except another fairy.'

'So,' said a still incensed Spiggot, 'you see what you've
got me into, Jack? Now I shall have an ulcugga fairy
after my tail. Raminago'bris? What was I thinking of,
giving you that name?' Spiggot's worried frown marred
his otherwise pleasant countenance. 'Every time I think
about what you made me do it feels like there's a cow
kneeling on my chest.'

'I'm telling you, Spiggot,' replied Jack, 'this fairy will
be so grateful to get back into Liöfwende, she'll kiss you
till you bleed. You don't know how distressed she is, just
fading into nothing. Hundreds of years she's been
trapped in that shop. Can you imagine how *bored* she is?'

'You don't know fairies. They do not know the
meaning of the word "grateful". Once she's here, all those
years will be instantly forgotten. What will be remembered is the horrid name I've given her.'

'Spiggot, dear, she will be in thy thrall,' said Rosamund,
seeking to bring the argument to an end. 'Now, Jack, wilt
thou not take thy magic crossbow and shoot for us an
hind for our supper?'

'A deer?' cried Jack. 'Shoot a creature with melty-
brown eyes looking at me? You've got to be joking, Rosy.
I'll go out and get us a hare . . . no, not a hare,' he back-
tracked hastily, when he saw Spiggot's horrified
expression. 'Hares are sacred animals, aren't they? And
they have to be hung for days on end, don't they? No, a
rabbit then, or a partridge or something. Don't you
worry, I'll find us some meat. I'm fed up with Spiggot's
mushrooms, too. The hunter is going hunting!'

Jack went to the cart, collected his crossbow, and
then set off over the white heather. Always keeping the

camp in view, for he was aware it was easy to become lost in Faerieland, especially when the ferns grew to head height and the ground dipped and rose as it did in Scotland. He saw one or two red stag and a lot of quail, but nothing he could really shoot. The stags were too big (and had those eyes) and the quail were too small. There were mountain hares, of course, which did not run in zigzag fashion like English hares, but in a sort of wide arc. Once he saw a wildcat and had to stop to let his racing heart catch up with itself. He did try to catch a salmon in a river, but it slipped through his fingers and he lost it, silver fish amongst silver water, wet-grey scales against smooth, wet-grey stones.

It was a pleasant walk though, amongst the aromatic hills.

Finally, he shot a rabbit. The arrow from the crossbow changed into hawk in flight, chasing the prey, then back into an arrow again on impact. This was the magic of the bow. Jack slung the dead rabbit over his back and set off towards camp again. As he was walking through some bracken, he tripped in a hole and his crossbow went flying. He searched for it, finding it at last amongst the ferns, cursing as he did so. Along with his bow he made a remarkable find: there amongst the heather, he discovered a cache, a horde of treasure.

There was a beautiful sword, a claymore so wonderful in its craftsmanship it took his breath away. There was also a golden torc which looked immensely valuable, a diamond necklace, a soft leather belt encrusted with emeralds and rubies, and a gold-dragon buckle, a bronze pin with an opal end, probably from a brooch or clasp, and finally a pair of silver shoes.

'Oh, wow!' whispered Jack, to himself. 'Like a trove or something!'

It was the claymore which fascinated him most. It was a weapon for more than a fairy king, with its caged hilt made of filigree gold. It had a long curved blade, thicker in the centre than at the two ends. Jack could see from the patterns in the blade that it had been fashioned from at least four different sorts of iron rods, beaten flat, but their shapes forming swirling forms.

'Oh, my,' said Jack, gathering up this bounty. 'I must show Spiggot these. He can have the silver shoes. And Rosy can have the necklace. Kling can have the golden torc. I shall keep the sword.' He put on the belt and stuck the sword in it. 'And if I meet any aggressor on the way back, I shall cut him down with my new blade, as if mowing grass.'

He did indeed meet two creatures. The first was a giant wolf with thick bristling hair and a row of teeth that looked as if they could crunch rocks to powder. Jack unslung his crossbow and he and the wolf gave each other a wide berth, one going to the left of the path, the other to the right, each keeping a wary eye on the other, neither wanting a confrontation.

Next, Jack met a grey-bearded dwarf, a powerfully-built creature, shorter than himself. They confronted each other, in the middle of a log bridge crossing a burn. The dwarf did not seem inclined to give way. Jack, too, was feeling rather bumptious and refused to back up. The pair of them stood there, glaring at one another.

Finally, the thick-set dwarf drew a hammer from his belt with one of his large hands. Jack immediately whipped out the claymore and stood ready to do battle.

The dwarf spoke. 'Hoots mon, oota-ma-wah, who d'ye think ye arrrrrgggghhh.'

The strength of the accent made Jack want to laugh.

'Who do I think I am? I am the steel-sword wielder, that's who I am, wild thing.'

'Oh,' said the dwarf in a less heavy accent, 'you're not the fachan. No, of course you're not. You've got two legs and the fachan has only one . . .'

'Like the Irish giants.'

'I don't know about that,' replied the dwarf, 'but you've got to talk to the fachan in his own language, or he'll spit fire at you. Anyway, mortal youth, if you'll just retreat, I'll be on my way.'

'How about *you* back up or I'll slice you in two?'

The dwarf blinked. 'You'd kill a child, just to cross a bridge?'

'Child? You look about a hundred-and-one with that grey beard and wizened face. I don't want to be cruel, but age has been harsh with your features, matey. You've got a fizzog craggier than the face of Ben Nevis, and slightly more ashen about the temples.'

'I'm only seven,' came the astonishing reply.

Jack found this difficult to believe. 'Seven? Seven years old?'

'Yes. Dwarves are born *looking* old, a bit like gnomes. My beard was grey before I was six. We can't help it, it's just the way we are.'

'Seven!' repeated Jack. He rallied. 'Yet, still, you've

got the body of a wild boar. You could give me a good fight.'

'I don't want to fight. I want to go home. If you're not the fachan, then you have to let me cross. I can't go backwards. My feet won't let me. Please, mister . . .'

Jack sighed and retreated. The dwarf-child crossed, said thank you in a very nice manner, and left Jack still holding the deadly blade he had found in the bracken. He stuck it in his belt again and continued on to the camp. There he found his friends waiting impatiently for the meat. He gave Kling the rabbit. Kling skinned and gutted it within record time, stuck it on a sharpened stick, and began roasting the meat over glowing charcoal. Jack, in the meantime, produced his treasures.

'Look at these,' he said, joyfully. 'You can all take your pick, but I'm keeping the sword.'

Spiggot went slightly pale and reached out. 'Show me that claymore, Jack.'

'I'm keeping it,' said Jack, eyeing his friend warily. 'It's mine.'

'I just want to look at it.'

Jack reluctantly handed it over. Spiggot took it as if it were a venomous snake and studied it carefully. Then he handed it back to Jack.

'It's a good job you didn't fight anyone with that weapon,' said the boggart. 'You wouldn't be here now, if you had.'

'I nearly did. Only he turned out to be an infant.'

'You had a lucky escape then, Jack. That weapon's name is "Greyblade". You can see it, etched on the metal. It's a famous sword – or rather, infamous. It always brings its owner ill-luck. It's fatal, going from hand to hand, but always the new owner is murdered or killed in battle. You should get rid of that blade now, Jack. Fling it into the heather. Let someone else find it.'

'Like you?' asked Jack, suspiciously.

'No, and thank you for the offer of the other presents, but they are all fatal gifts. That necklace is from the throat of Queen Bridey, who cursed it on her death. It burns the neck of the wearer. The golden torc will strangle. It was fashioned as a slave torc by a spiteful fairy princess who could only keep her lovers by force. If they tried to run away, the torc shrank, and kept shrinking until it had cut off their heads. The silver shoes! Ah, yes, made of course by the leprechauns we have just left behind in Eri-innis. The wearer puts them on and again the shoes shrink until his feet have been crushed to a pulp and he is crippled for the rest of his life.'

Jack looked down at the shoes. 'Nasty,' he said at last, beginning to believe his friend. 'Those shoes, eh?'

'Believe me, Jack. The golden pin? Use it and it will worm its way through your clothing, into your flesh, and eventually find its way through your body until it reaches your heart, which it pierces without mercy. The waistband I do not know.' He peered closely, while Jack, realising he was still wearing the jewelled belt, took it off in a panic, expecting to be cut in half at any second.

'Well, what shall I do with all this stuff?' said the disappointed mortal youth. 'I can't just chuck it away, can I?'

'Best thing, Jack,' advised Kling. 'Kling agrees with the master's son.'

'Ay, Jack dear, do as they say,' said Rosamund. ''Tis not wise to meddle with poisonous magic.'

Jack shrugged and took the items to the edge of a clearing, where there was a waterfall dropping into a pool. He threw everything but the silver shoes into the pool. Within seconds the crystal clear waters turned to blood. Jack went as pale as the moon just rising above the mountains. He felt sick. What if he had used the sword? That would have been fatal. He didn't like word *'fatal'*. It had a sort of final ring to it. Lucky for him he was travelling with a boggart who knew his magical, mythical stuff. Jack put the shoes in his backpack and then went back to the others.

'Thanks Spiggot,' he said, quietly. 'Good job you know about these booby traps creatures leave lying around.'

'You can't live in Liöfwende without knowing, Jack. I mean, you're just a visitor here. You can't be expected to know. It would be a disgrace if I didn't.'

They all tucked into the rabbit with great gusto. Afterwards, Kling cut a reed, fashioned a flute, and charmed them all with his repertoir of ancient rat tunes. They were weird, but haunting in their melodies – the ghosts of songs, rather than the songs themselves. Jack wondered when rats had had the time, or the inclination, to write such music, but Kling told him nothing was written down.

'It's all in the head,' said the water rat. 'Or is it the tail?'

Now that Jack had heard the songs, added Kling, he would never forget them.

It was true. As Jack was trying to sleep that night, the tunes kept invading his privacy, intruding, wouldn't go away. He got up, walked about, tried to think of other things, but the songs wouldn't leave him alone.

In the middle of the night, he did manage to cast them off. It was shock that did it. The seelie court came and roused them from their birch-twig beds. One moment the camp was quiet, with a lifeless pallid moon peeking through tors, and the next it was seething with thin sharp-eyed creatures whose breath hissed from their mouths.

The seelie court, unlike the unseelie court, are wingless fairies. They are said to be not as vicious or viperous as their winged cousins. But Jack still found them a terrifying set of creatures.

They carried the four companions off, literally, to a mountain fastness, where they left them until the dawn came. Then Spiggot, Jack, Rosamund and Kling went through a frightening ordeal. Forced to run the gauntlet, they were prodded through lines of fairies with angled bones, whose breath smelled of lavender but who spat at them with their eyes. The tongues of the seelie court lashed out, stinging the flesh at which they struck. The nails on their hands and feet were talons. They used these to prick their victims, to spur them on. Jack was told by Spiggot that the points were poisoned. Any hesitation and a seelie court nail would break the skin. The pierced victim would end up writhing on the ground, in terrible pain.

'Nice fairy folk,' said Jack, bitterly. 'Nice hospitality. I wish I'd saved some of those *nice* booby traps I found.

It would do my heart good to see that one over there choked by a golden torc. Or the one with the long hair scalded by a red-hot necklace. Or him standing on the rock chopped in half by the belt with gems round it. Wee gifties for the nice fairy folk. Yeah, that would have sorted one or two of them out . . .'

At these words, all festivities ceased. The seelie court fell as silent as death all around them. Jack was the centre of attention.

THREE

They stood on the hillside, in the clean clear air amongst the scented heather, amongst the bracken brakes and the tall perfumed pines. Then, out from behind an outcrop of rocks, through the crowd of lean, hard-looking fairies, came another of their number. His red hair seemed to crackle with each flick of his locks. Tiny white sparks flew from his eyes. There was such grace in his movements he could have been a dancer. Yet there was also strength there, of body and spirit. Clearly this was the clan chieftain, for he was a head taller than the rest of them and had an imperious air about him. He strode forward and fixed Jack with an unflickering gaze.

'Whut *belt*?' he asked.

'The – er – a jewelled belt.'

'A jewelled belt wi' rubies an' emeralds? A jewelled

belt wi' a gold buckle in the shape of a dragon? A belt of
the finest leather that was ever softened by squirrels'
teeth? Was *that* the belt?'

'Yes, that was the belt thee had, Jack,' said
Rosamund. 'Thee must remember the shining red and
green stones?'

Jack was unsure of himself now. 'Well, it was just one
of a number of fairy booby traps I found in the bracken.
I can't be sure that the gems were rubies and emeralds.
Or that the buckle was made of gold. I threw it away
with the rest of the booby traps, of course, as Spiggot
told me to.'

Spiggot sucked in his breath and shook his black
mane.

'Oh, I didn't tell you to, Jack. I don't think I even saw
them,' the boggart's face was deathly white. 'I'm almost
sure I didn't. That is, *I saw* them, but . . .' His voice
trailed away.

Jack was incensed at this betrayal. 'What a liar!' he
said. Then he remembered that most faerie folk regarded
lying as a proper means of weaselling out of responsibility, so he added, 'And a traitor, too!'

'Traitor, is it?' said the chieftain, turning his terrible
gaze on Spiggot, whose head now hung lower, his hair
over his boots. 'Ye'd betray yer own servant and his slattern, whud ye?'

Jack was about to protest that he was no servant, but
he wisely kept his mouth shut. Rosamund was not going
to let *anyone* call her a slattern, though, fairy chieftain or
not.

'Slattern?' she cried. 'No kitchen slut am I, but a

baron's daughter, high-born. Thou hast the manners of a hog and art an oaf besides.'

The seelie court let out a unified, horrified gasp, but the chieftain merely smiled.

'If ye can return my belt to me – for 'tis certainly the belt which was stolen from me, probably by some boggart thief from south of the border – I shall forget the insult from the pretty lassie.'

Jack hastily described the pool into which he had flung the booby traps and the chieftain sent several seelie court to investigate. The fairies returned, triumphantly waving the belt. The king put it on and seemed to grow in stature. Once again he put his gaze upon the prisoners.

'Ye think we're no hospitable, is that it?' said the seelie court king, stepping forward. 'Is that whut ye were trying tae say earlier?'

'That's the gist of it,' Jack replied, folding his arms in defiance. 'That's the plain truth of it.'

'Oh dear, Jack's going to be given the head of a pig,' groaned Spiggot. The boggart stepped bravely forward. 'Look, he doesn't know what he's saying. He's just a mortal, after all. Now, I'm faerie, and I'll fight any one of you in single combat, if you'll ignore what my friend has just said. Any one of you.'

Spiggot went to Kling's cart. The fairies parted for him, letting him through. He began to put on his armour in a determined way. The seelie court chieftain's eyes lost a little of their fierceness. He shook a wicked shock of red hair which hung to his waist. He turned his intense gaze, first on Jack, then on Spiggot.

'Tak off yer armour, boggart,' said the king at last, in a voice of flint. 'This mortal says we're no hospitable. Why, ye only have tae ask. Have ye no a tongue in yer head, mortal?'

Jack gulped. If he was not afraid before, which of course he had been, he was terrified now. Now that the king's demeanour had softened, he appeared even more terrible. It seemed there were mountains growing from his shoulders. It appeared there were forests in his face. And all up and down his long body were elongated rivers flowing with torrents of water. This was the most powerful of fairies and Jack had the feeling he could be physically crushed by a mere stare. He gulped again, and said in tremulous tones, 'Could – could we avail ourselves of your hospitality, sir?'

'Huh!' muttered the king. 'Sassenachs and their "sirs". Time was we used tae eat sassanachs, if they wisna too stringy. Well, laddie, ye can have yer hospitality. The seelie court are not known fer meanness, not like the unseelie court, who whud eat ye whether ye were stringy or no.'

'Actually,' said Jack, growing bolder again, 'we have a friend amongst the unseelie court.'

'A friend, ye say?' replied the king. 'Ah think not. Ye may *know* some fairy amongst 'em, but he's no yer friend, ah can vouch fer that wi'out even speakin' to him. No unseelie court whud befriend a mortal.'

Jack admitted, 'Well, he travelled with us.'

'That's different, laddie. Travelling. Huh! Well, now, be on yer way, back to Liöfwende wi' ye, travellers.'

'But, sire,' said Rosamund, 'we came to seek thy help. It was thee with whom we came to speak. Liöfwende is in the thrall of underground faerie, called the thrum. They are eating all the oaks and must soon begin on the elms and other trees. Not only must they be stopped, but a plug must be placed on the cairn from whence they emerge. This is in the hands of a wicked sorcerer named Mallmoc, an ancient magician from the Aquitaine court of my own time, who has somehow discovered a passage to Liöfwende. Mallmoc is protected by the ulcugga fairy race, one of the most numerous here in Faerieland, so I have been told. Canst thou not assist us?'

The chieftain peered at the distracted way in which Rosamund was addressing him. She appeared to be staring over his left shoulder.

'Whut's wrang with the maid's eyes?'

Spiggot answered the seelie court chief, 'She loaned them to the west country pixies and they have not returned them.'

'They widnae. Yet she sees a wee bit?'

'She was given the power of shadow-sight.'

'Well, I think we can do better than that, hen,' said the chieftain. 'How whud ye like the eyes of an eagle?'

'Any eyes would be better than none,' replied Rosamund, 'if it please thee, my gracious lord.'

It seemed that a golden eagle had fallen, like a thunderbolt, from the sky just a week ago. The fairies, who waste nothing, had taken its claws, beak, feathers and eyes. The eyes had been preserved by enchantment and were now to be given to Rosamund. One of the seelie court stepped forward and pressed them into her head. The fairy magic did its work. Rosamund stepped back, blinked several times, and announced she could see.

'Not only can I see, dear Jack,' Rosamund cried, 'but mine eyes are sharper than light. On my oath I can see for a hundred miles! These are good eyes, keen eyes, eyes that can see almost into for ever. Oh, I thank thee, sire, for thy kindness,' she said to the fairy chieftain.

'Hazelly eyes,' said Jack, disappointed. 'I liked the blue ones.'

'Well, Jack, this is still me.'

'Yes, and a beautiful you, but I just liked the blue eyes. It doesn't matter. The hazel ones will do. As you say they can see into eternity or whatever.'

Spiggot said, 'Mallmoc? Does he really come from your time? Did you know him then?'

'I have recalled there was one Mal du Morc, a wizard or magician as such, in the Aquitaine. This creature, I was told, was an evil being. The queen of Aquitaine had ordered him to be hung, drawn and quartered, but Mal du Morc disappeared in a sudden storm with his guards, when they were escorting him to the execution gallows. When the storm abated, Mal du Morc was gone, leaving four soldiers of the queen dead on the ground. Their heads were twisted back-at-front, as were their arms and legs. Their eyes, tongues and – and other bodily parts – had been torn from their roots. Their hair had turned a ghostly white and the tragic expressions on their faces showed they had seen something of great horror, for their teeth protruded from their mouths as if forced outwards by some great exhalation of air, or perhaps because their spirits were forced to flee their bodies in great haste.

'Thou hast never seen such horror. Even their black-ened fingers and toes attested to the fear that had overcome them, like a blast from hell. Not long after this event, the queen mysteriously collapsed from within herself, her skin left hanging like a flaccid sack upon her bones. The fetid corpse was sent to Rome, to be exorcised by the pope, for it was said to jump to its feet and perform a grotesque dance every time the moon was full and witchboys roamed the hills around the new monarch's palace.'

'Well, there's a thing,' said Spiggot, amazed by the story, as were the seelie court, who had stood there silently listening to this maid's astonishing tale of evil. 'You kept this dark, Rosamund.' Spiggot became stern. 'Why?'

'I was afraid of thee, dear Spiggot. Afraid thou would turn me from thy side, and Jack too, for he was my confidante.'

'You knew about this, Jack?' Spiggot's unusual sternness was now turned on his friend.

'Yes, but Spig, it makes no difference, does it? Good lord, Rosy's given her *eyes* for you. You can't think she's anything but loyal to our cause, now can you?'

The boggart considered this and nodded. 'You're right, Jack – but no more secrets, Rosamund. Eh?'

'No, dear Spiggot, none.'

'So, Mallmoc was a medieval sorcerer and now he's in Liöfwende.'

'Aye, it seems so,' said the seelie court chieftain, 'yet this is no a problem for the seelie court, nay, nor for the unseelie court, for this is Thristlac, not Liöfwende. This fair country holds more pines than oaks, more firs than elms.'

'Still,' replied Spiggot, 'the thrum will eat the roots of those too, once they run out of deciduous trees.'

'Is that a fact?'

'It is indeed, sire,' replied Spiggot, following Rosamund's lead. 'Ask any goblin pedlar that comes this way. You stand to lose your forests, just as we will lose ours, if nothing is done. The thrum will eat through trees until there are none left in any of the faerielands.'

'Then it's mair serious than ah had been led tae believe. It may be we seelie court will hae to join this army o' yours tae fight the ulcugga. They're aye numerous beasties, the ulcugga though. We'll need mair than seelie court tae match them.'

'We already have the promise of the Eri-innis fairies,' said Jack, 'and we're hoping to get the unseelie court too. Then there's King Cimberlin's fairies. Not a lot of them, I know, but they can help.'

'We'll fight alangside the tuatha dé, and the Liöfwende fairies, but no wi' pixies or elves, mind,' said the chieftain, firmly. 'Ah draw the line at pixies and elves. And nae fenoderee, bendith y mamau or tylwyth teg. Well, maybe tylwyth teg, but not the black-hearted mamau. The leshy willnae fight, and the gwragedd annwn are all watery females and dinnae approve of battle. Whut about that there Robin Goodfellie, Puck, as he calls himself? Will he no come to the scrap wi' us? He's a bonnie wee chap, and he's aye gude in a tussle, so ah've heard.'

'We might get Puck. You never know,' said Spiggot. 'If he wakes up in a bad mood that morning.'

'And who will lead this mighty army?' asked the

chieftain, his long red hair flowing in the breeze. 'Who will be our battle-king?'

'I have been appointed to that post,' said Spiggot, a little pompously. 'I am your leader.'

The hooting of laughter from seelie court woke moles a hundred miles away, as they slept in their Earth-caverns deep below the ground.

FOUR

Spiggot said nothing further. He simply continued to put on the armour which he had begun to don when he thought Jack was in trouble. The seelie court fairies watched him in amusement. When he was fully accoutred, he unsheathed his sword and stood there, his helmet plume waving in the wind, his golden armour gleaming.

'Produce a champion,' cried Spiggot. 'I will fight him in single combat. If I win, you will accept my leadership. If I lose, you – you can throw me in the nearest tar pit. I will prove to you that I am a warrior of the first order. I may look like a smithy's son from the outside, but inside I am as fierce and skilful as any fairy knight, now or then!'

'Nice armour,' said the chieftain, nodding. 'Yer ain?'

'Given to me by King Cimberlin of the Northumberland fairies.'

'Right. Yer on. Back up, seelie court. Make room.'

The seelie court became excited, forming a great circle. Here was a bit of sport! A boggart was ready to do single combat with any mythical beast or hellish creature that the clan chief might summon! What was it to be? A one-eyed ogre with a giant club? A terrible creature from the mind of a madman: half-lion, half-eagle? A dragon, perhaps? Or some huge venomous serpent? Or even a three-headed savage dog, with a spearpoint tail? It was good fairy fun, just waiting to see what the chief would call forth.

Jack, Kling and Rosamund joined the circle. They had every faith in their boggart friend. They had seen him fight before. Above them, the night was now hard with sharp, cold stars. Supernatural darkness had fallen swiftly on the scene. Yet there was a faint green glow, coming from the hillsides, which lit the area with an eerie, unearthly light. The seelie court chieftain stepped forward, into the ring, to formally begin the battle.

'My name is Cragfeggian, clan chief of the seelie court,' he said, holding up his thin pale arms, the red hair on them glinting in the weird light, 'and I call forth the Abyssinian cat!'

There followed a whirling of dust and grit in the middle of the combat zone, and when it had settled a cat the size of a human stood there on hind legs wearing breastplate and helmet. It carried a huge round wooden shield, with a boss of iron. In its weapon paw was a great mace, its spiked iron ball as large as a man's head. When this warrior from regions unknown saw its opponent standing there, sword in hand, it let out a horrible howling screech, which hurt the ears of the mortals sitting amongst the spectators.

'Ow,' whispered Jack to Rosamund. 'I hope its battle skills aren't as sharp as its tongue.'

The great cat immediately attacked the armoured boggart. The mace came up and fell. Spiggot skipped out of the way. The head of the weapon struck the ground with such force it caused all the spectators to be jumped into the air. A huge dent was left in the turf. The cat whined, raised its club, and brought it down again with great force.

Spiggot had not even had time to get in a swipe with his sword. He was too busy ducking and weaving, trying to stay out of reach of the agile cat. Finally, he turned and stood his ground, to great cheers from the spectators. The talented boggart hacked repeatedly at the shield of the Abyssinian cat, until the wood splintered and split open. The boss was struck by the sword, but instead of shattering the metal blade, as the seelie court expected, the iron boss flew off the front of the shield and went spinning into the crowd. Jack's steel blade was having a devastating effect on the feline's protection. Finally the cat threw away the remnants of the shield and took the mace in both hands. It now proceeded to chase Spiggot around the ring, trying to crush him with some immensely powerful blows.

'Stand yer ground! Stand yer ground!' came the yell from the crowd. 'Skin the cat! Skin the cat!'

Spiggot was doing his best to 'skin the cat' but could not get in a good thrust or slash. Despite being large, the cat was like any other cat. It was very, very agile. Its movements were lithe and supple, and it moved with great speed and skill. Once, the mace bounced off Spiggot's helmet and the boggart spun completely around, before getting his balance again. One thing Spiggot did notice, after a while, was that the cat could be distracted. If he threw out his left hand, the cat's eyes tended to follow the movement, leaving Spiggot the opportunity to thrust. He made this move twice, the second time managing to prick the fur of the great cat and cause it to yowl.

Spiggot finally found victory by carrying out the movement the other way around. He flashed his sword over his head. The cat's eyes followed the blade. Spiggot then reached forward and spun the cat's helmet back to front. The poor creature was now blind. It screeched with anger, dropped its mace, and tried to turn its helmet back again. At that moment, Spiggot could have run the giant cat through. Instead he chose to kick away its legs so that it fell thrashing to the floor. Without its weapon, without its shield, it was now helpless.

'Do it!' yelled someone from the crowd. 'Run it through! Do it now! Kill the cat! Make it dead!'

Spiggot recognised the voice. It had an urgent tone to it, as though there were several generations of hate behind it. Kling, of course. Kling was a rat and everyone knows what rats think of cats. Cats had shown no mercy towards Kling's kin. Cats killed rats for sport. No wonder the voice sounded so anxious, so desperate for the moment of truth.

Yet, Spiggot could not do it. It was not in him to kill a creature who lay helpless before him. He stepped back and lifted the visor of his helmet. The cat, seeing its chance, sprang forward. Its claws were out: a fantastic array of sharply-pointed hooks. Its teeth were bared, the yellow fangs prominent. But before it could use any of these natural weapons, it disappeared into the ether. The seelie court chieftain had sent it back from whence it had come.

'Och,' said the chieftain, shaking his red head in disappointment, 'ye won, but ye didnae finish the job.'

Spiggot thought he had failed. 'If it had been an ulcugga fairy, I would have done, but the cat had done me no harm.'

The chieftain stood staring at him for a while, muttering incomprehensibly. 'Buts and bens, oor wullie, the broons, jings, crivvens, and aw that.'

Then finally he lifted his head. 'Ye have honour in ye, boggart. Ah'll follow a leader with honour in him. There's nay much o' it aboot these fairy days and it's aye remarkable. Ye have mah word on it.'

Jack thought Spiggot would say that a fairy's word wasn't worth all that much, but the boggart simply gave a huge sigh and said, 'You won't regret it.'

'Well, ah might,' said Cragfeggian, 'but ah've said it now. And ah'll dispatch a fairy to the unseelie court. Ye won't want to go there, now, will ye?'

'I'd prefer not to,' said Spiggot.

'Why not?' asked Jack.

'You've met one of them,' Spiggot replied. 'And he was probably the mildest unseelie court in the clan, being chosen for ambassador. You wouldn't want to meet the host, not face-to-face. They're a terrifying group of fairies.'

'If they're so bad, then why don't they rule the world?'

'Because there are so few of them, that's all. No, it's best it's done this way. That's why I wanted to come to the seelie court first. Now, I'm going to get this armour off and have a rest, Jack. You can come and chatter to me if you want, but I'll probably drop off to sleep.'

'I'm tired myself,' said Jack. 'It's been a long day. It's been a long six months. I could sleep for a week.'

Rosamund too, stated she was 'fatigued', and was asleep within a few minutes. Jack covered her with a blanket from the cart, then found a mossy spot for himself amongst the ferns. Kling came and lay beside him, which slightly irritated Jack, because the rat continually scratched at his fleas.

'He should have run him through,' muttered Kling. 'He should have finished the job.'

'You would have done?'

'Kling would have no hesitation in sticking a cat.'

'No, I suppose not.' Jack turned over and looked up at the stars. They didn't seem so sharp and prickly now. 'Have you ever been chased by a cat?'

'When Kling was a ship rat, yes. All over the decks, along the gangways, up and down the rigging – everywhere. Blamed ship's cat used to chase Kling until he was mad with fear. But Kling was a young rat in those days. Kling could move fast.'

'You were a ship rat?' said Jack, interested. 'I thought you were a water rat? That is, a rat who lived in the water, not sailed on it. Where did your voyages take you?'

'Oh, Singapore, Hong Kong, Cathay, all over the world, really. That was when Kling was in a British man-o'-war.

Then Kling transferred to a Chinese junk, a grain boat. That was after Kling got fed up with being chased by the ship's cat. The Chinese captain didn't have a cat. He had this terrier who was half-blind and only made a show of chasing rats. Then the Chinaman was attacked by junk pirates, and so Kling became a pirate on the *Pearl River*, and saw lots of blood and fighting.'

'A *pirate*!' repeated Jack, impressed. 'You really have seen life, haven't you, Kling?'

'In the raw. Kling has seen it all. Kling was five days at sea when the pirate ship was blown from the water by the Emperor's battle fleet. Kling clung to a piece of flotsam all that time, while his friends were being taken by sharks and barracuda. Then Kling was washed up on a desert island and spent seven weeks waiting for a ship, fighting the land crabs to get at the coconuts. Nasty beggars, land crabs. Like armoured tanks. When a ship passed by Kling swam out to it. This time it was a tea clipper, on its way back from India. That tea tasted mighty good, Kling can tell you.'

'You ate tea leaves?'

'Lovely, when they're still green and freshly picked.'

'Listen,' said Jack, turning over to look at the giant rat beside him, 'you're not telling a big story, are you?'

'Fibbing? Kling?'

'It's not been unknown.'

'When Kling retells his history, he cannot lie, or his tail grows to an enormous length. See,' he swished the item in question, 'still the same.'

'If you say so.'

*

The following day Jack sought Cragfeggian. The seelie court were not early risers. They slept amongst the bracken and did not get up until the sun made dead ferns crackle. It was the noise that made them rise, or they might have stayed there all day. Once up, though, they were full of energy, and played a game of chasing red deer. The idea was to touch the deer's scut on the run. They loved the waterfalls, spending hours under the tumbling burns. They climbed the trees and shook the corbie nests to make the birds screech in alarm. This was where Jack found the chieftain, who was as childish as the rest of his clan when it came to games.

'Whut?' snapped Cragfeggian, as he was accosted during 'stane hopping', a game using the slippery stepping stones which spanned a wide burn. 'Ah'm *really* busy.'

'I need the help of your magic to get a friend of mine from Mortaland into Faerieland.'

'Some bonnie lass, is it?'

'No, well, it is a *she*. An ulcugga fairy, trapped in a shop called Polkinghorne's Antiques.'

'Och, man,' the fairy chieftain shook his head sadly, 'd'ye not know better than to fall for a fairy? Ye'll only find grief.'

'I haven't fallen for her . . . look, it's your go.'

Cragfeggian turned and skipped over the wet stones, first on his toes, then on his hands, and finally on his bottom.

'Easy,' he said, coming back to Jack's side. 'Now, an ulcugga, ye say? Ah thocht you and your boggart were no fond of the ulcuggas.'

'This one did me a great favour and she's trapped in Mortaland – has been for centuries – and can't get back. She's fading away, fast. If she doesn't get here soon, she'll be nothing but blown mist.'

'Och, one of they? Ah'm not promising anything, mind, but ah'll do mah best. Ah cannae say fairer than that.'

'It's all I ask.' Jack gave the chieftain the name of the town, the name of the street, and repeated the name on the shop front. Then he left the seelie court to their important highland games.

FIVE

'The trouble is,' said Jack, 'I can't tell the difference between the men and women – that is, the male and female seelie court. They all look the same to me.'

''Tis true, Jack. Their raiment is much the same, they being clad in green hose. I, too, have no notion which are maids and which are squires. 'Tis a strange world we have found ourselves in, full of dragons and fairies and giant creatures. Yet, I am glad to be here, Jack.'

The pair was sitting at the mouth of a cave. Below them the loch waters were calm and peaceful. Dragonflies skimmed the surface, and damselflies, with flashes of blue. It was a peaceful day in Faerieland, with only the ever-present clouds of midges to mar the tranquillity. These nasty little creatures did not seem to bother the faerie folk, but they certainly took chunks out of Rosamund and Jack. Every so often one or other of

the pair would slap and clap and try to kill as many
insects as possible.

Still, they were as happy as any young couple who
were falling in love. They were lost in a foreign world
and they were quite foreign to one another coming from
different cultures, different eras in history. But to those
young people caught in the first flush of love, nothing
really matters except that the love they feel for the other
is returned in full measure.

They had said nothing about how they felt, but they
each knew it. Rosamund looked into Jack's eyes and saw
adoration. Jack had to go by Rosamund's demeanour
and body language, for her eagle eyes often peered at
him in a sharp, startling way, which made him feel like
raptor prey. Sometimes he had the idea that she was
going to stoop on him from a great height and carry him
off in her ivory fingers, then tear him to bits with those
fine white teeth of hers.

He got the feeling now, as those sharp hazel eyes were
turned on him, revealing Rosamund's innermost thoughts.

'Jack, what ails thee?' cried Rosamund. 'Thou art
afraid?'

'Oh,' he tore away from her gaze, 'it's – it's nothing. I
guess you're hungry, aren't you, Rosy?'

'How dost though know that?' she said, delighted, her
eyes opening a little wider. 'I starve. Yet thou knows this
for a fact, Jack? Canst thou read my mind as two court-
ing lovers are like to do? Is it that we are twin stars, dear
Jack, who share the same heaven?'

He didn't want to tell her that her naked hunger was
evident in the eagle's eyes. That she was at that moment

looking at him as if he were a rabbit getting ready to run. He *felt* like a rabbit about to bolt. In fact, if she moved suddenly, now, he would be off, down the hillside, zigzagging in panic, waiting for the thunderbolt to fall and break his back.

'Yes,' he said, 'we're twin souls all right, Rosy.'

Happily, at that moment, they were interrupted by Cragfeggian, who suddenly appeared out of a crack in a lightning-blasted tree. The Highland chieftain of the seelie court looked very pleased with himself. There was someone behind him, someone Jack couldn't quite see.

'Laddie!' he cried, 'Ah've brocht ye a friend. Raminago'bris, of the ulcugga clan, a Sassenach fairy.'

And there, in the clear light, stood an ulcugga. Jack would not have recognised her as the fading fairy in the antique shop. She was fully restored to her original shape and form. The dust and weariness of centuries amongst old furniture in Mortaland had gone from her. She was bright and colourful, with crystalline eyes and a pouting mouth. She was, in fact, quite beautiful in the way of precious stones: a hard, gem-like quality.

She was also out of temper: that was very obvious.

'Raminago'bris?' she shrieked. 'You gave me that name? How could you give me name of a despised cat? I am all wind and fury! Do I look like a bad poet to you? Do I look like someone who stops travellers and bores them to tears with bad rhymes? What stupid fools you mortals be.'

'Pleased to see you too,' replied Jack, 'and I'm so glad you're grateful for your release from your Mortaland prison.'

'Never mind that,' she snapped, running her eyes up and down Rosamund in an ill-mannered way, 'how do I get rid of this foul name? And tell the wench not to stare at me in such fashion or I will make her skin smart, or worse.'

Spiggot had been right. It had been stupid to think that a fairy would be grateful for any favours. Now here was the same fairy who had begged him to help her and who said she would be eternally in his debt if he got her out of Mortaland. Yes, that very same fairy railing at him, hurling insults, not in the least bit pleased at her good fortune.

'Speak not to my Jack in that fashion,' spat Rosamund, coming to the defence of her friend, 'or I shall tear the very eyes from thy head.'

'One more word out of *you*,' replied Raminago'bris, happy to have yet another target for her wrath, 'and you'll spend the rest of your life as a toad under a stone.'

'Whoa, whoa,' muttered Cragfennian. 'Ulcugga ye might be, but I rule here, southerner. Ah say what gets toadied and what disnae. Was it no Spiggot the boggart that named ye, anyway? That's the story ah heard. Not the mortal Jack, but the faerie blacksmith's son. It's him ye want to toady, no the laddie here, or the maid. The boggart.'

'Is that true?' snarled Raminago'bris. 'It was the boggart?'

'It was me who asked him to find you a name,' replied Jack, 'and I take all the responsibility. You wanted to get out of Mortaland. You couldn't remember your name. So we had to find another name for you, and this is what came up. You don't like it, hard cheese. I went to a lot of trouble to get you back here. I hope you've thanked Cragfeggian here, as well, because he put himself out, using his magic and everything to make a passage for you. If all you can do is spit fire at us all, I suggest you go back to where you came from. Maybe a few more centuries back there will improve your manners.'

'Tis well said, Jack,' Rosamund chimed in. 'She has the manners of a hog.'

'Bah!' cried Raminago'bris, still steeped in fury. 'You stupid mortals.'

With that, she vanished.

Jack looked around him. 'Where's she gone?'

Cragfeggian replied, 'Ah sent her hame. Her blether was aye getting on mah sair nerves. Ye willnae see her again.'

'I thought her magic was as powerful as yours?'

'It may be, laddie, but this here's Thristlac. Ah say whut's whut here in the bonnie hills of Thristlac.'

'Oh, I see, territorial advantage. That makes sense. Well, I hope we don't run into her again. She was a right harpy, wasn't she? Reminded me of Jenny on a bad hair night.'

The clan chief left them then and the pair went down the hillside to where Spiggot was arguing with Kling.

'Master's son, we cannot risk going down the centre of Liöfwende – the landscape is crawling with ulcugga.'

'Time is of the essence, rat,' said Spiggot, scratching the spark burnmarks on his arm, a sure sign of nervousness in the boggart. 'I'm the leader of the expedition. I say what goes and what doesn't go. If we stick to the ridges we might not even see an ulcugga. You know they like the valleys and dales, rather than the heights. We'll be safe enough.'

'What's all this?' asked Jack. 'Difference of opinion?'

'There's no opinions. I say what goes,' repeated Spiggot, expecting argument from a second quarter. 'I'm the leader.'

'I agree,' said Jack. 'He's the leader, Kling.'

Kling shrugged his rodent shoulders and swished his tail to show he washed his hands of the affair.

'All right. Don't say Kling didn't warn you.'

That evening, the messengers arrived from the unseelie court. It appeared they had heard from their ambassador, the burgundy knight, in the place Jack called Standing Stone City, where King Cimberlin held sway. The unseelie court were ready to join the army of fairies to fight Mallmoc and his hordes of ulcugga fairies. Thus Spiggot had almost accomplished his mission. He had fairies coming from Eri-innis, from Thristlac and from Liöfwende. Now that these three powerful groups had joined together, an uneasy and unlikely alliance it had to be said, other smaller clans too would join. There would be fairies from the islands of Wight and Man, from the Shetlands and the Orkneys, from other parts of Liöfwende, including the south. A mighty army, to be led by a common boggart. It was unprecedented: but these were uncommon times. Such dangers as the mortal wizard Mallmoc created called for unusual counter-measures.

'We will begin with the defeat of the ulcugga army,'

said Spiggot to the seelie court. 'Then we will take Mallmoc's castle and destroy it.'

'Destroy the Red One? But it is fashioned of iron?' said a fairy.

'Somehow, we must destroy it. Perhaps Jack could help there? He is what is known as an engineer. He works with engines . . .'

Many of the seelie court held their noses, as if a great stink was in the air.

'. . . and as such he will know how to destroy engines, for the Red One, Mallmoc's Castle, is an engine. See how it sucks the birds from the sky to its walls and burns them there on its hot plates! Jack will assist.'

Spiggot paused for breath, then continued, 'Finally, we will force Mallmoc to return to us the locking-stone to the magic cairn. We will then drive the thrum underground and lock the cairn, thus preventing them from pouring forth again to eat our precious oaks, elms – and pines. This is a good plan. I thought of it myself. It will work, I know.'

'Sounds OK to me,' said Jack. 'How about you, Rosy?'

''Tis a wondrous and fantastical scheme, worthy of an alchemist or mayhap an apothecary, who are wise men indeed.'

'Well said, Rosy. What about you, Cragfeggian?'

'Och, if it works as well as it sounds from the mouth of the boggart, then we're aye on the right road.'

Satisfied that everything was now in place, Jack, Rosamund, Spiggot and Kling got a good night's sleep before setting off the following morning. With the prevailing south wind in their faces – on most days not much more than a breeze really – they began the long walk home. They followed the winding paths of woodland trails and when they left the trees they took to the ridges. Once or twice, a flight of owls and nightjars went overhead, with bogles on their backs. The group hid themselves in case these were Mallmoc's creatures. They could afford to take no chances.

Once, too, a spriggan with its parasite ventured into the camp while they were asleep. Spiggot woke to see the spriggan walking off with his golden helmet and had to run him down while getting prickled by the spriggan's parasite. The parasite had a skin like a horsechestnut case and it was extremely uncomfortable to be attacked by such a creature.

They also had to pass through villages of goblins and gnomes, thereby running the risk of having their position revealed to Mallmoc. Goblins and gnomes are not the most discreet of supernatural beings. They would sell their grandmother's shoes for a crooked sixpence.

Indeed, the news of Spiggot's march south was quickly taken up by the stray zephyrs which are torn from the prevailing wind in its long journey northwards. These zephyrs carried the information to the ears of Mallmoc, who sent out his ulcuggas to search for his enemies. Kling's prophesy was about to be fulfilled, though the rat himself would have preferred to be wrong.

You could not go about the countryside whispering in the ears of fairy kings and hope that Mallmoc would not hear it. He had spies everywhere. And Mallmoc left nothing to chance.

A great storm was created, and within the darkness and chaos of that storm, out of sight of any good and noble eyes of Liöfwende, nefarious forces were unleashed. Beings of unimaginable malevolence were let loose, sent forth, to scour the landscape for the boggart and his friends. Their instructions, whispered in the dead of night, shocked even those ghastly creatures. Evil as they were, they were sickened by the horror of their orders. They flew out, ragged and foul, to sweep the ridges and hills around Mallmoc's castle: a demon swarm with a single purpose.

The ever-toiling Spiggot knew nothing of this, of course, and he and his companions trudged determinedly south.

PART SEVEN

The scullery of hell

ONE

'I forgot to ask the seelie court something,' said Jack to Kling. 'I wanted to ask them what they called hopscotch in Scotland. Is it hopenglish, do you think?'

Kling, lugging the cart over yet *another* hill, rolled his eyes and sighed heavily. 'Is that all that Jack has to occupy his mind?'

Jack never failed to be nettled by Kling's lofty attitude towards life. Surely things weren't always serious? Sometimes there had to be a lightening of the spirit.

They were at that moment cresting a hill in a most dangerous border area between Lancashire and Yorkshire. It was here the ulcugga operated in great force. Already there had been three sightings – Rosamund, using her eagle's eyes – and three times the companions had managed to hide or give the ulcugga the slip. However, the ulcugga had received numerous

reports from their ethereal spies, those spirits of the wind
and still air, and were now waiting for the group in large
numbers. Eagle's eyes or not, Rosamund could not see
round corners, or through the next hill.

Spiggot, in his suit of fairy gold armour, was the first
to reach the top. He looked down the slope on the other
side with dismay. Ulcugga fairy troops swept in a great
semi-circle below him. Turning, he saw that their retreat
had been cut off at the bottom of the hill up which he had
just come. There was no escape. It was useless to fight.
There were far too many of the creatures for a knight
and three squires to deal with, even if one of those
squires was carrying a magic crossbow. Jack and Kling
were arguing about something. Rosamund had her head
down and was looking where she put her feet. Spiggot
waved them all to a stop.

'We're surrounded,' he said, quietly. 'I can see the
pale face of Prince Rincortle, my deadly enemy. His
magenta eyes are smiling for once. He knows he has us
trapped.'

Jack stepped forward with the crossbow. 'I can kill
him from here,' he said. 'Maybe without their leader . . .?'

'Fairies don't work like that. They will take us
anyway,' replied Spiggot, quiet again. 'Rosamund. Can
you see a way out, with those eagle's eyes of yours?'

Rosamund scanned the whole three hundred and
sixty degrees of horizon with her sharp, superior vision
and shook her head sadly.

'There are more ulcugga on the ridges. I fear there is
no escape, Spiggot.'

'Then we are done for,' said Spiggot, in despair. 'I shall

do what I can to get him to let the rest of you go. He might just be satisfied with capturing just me . . .'

Rincortle spurred his white horse forward. A prince of the ulcuggas, he was truly a beautiful being. His long blond hair fell like silken rain about his stately form and down the flanks of his handsome stallion. Riding bare-back, like all fairies, he was slim, lithe. His face was the face of an angel, divine in appearance. The magenta eyes in that visage were soft and warm. If someone like Rosamund had met this creature alone on the highway, she would have been amazed by his comeliness, she would have been delighted by his charming company. It was difficult to believe that this was truly a bad fairy, one who would have no compunction in destroying a whole village of boggarts, if his master desired him to do so.

'So, cousin of vile goblins, I have you at last,' said Rincortle, coming up alongside Spiggot. 'I am tempted to split you with my sword this very moment, for causing us so much trouble. Yet, it would be a mercy and I think you would be disappointed if I showed mercy, would you not? Better to take you back and put you to work ham-mering iron plate for the rest of your days. Plenty of time over the next few hundred fairy years to reflect on the error of your judgement.'

Rincortle's eyes scanned the rest of the group; they came to rest on Jack.

'Ah, this is the mortal who stole the maid from us? Well, then, you will have told him his fate, will you not, boggart? To feed and stoke the forges for the ironsmiths of Mallmoc. A noble work, mortal, yet you need a stronger form in order to carry it out . . .'

Some shining dust left the hand of the fairy prince and settled on Jack's shoulders, like golden snow. Jack felt a ripple go through his body, then a jolt which made his eyes start from his head. His heart seemed to shoot upwards into his throat, then it sank slowly back down deep into his chest again. Finally he felt as if he were being pressed by a mighty weight, or giant hand, pushing him down on the top of his head, so that his torso, legs and head folded in on themselves.

Rosamund gave a little scream and stood back from him.

'What's happened?' cried Jack, afraid. 'Why are you all looking at me like that?'

His voice sounded strange to him: deep and guttural. When he looked down he saw that his legs, arms and torso were much fatter than before, and shorter. All four limbs were like stumpy logs, stuck to a thick stubby trunk. When he inspected himself he saw that he was corrugated all over from head to toes: ridges and rolls of flesh now covered his shortened bones. He had indeed been squashed into himself, so that he was half his original size and covered in furrows of blubbery muscle and fat.

Looking up, he could see Rosamund staring down at him with revulsion on her face.

In that hoarse voice which he did not recognise as his own, he cried, 'I'm a dwarf!'

'Oh,' said Rincortle, 'I think that's being a little unfair to the noble brotherhood of dwarves, don't you? Dwarves are quite handsome creatures, in their way. I've simply caused your body to concertina to concentrate

your strength into your torso and limbs. You are now a
compact working animal, like a strong donkey, and will
be useful to us. And for a little decoration, I've given you
a pair of bat's wings, just where your thick neck meets
your flattened head. Adds a little absurdity to the whole
image of your friend, don't you think, boggart? Jack,
isn't it? That's it, Jack, flap those little black wings. It
makes you look even more ridiculous.'

Jack realised he was doing what the prince wanted
him to do and I stopped trying to fly away. Utter misery
flowed through him. Rosamund would never look twice
at him now. He was a monstrous creature, ugly in every
part, and subject to the mirth of every other living creature. Any happy days on Earth were over. His body was
a walking horror, good only for one thing, to stoke the
fires of the furnaces of hell within Mallmoc's iron castle.

Rincortle satisfied himself with merely verbally chas-
tising Rosamund. Since she was a lovely maid, and
fairies enjoy beauty as much as mortals, she would be
allowed to retain her own form. Spiggot, who would be
chained to the other ironsmiths and forced to make metal
plate for the walls of Mallmoc's iron castle, would also
remain as he was. Kling was released from his harness
and told to begone. It was not that Mallmoc was against
using animals as beasts of burden, but he particularly
disliked having rats around. The made him shudder with
revulsion. He didn't like spiders or snakes, either. In his
fears he was much like any other mortal.

The others put their possessions in his cart –
Rosamund, the hurley slitter; Jack, the silver shoes with
the horrible secret, his magic crossbow, the strange

green bottle he had found in the inglenook of Mallmoc's chimney in Mortaland; Spiggot, his armour and his sword. The ulcugga were not interested in these objects. They were a race of fairies who prized power rather than possessions.

Without looking back the rat left his master's son in the hands of the ulcugga, unable to do anything to assist Spiggot, Jack or Rosamund.

'Now, march!' ordered Rincortle. 'Your days of rebellion are over, boggart.'

The group was herded along the paths and byways of the north, until Mallmoc's castle, the Red One, came in sight. It was an ugly object, covered in flakes of rust. There were no windows. Around its walls were dead and stunned birds which had flown into it in the full force of their flight. They seemed to be attracted to the vast metal structure in some way. Rincortle led his prisoners down the bare slopes of the surrounding hills, to the great doors of the castle. There was a loud clanking of machinery, a grating of rusty chains on capstans, and the doors opened: two huge studded squares of iron that lifted upwards, allowing entry from below.

The three friends were thrown into an airless dungeon, the floor of which was covered in dirty straw which smelled of the previous occupants. The only opening to the cell was the small grille in the door, which let in a little air but no light. There were rats – real rats – scuttling around in the straw. Jack could find no furniture: there was only the stone floor covered in that fetid straw on which to lie. He felt utterly depressed and kept himself apart from the others. Even if Rosamund was treating him kindly, he felt she must find him a revolting sight and that of course upset him.

After twenty-four hours without food and water (they had to lick the condensation running down the slick walls of the dungeon) they received a visit. Mallmoc himself came to see these creatures who had given him so much trouble. He was preceded into the cell by a goblin carrying a huge tray of lit candles.

If Jack now thought his own form revolting, he considered Mallmoc beat him hands down. The sorcerer was dressed in a huge sweeping gown of black silk. The gown had a hood, which covered the wizard's head. Underneath the fabric the body was so old it was rotting like a corpse. It smelled musty and rank – the smell of a rubbish tip combined with stained grave earth – and all the occupants of the cell gagged when he came close to them. This did not seem to bother the sorcerer one bit: in fact he smiled, a ghastly smile that merely opened up holes and hollows in his face.

'You find the stink offensive? Well, well, we can't all smell of lavender and roses, can we? This poor shell of mine has been around several centuries and it was only meant to last a hundred years at the most. Poor design, in my opinion. If I had been its creator, I should have made it of iron, or stone, something a bit more lasting. I could of course *change* it, with some spell or other, but it wouldn't feel right. One never feels right out of one's birth chamber. It's like sleeping in another bed.'

'You could try using deodorants,' croaked Jack.

The sorcerer's eye sockets were turned on Jack. The

youth gulped in fear as he stared up into those pits of hell. They were fathomless and brimming with waste horror. There was enough terror in there to spread amongst a thousand Jacks and still have some left over. Jack stumbled backwards, tripping over his own huge feet.

'Ah,' murmured the sorcerer. 'The squashed one speaks. Well, well, we shall soon see how sarcastic your tongue can be once you have a shovel in your stunted little hands. It's hot work you know, but very rewarding, shovelling coke and coal into my furnaces. The reward is that you won't be whipped if you work hard enough. Slacken and you will be flayed to the bone, that's a promise. We don't like slackers here, Jack.'

Somehow Mallmoc managed to sound like a solemn schoolmaster when he spoke those words. In fact, with his black robe and his tall lean demeanour, he *looked* the old fashioned schoolmaster. Jack was about to be given a lesson in terror.

TWO

Next, the sorcerer turned his attention on Spiggot.
'Now, the boggart who thinks he is a king.'

'A knight,' protested the modest boggart. 'Only a knight.'

'Well, then, above his station, whatever his ambitions. We're about to pull you down again, my little blacksmith. Pull you down and fit you firmly in your round hole. You will lead no armies against Mallmoc, and without you they will fritter away and leave me in peace.'

'Why did you steal the locking-stone to the magic cairn?' cried Spiggot. 'Why did you release the skaggs and the thrum?'

'I?' replied Mallmoc, loftily. 'I have done nothing of the kind. I merely continue with my own ambitions. To build an impenetrable castle, so that when I melt the walls between Mortaland and Liöfwende, and the mortals come pouring into Faerieland, I shall be the unassailable ruler of all. Yes, boggart, it is my intention to make Mortaland and Faerieland into one indivisible place, over which I shall hold sway.' He went off into some sort of dreamy reverie. 'I shall visit pain and death upon those who forced me to flee to this devilforsaken land. They will be sorry they ever heard the name of Mallmoc . . .'

Spiggot was aghast. 'You will do *what*? But there will be utter chaos. All people from all times? Liöfwende, Thristlac and Eri-innis cannot hold so many mortals and faerie, not all at once. It will boil over into complete anarchy. Even a lowly boggart such as myself can see that.'

Mallmoc came out of his dreamy state. 'I can control all that,' he snapped. 'I have the power. Besides, once I've finished with most of the mortals, there won't be *that* many left. And those that are will be in a such a sorry state they'll spend their time rooting for grubs and worms to eat. You faerie will be helping me round them up, like wild dogs. There'll be plenty of work for you to do, don't worry. You won't have *time* to descend into mayhem. Into a little madness, perhaps, but not chaos.'

'He's insane,' whispered Jack to Spiggot. 'Completely insane.'

'Bah!' exclaimed the sorcerer. 'If by insane you mean out of the ordinary, yes, that's what I am. Now, the maid.' He turned his attention on Rosamund. 'What a beautiful little butterfly! What a delightful visage. The eyes are a little strange, but I enjoy strangenesses. I think I shall keep her for my own slave. You shall be my personal servant. You shall be my water girl. I drink gallons of water, you know. In here it is as hot as hell, and it dries the juices in this rotten old corpse. Yes, you will look very sweet with an urn on your shoulder. See to it, goblin. Bring her now.'

The goblin with the candles called for assistance and more goblins came, to drag Rosamund from the cell. Jack tried to stop them, but was beaten to the floor. He cried after Rosamund, who was strangely silent, not weeping, not protesting. Jack remarked on this, once Mallmoc had gone, to his companion.

Spiggot said, 'You forget, Jack, that she comes from a time when maids were treated like cattle. She's used to it.'

'I suppose she is,' croaked Jack, thoroughly upset. 'Oh, what have we got ourselves into here, Spiggot? And what a liar that Mallmoc is. Why does he keep on denying he's got the stone to the cairn? I don't understand that bit. You'd think he'd be crowing about it, the way he is.'

'Who can fathom the mind of a wizard?'

'I suppose so. But he likes to brag, doesn't he?'

Spiggot went quiet for a while. Then he said, 'Oh, Jack, his plans! He will destroy us all, that sorcerer. How do you mortals manage to produce such evil creatures? A faerie would never have such terrible schemes in his head. Most of you mortals are nice people, I know, but just occasionally you make one of these ghastly creatures who are intent on destroying everything and anything in the pursuit of power. You've had a few of those in your world history, you must admit, Jack.'

'It's true,' croaked Jack, in that harsh voice. 'You're right, Spiggot. But your being right doesn't help us here. We've got to find a way to escape. We've got to get out and do what you set out to do – marshal Faerieland – get the fairy armies together, and attack this madman. Destroy him before he has a chance to destroy two worlds and all the creatures in them. What about telling Rincortle what he's planning? Surely even the ulcugga won't want Faerieland bubbling over with terrified mortals?'

'It's too late for them. The ulcugga have thrown in their lot with the sorcerer and they'll sink or swim with him. You don't understand faerie, Jack . . .'

'You're so right, I don't.'

'We must just wait our chance. Perhaps we're allowed to go out once in a while? We could make a run for it.'

Jack said, 'Doesn't seem very hopeful. And what about Rosamund?'

'We might have to leave her behind, Jack. Set her free once we've defeated Mallmoc.'

Jack didn't like the sound of this. If there was to be an escape, he wanted Rosamund to be with them. But getting out of the castle seemed an impossibility anyway. It was a pipe dream. They were locked inside a windowless ironclad, with guards and sentries all around them. There did not seem to be a hope in heaven of getting out. Jack didn't ask Spiggot if anyone had ever escaped from the Red One. He didn't want to hear the answer.

'Well,' he said, 'maybe the fairies will get together anyway, and fight him without you. They know where he is. They can concentrate their forces on this valley. It wouldn't take much planning.'

Spiggot shook his head in the darkness of the cell. 'You don't understand, Jack. When you called this castle an *ironclad*, you were closer to the truth than you knew. It is indeed like a boat. It can float over the ground, if Mallmoc wishes it to. It sails through soil as a ship sails through water. Overnight it can be somewhere far away from where it is now. Mallmoc has more tricks up his sleeve than a card sharp like yourself . . . we're doomed, Jack. Doomed to a life of hard labour and no reward.'

What a gloomy prediction! Yet Jack knew it was true. They might hold on to hope for a little while. Perhaps for a long while. Hope dies very slowly in the human breast. It sort of hangs on there, hoping. But eventually it will turn to smoke and drift away. Jack couldn't imagine a life without hope: it was so terribly dark he couldn't see through to it.

Later that day they were fed, then Jack and Spiggot were taken to the heart of the Red One. On the way, Jack saw his battered motorcycle, leaning against a wall. It was rusty now, and full of dents. Rats had torn the plastic seating to pieces and the stuffing was hanging out. He stared at the machine which had got him into so much trouble. A smirking ulcugga guard told Jack that the machine would eventually go into the melting pot, along with the molten metal.

'Your chariot will become part of the iron castle, mortal.'

'Good riddance,' muttered Jack.

Spiggot whispered, 'Jack, the quivvel. Look at my pocket.'

Jack looked down and saw that Spiggot's pocket was jumping about as if he had a live frog in there.

'The locking-stone is in here somewhere,' whispered Spiggot. 'I knew it. Mallmoc has it hidden in the castle . . .' He suddenly received a blow to the head, and an order. 'Quiet, boggart! No speaking.'

In the great foundry, the place Mallmoc called his 'scullery', Jack and Spiggot were shown their places. Over the vast, dark earthen floor, lit only by the light of furnace fires, were hundreds of pits. In each of these pits stood two boggarts, stripped to the waist, wearing leather aprons. One of each pair held a heavy hammer, the other a pair of long iron tongs. There was an anvil beside each pit. Red-hot and white-hot iron would be wheeled in barrows to the pits by shrunken mortals, who delivered it to the boggart smith pairs. The boggart with the tongs would grasp the hot shapeless iron, hold it on the face of the anvil, and the other would hammer it flat. It was as simple as that. Highly-trained boggart blacksmiths, proud of their heritage, who had an inherent instinct for metalwork, spent their lives denying their skills. Instead of using their talent to make things in metal, they merely hammered it into flat plates, to be welded to other such plates.

The work was deadly dull for sparkling creatures and all the lustre had gone out of their eyes. They worked in a mechanical way, their movements entirely economical. Occasionally some newly-taken prisoner would glance towards the furnaces, where the mortals threw iron ore into great cauldrons, melted it down, refined it, then poured it on to trays to solidify, before wheeling it to the boggart smiths in thick rough form.

The flare of the great fires, the sight of flying sparks, fountains of white metal, waterfalls of molten iron, caused the spirit of the recent captive to flutter. But it was the flutter of a dying moth. Soon that spirit would be dead, alongside all the other dead spirits, and the boggart would glance no more at the furnaces, where even iron had more movement, more dance, more soul than that of faerie or mortal. This was the scullery of hell, where scullery maids were boggarts and mortals, whose work bored them into nothing but shells of what they once were. The labour was so repetitive, so simple, so exhausting, they died within themselves.

Jack was given a metal barrow. When a dwarfed human like himself lifted a rough plate of hot iron with a winch and dropped it into the barrow, Jack had to wheel it to the nearest pit with idle boggarts. This he did, finding the heat of the plate so intense it burned his face and chest. They had given him thick sackcloth mittens to cover his hands, but still the heat went through the handles of the barrow and burned the skin on his fingers and palms. It was terrible work. Every so often a goblin would pour water over him, to cool him down, and he was given a drink, but these were his only luxuries in this dreadful place. Food came once a day, halfway through his shift, and when his work period was over he simply fell in a corner of the great, dark hall, as far away as he could from the fires, and fell asleep.

On waking, the nightmare began again. At first he tried speaking to some of the other mortals, wondering from which place, which time, they came. There might even be famous people amongst them, for all Jack knew.

But whenever he was caught trying to speak to one of them, a whip descended on his back. There were goblin overseers everywhere (for ulcugga fairies would not come into the foundry) who were only too willing to flay the skin off the back of a mortal. Of course, in the world at large there were good goblins, just as there were good fairies, but these were the dregs of faerieworld, gathered for their viciousness, for their spite.

Once, before Jack fell asleep, he whispered to a squashed mortal beside him.

'Who are you? Do you speak English?'

'I am Joseph, of Spittlegate,' came the whispered reply. 'Former cordwainer to the great and wealthy of the City of London. Speak to me not, sir, for we will be sorely punished.'

That was all Jack got out of him, and the next time it was someone else beside him, a stunted woman in rags. She merely stared bleakly with empty eyes when he asked her who she was, and shook her head. This time Jack was heard and was warned that if he did not cease trying to speak to other inmates of the prison, he would be thrown into one of the furnaces without any further warnings. Jack shut up. From that moment on he did the work he was expected to do, getting blisters for his reward, and left the other mortals to theirs, knowing he was putting everyone in danger.

Jack's hopelessness increased when he lost all sight of, and contact with, Spiggot. He knew the boggart smith was somewhere out there, in one of the pits, amongst all the other ironsmiths, but it was impossible to tell where. Jack always looked keenly at every two boggarts when he visited a pit with his rough iron. They invariably looked as miserable as he himself felt. Their thick sturdy bodies were covered in dirt and sweat, they had lacklustre eyes and there was a deadly dullness about their work. Jack's spirits sank lower and lower, until, after many days of this work he was as lifeless as all the others under Mallmoc's iron roof.

THREE

Once in a while a boggart was taken from the iron-pits to a different area of the castle. Here, in one of the workshops off the bailey, was the forge where swords were made. The ulcugga fairies needed weapons just like any other army or group of hunters. Being fairies they liked the best. Spiggot's father, Gnomon, was known throughout Liöfwende as a craftsman of great skill. Faerie folk are great believers in hereditary talent and Rincortle believed that Spiggot would have inherited his father's fine hands and sharp brain for fashioning fighting blades. When the fuss of the capture had died down and Mallmoc was engaged with other affairs, Rincortle had Spiggot transferred to the sword-making forge.

Spiggot entered the forge in chains, wondering whether something terrible was going to happen to him. He was greeted by the trusty boggart, a thickset, barrel-chested faerie with a broad stupid face. The trusty was named after a particular duck, called a Smew, because his mother had eaten one for lunch just the day before he was born, and liked the sound.

Smew had a bunch of keys attached to a broad leather belt. To the annoyance of everyone who worked in the forge and several who did not, he jangled these keys continually. It was with great gravity and solemnity that he used one of these keys to remove Spiggot's manacles.

'Now don't you go and try to run away on me,' said Smew to Spiggot. 'I'm responsible, you know.'

'Responsible for what?' asked Spiggot, rubbing his sore wrists, glad to be free of the chains.

Smew frowned. 'For all you boggarts. I'm the chief boggart. Didn't they tell you?'

'No, they didn't. I haven't even been told what I'm doing here. I thought they were going to shoot me full of poisoned arrows. What is this place? Are we making iron bricks? Or iron roof slates? What?'

'Swords!' exclaimed Smew, reverently. 'They must like you, to put you in here. This is the best job in the whole castle!'

'Next to Rincortle's, of course,' replied Spiggot, dryly, and the rest of the weaponsmiths laughed. This disconcerted Smew, who wasn't used to boggarts answering him back, any more than he was used to laughter.

'Rincortle doesn't work,' said the shocked Smew. 'He's a fairy.'

'And don't we all know it? Well, then,' Spiggot put his dirty hands on his hips and surveyed the forge, 'what's to do? Swords, is it? Swords to put in the hands of those dark-hearted fairies. So, what do we do, when we're not being supervised by an ulcugga? Deliberately put flaws in the blades, so that they snap the first time they're used in anger?'

Smew drew himself up indignantly and rattled his keys to show how emotional he felt. 'No, we do not, Spiggot. We make the best blades in the whole of Liöfwende. Better even than the claymores of Thristlac.'

'Why?' Spiggot's hands were still on his hips. He had the attention of the whole forge now. They were staring at him in an interested fashion.

Smew was getting out of his depth. 'Why what?'

'Why do we make strong steel blades for fairies who constantly kidnap boggarts and work them to a frazzle?'

'Because . . . because we're told to. Because we have to. Because if we didn't, we'd be put back in the iron foundry.'

'Yet, if we *did* introduce hidden flaws in the blades, no one would know until the swords were used in earnest, which might be never, or it might be when your clan go to war against the ulcugga.'

At that moment Rincortle arrived. He had taken time out to pass by the forge to see how Spiggot was getting on. It naturally incensed him to see that his trusty was keeping everyone talking and no work was being done.

'Smew,' cried Rincortle, 'if my own overseer can't see the need to keep up the pace of work, how can the workers see it? Do you want to be replaced? I can do it now, you know.'

Smew rattled his keys again. 'This – this – this *new* boggart is upsetting the others. He wants to make bad swords. I was telling him he must make *good* swords. That's what I was doing.'

'Causing trouble already, Spiggot? Well, well, I can put you back in the foundry, or you can buckle to. Which is to be?'

Spiggot replied, 'I don't have much choice, do I?'

'You have no choice whatsoever.'

'Then I shall buckle to.'

Spiggot joined another boggart at the furnace and the whole forge began working once again. Prince Rincortle watched them for a short while, then left, but not before warning them, 'I shall test the blades, to see if they are defective. For every sword that does not pass inspection, one boggart will return to the iron foundry. Make up your minds.'

Spiggot got stuck into the job. It was not in his nature to fashion poor objects from the fairy iron ore, but he wanted to now. If only he could have kept his big mouth shut! Kling would have told him that. Jack would have told him that. But he had to go and let it out like some braggart. Of course, he had not expected that Smew would be the traitor he had now showed himself to be. He had thought that the trustyship had been thrust on the stupid boggart, rather that being sought by that individual. But it seemed that Smew was a puppet of the ulcugga fairies – their pet dog.

Spiggot did as he was told and produced good swords. He did not want to be responsible for a boggart going back into the foundry. The work was not difficult, nor anywhere near as tedious as flattening iron plates, but of course like any trapped faerie he yearned for freedom.

This was always at the forefront of his mind, though he worked diligently enough, and even made some suggestions to Smew to improve the quality.

Rincortle was not totally convinced of Spiggot's loyalty to the forge, so he sent an ulcugga to watch over them while they worked. During the first week it was a male ulcugga with a gabby habit: he couldn't resist chatting to anyone who would listen about his herb garden. You would think this creature had the only herb garden in Liöfwende. Certainly, it had to be the best, for no other could match it. Rincortle caught him trying to engage his charges in conversation and removed him, replacing him with a female ulcugga. Female fairies were less inclined to chat away their idle hours, preferring instead to count the clouds in silence.

This particular ulcugga watched the group intently, presumably to make them realise they were under scrutiny and had to work. Her eyes however were almost always on Spiggot. Spiggot wondered whether Rincortle had singled him out for close observation.

'It's the prince, isn't it?' snapped Spiggot one day, as he passed by the fairy to reach the tempering trough. 'He's told you to stare me out.'

'No, it's not Prince Rincortle.'

'Who is it then?' asked Spiggot, indignantly. 'I'm working as hard as I can.'

'I know you are. It's not him, though, it's me.'

'Why are you so interested in me?'

The fairy shrugged. 'You were the boggart with that mortal who brought me back from Mortaland.'

Spiggot stared at the fairy. 'You're Raminago'bris.'

'That stupid name,' flared the fairy. 'Yes, I am she.'

Spiggot came clean. 'It wasn't Jack who suggested that name, you know. It was me. It was just a joke, but Jack took it seriously. I'm sorry you ended up with it, but it wasn't deliberate. Jack was very fond of you. You helped him get back here, to Liöfwende, and he was grateful for that. That's why he spent time in helping you get back too. You know as well as I do, if he'd been a faerie, he would have forgotten about you the moment he returned to Liöfwende. We are not grateful beings, us faerie. Jack, on the other hand, always honours his promises. It's a thing with mortals. They remember to honour their promises. They *are* grateful.'

Raminago'bris appeared a little moved by this. She said, 'You can't spend time in Mortaland and not have a little mortal rub off on you. I slept in their chairs. I lived in their lamps. I sometimes wore shoes and raincoats, to keep my spirits high. I find it hard to feel *gratitude* towards any mortal but I do have a few wisps of feelings for Jack. He is a handsome young man, and after all, I am female. Fairies have been known to fall in love with mortals and marry them. I'm not *that* fond of Jack but I hate to see him in such straits.'

'I see. So – you feel – something – towards Jack?'

'Why not? And he did get me out of that place. Several hundred years. It was deadly. It was worse than deadly. Stuffy sofas, old oil paintings, brass clocks. These do not make wonderful companions. Yet within a few hours Jack had me out of there and back in my comfortable form of ulcugga, fully-fleshed, my mind alert again. I think that was some feat he performed. To release me. And –'

'And?' asked Spiggot, his heart racing a little.

'And this place,' the fairy looked around her in loathing, 'is nasty and ugly, far worse than the shop. I can't stay here. I won't. I shall get you out of here and leave at the same time, find an island somewhere, perhaps the Hebrides, or the Orkneys, or whatever we call them. I've forgotten. But a place with clean fresh air would be nice. Better than inhaling the fumes of molten metal and choking on coal dust! We shall leave one night, when the others are asleep. Keep a watching wake for me.'

'We have to take Rosamund – the maid – with us. Jack would never go without her. It's that honour thing I told you about.'

'But she's constantly with Mallmoc. She washes his feet with oil. She brushes that vile coarse hair, or what's left of it. We'll never get her away.'

'We must. There's got to be a time when she's not close to him.'

Raminago'bris sighed. 'I'll see what I can do.' Her eyes lit up for a moment. 'In fact, there is something we need in order to get out of this place. A spell in the *Book of Diabolical Magick*, which is essential to our escape. I thought to get it myself, but she would have easier access to it. Can she read, do you think?'

Spiggot shrugged. 'Who knows?'

'Ummm. Mortal maids from her time were often kept ignorant. Of course the youths weren't much better, being thick-headed and interested only in battles and brawls. Clerics and holy men did all the reading. Still, you never know, she might have been a pious young creature, keen on discovering what the illuminated texts had to say. There have always been maids brighter than the rules that bound them.'

'Good. When shall I expect you?'

'It is to be hoped in three nights.'

Spiggot went back to the other boggarts, who had been watching him deep in inaudible conversation with the ulcugga fairy. Smew was particularly interested in what had been said. Spiggot muttered in a disgusted tone, 'She thinks I'm not working hard enough. She said if I don't buck my ideas up she'll report me to Rincortle. I hate these ulcugga, don't you?' Unable to resist it, Spiggot added with a significant nod towards Smew, 'And she says she's going to hold you responsible!'

'Me?' cried Smew. 'I haven't done anything.'

'That's the problem. You haven't. You should, you know. You should shout at me, tell me not to be so lazy, yell at me with great fury in your voice, scream at me. It would show you cared.'

'So it would,' replied Smew, with a quick glance at Raminago'bris. He then proceeded to lambaste Spiggot, jangling his keys in the boggart's face. Raminago'bris was surprised at this violent behaviour, but believed it was something to do with boggart protocol. She turned her back on the scene, thinking it unseemly, which fuelled Smew's fears even further. The trusty increased his mock rage. His voice got louder and louder, and more strained, until he was so hoarse he lost it altogether.

FOUR

Midnight in Liöfwende. Since there are no clocks to mark the witching hour owls do the job for them. Hoots replace chimes and bells. Not to the right number of course, for owls can't count, but all over the land the sound of their hollow notes tell the hour. Then it is silent again. The moon can relax and wane the rest of the night away. Foxes, stoats and weasels are up and about, this being a time for hunting. Busy, busy, carnivores. It would be unthinkable *not* to score the passing of midnight. Even the supernatural world needs its audio milestones, its calls to attention. Who would know that the year had ended and a new one begun without clocks and owls? The owls could be heard, even though their voices sounded faint from within the walls of the iron castle.

Spiggot's eyes opened. He was curled up with the rest of the boggart swordsmiths, or waylanders as they are sometimes known. The only light was the dim glow from the furnace, where the embers were dying. Spiggot glanced towards the doorway. Sure enough the two wooden doors had been unlocked and one was open.

Raminago'bris had earlier given Spiggot a key, which he had hid in his hair. He now took this out and unlocked the manacles which held him prisoner. Smew, like the other boggarts, was fast asleep. Spiggot placed the manacles around the trusty's ankles and wrists and clicked them shut.

Smew woke up at that instant. He stood up and tried to walk but found himself held by chains. He opened his mouth to scream for help, only to find his voice gone. What came out was a thin squeak, not much louder than that of a mouse. One or two of the boggart prisoners woke and opened their eyes, but on seeing what was occurring wisely closed them and feigned snoring. Smew rattled his chains, frustrated, angry, and tried again. Again the mouse's squeak. Spiggot smiled at him and patted him on the head.

'Farewell, Smew. I hope you like the foundry. That's where you'll be sent, for letting me escape. Have a good century.'

Once Spiggot was outside, he found Raminago'bris waiting for him.

'Quickly,' she whispered, 'put this on.'

Raminago'bris was carrying three robes over her right arm. She handed him one of these, much like a monk's habit with a hood, which Spiggot immediately put on. When he was wearing it, it covered him completely. Raminago'bris then motioned for Spiggot to follow her.

The boggart did as he was told. They passed through a maze of passageways, walking slowly. On occasion they came across ulcugga fairies, but Raminago'bris merely nodded to them. If they glanced too hard at Spiggot, whose face was hidden by the habit's hood, she murmured, 'Holy man' or 'Mad monk'. Fairies, being pagan, have a horror of coming too close to members of mortal religions. They instinctively shied away from this mortal in a monk's habit. The ulcugga knew that Mallmoc, being mortal, sometimes used the potency of renegade monks and unfrocked priests to assist him in his darker magic, so were used to seeing such creatures wandering the halls and passageways from time to time.

Finally the pair were outside the inner sanctum of the sorcerer himself. Here Raminago'bris paused. Earlier she had managed to whisper some instructions to Rosamund, as the young maid was exercising in the central yard. However, Rosamund was supposed to be here, in this spot, waiting for them.

'Where is she?' hissed Raminago'bris. 'Mortals! Never on time.'

At that moment a sheet of iron moved as if it were a curtain. It was lifted, and under it came a furtive-looking maid. Rosamund had managed to get away from her master. What was more, as suggested earlier by Raminago'bris, she had stolen and used a spell for turning iron to velvet. This was to be the means of their escape. Rosamund was very pleased with herself. The spell had not been easy to steal and even less easy to work, but fortunately the language had been Latin, which Rosamund knew.

'Wherefore hast thou not woken Jack?' murmured Rosamund, looking around.

'That's next,' answered the ulcugga fairy, looking anxious and agitated. 'Is the wizard asleep?'

'He rests. He never sleeps,' answered the strong-willed Rosamund, 'or I would have burned out his eyes with a hot poker ere he woke. His resting is light and uneasy. We must be gone, quickly.'

It was almost as if Rosamund had assumed command of the escape. She donned a robe and then bid Raminago'bris to lead the way. As they found their way down to the iron foundry, by way of countless stairs and passageways, Spiggot asked Rosamund, 'How did you learn to read? Raminago'bris said maids of your time were ignorant.'

'Most were,' sniffed Rosamund, 'but not I.' She paused, before telling Spiggot, 'There was a young novice monk. He fancied he was in love with me and to be close to me he suggested to my father that he read me the holy scriptures. When I was a youngling, my father considered me to be a humgriffin, too boyish and rowdy, and it was suggested to him that the holy scriptures might calm my spirit and make me more the maid. Thus I was read to, but became fascinated in the illuminated letters of the great books. Then in the writing itself. The young noviciate, whose name was Solomon, though he was more passionate than wise like his namesake the ancient king of Israel taught me to read, while trying to steal kisses . . .'

'Might I suggest that you don't tell this story to Jack,' murmured Spiggot.

'Oh, no. Jack would be very jealous. And I was never in love with the youth, though he had pretty lips. I did nothing to encourage his ardour.'

They continued their journey through the corridors of flaming torches. Spiggot finally thought to ask, 'What happened to the young monk?'

'He was burned at the stake by my father, who then locked me in the chastity belt that I was wearing when I came to Liöfwende.'

'Ah, poor young man.'

'I pleaded and wept, but my father has a soul of iron.'

'I can imagine.'

They came at last to the foundry. Spiggot and Rosamund waited at the entrance while Raminago'bris went inside. She had a story for the guards, who at this time of the night were overseer goblins. Jack was to be taken to Mallmoc, his body parts to be used in some spell that required the fresh eyes and liver of a mortal. There was no suspicion attached to the time. The goblins had no idea when Mallmoc worked or rested. They released Jack into the charge of the superior ulcugga fairy.

Jack was led from the foundry hall, trembling, believing he was going to be dissected. He was now determined to make a run for it, believing he was about to be cut up and thinking he had nothing to lose, anyway. Once they were outside the hall he took to his heels. The others raced after him, charging pell-mell through the passageways, until Spiggot finally managed to run him down.

Jack fell on the floor and sobbed, 'You fiends! All right, chop out my liver. Pluck out my eyes. See if I care.'

'Jack, Jack, it's us,' said Spiggot, trying to catch his breath. 'Quickly, we're escaping. We must get out of here now.' Spiggot threw back his hood, as did Rosamund. Jack saw that he was in the hands of friends. His sobbing turned to joy. Raminago'bris now caught up with them. She told Jack to don the garment she gave him.

Jack put on the habit, saying to Rosamund, 'Sorry I look so filthy . . .' But Rosamund came from a time of mud and dirt and was used to seeing young men covered from head to foot in grime. She cared not a fig for such things.

The group were then led to great iron gates by Raminago'bris. The gates were unguarded, being as secure as any other part of the iron castle, they simply being plates of iron and there being no means of opening them except by Mallmoc's magic. With swiftness and great precision, for she was an intelligent maid and knew the art of ceremony and ritual, Rosamund turned the gates to velvet curtains. The four friends and the renegade fairy swept through and into the darkness of the open countryside. They were free! Their hearts soared. Each one of them vowed, individually, that they would never enter the iron walls of the castle again.

'I'll die first,' said Jack. 'I swear.'

'I, too, make the same oath,' said Rosamund.

They kept running, racing for the dawn. Over hill and brake, through vale and woodland. Occasionally they came upon small hamlets, of goblins, or boggarts, or pixies. One or two cottage lamps were still on, but the

four kept on going, moving silently through the single
street, not wishing to arouse the inhabitants for fear that
when the chase came their route would be revealed to
the ulcuggas. Finally they ran themselves into exhaustion
and crawled into an old badgers' sett to sleep away the
rest of the night.

When they woke and went out into the new day
Raminago'bris used some glittering powder on the
stunted form of Jack to make him into his old self once
again. He stretched instantly, the folded flesh and wrin-
kles disappearing with his growth. Then she declared she
had to be on her way, to some remote place where
Mallmoc would not seek her.

'I shall find a swan,' she said, 'to take me to one of the
outer islands of the north seas.'

Jack said, 'Thank you. I'm – I'm sorry we gave you
such a stupid name. At least, I don't think its stupid, but
everyone else seems to. Anyway, it won't matter where
you're going. No one will have heard of it there.'

'What is done, is done, Jack. We have helped each
other. Now we have no obligations. Goodbye – and good
fortune.'

'Good luck to you, too.'

She left them then, heading west, for a lake of white
swans.

The group was left to gather itself and gird its multiple
loins.

'Well,' said Jack, after he had washed in a stream,
'that was pretty brainy of you, Rosamund. To get that
spell. We could probably use it, when we eventually
attack the castle.'

'I don't think so,' said Spiggot. 'Mallmoc will destroy the spell and devise a counter-spell to stop it happening again.'

'I thought of stealing the *Book of Diabolical Magick*,' muttered Rosamund, 'but it was too large, too heavy, much like the weight of a tree and seemingly rooted to the Earth. Even so, it burned my fingers when I turned the pages.'

'You would have been destroyed, had you tried,' replied Spiggot. 'There will be a terrible curse on any thief who attempts to remove Mallmoc's book. It's his life's work, a thousand years in the making. Anyone who attempted to remove it would fall to dust, or worse.'

'Let me see your hands,' demanded Jack of Rosamund.

She showed him her palms. There were ugly red blisters all over her normally pale skin. Jack let out a cry of dismay.

'Oh, you poor thing. That must have hurt.'

''Tis nothing, Jack, compared with freedom.'

Spiggot said, 'I shall gather some herbs and wildrose petals, make some healing balm, and treat your wounds, Rosamund. Then we must be on our way south. I wonder what's happened to Kling? I hope he got back to my father all right.' Spiggot then realised the news of his capture would be abroad and his mother and father would be distraught.

'We must send word home as quickly as possible, when we reach the Northumberland fairies. Some bogle will carry the message on the back of a nightjar. Oh no, look at those oaks on the skyline! Dry and dead. The thrum have been here. We'll have to be wary of skaggs, too. They usually follow the thrum around. We don't have any weapons to fight any skaggs we come across . . .'

They walked south as quickly as their feet would carry them. Rosamund continually scanned the horizons for ulcugga. Indeed she was able to warn her group several times and each time they took a detour in order to avoid capture. The maid was a great asset to them, having marvellous vision. It was Rosamund who saw the two figures first, from a long way off, with her eagle's eyes. The others could see nothing and marvelled at the keenness of her sight. When they were nearing the City of Standing Stones, a giant rat at last came into sight. The rat was pulling a cart. A figure was walking alongside the cart dressed in the habit of a monk. Jack noticed that Rosamund had become increasingly agitated and wondered if she knew the person in the hooded garment.

'Kling!' cried Spiggot. 'It's Kling.'

They called to the rat, who turned and waved, almost upsetting the cart. When they reached him, he was almost in tears.

'Oh, master's son. Kling was dragging his claws along the highway, not wishing to be the creature who had to send word to your father with the terrible news. Yet here you are, all safe and sound.'

'You knew we would come this way?'

'Of course, master's son. Where else would you go? You must report to King Cimberlin. When did they set you free?'

'We weren't set free,' said Jack. 'We escaped.'

Kling looked over his shoulder, fearfully. 'Escaped? Then they will be after you.'

'Yes,' replied Spiggot, 'which is why we have to get to the Standing Stone quickly. But who is this? Your companion?'

'A mortal. We met on the way. He was starving and I had some chocolate . . .'

The figure in question had stepped forward a pace or two and stood before Rosamund. Suddenly the mortal threw back his hood to reveal the head of a handsome young man with golden curls. His hair was wild, his eyes were wild, but his expression was one of pure joy. He threw himself on the ground, bowing low and kissing Rosamund's feet.

'My lady,' he cried. 'It is my lady.' He looked up and then seemed a little fearful. 'Oh, she has the eyes of a loon . . .'

'Eagle,' corrected the maid sharply. 'Not a loon. Solomon? It is thee, then, beneath that thick woollen garb?'

'It is indeed, my lady,' replied the youth, raising a tear-stained but shining face, after thoroughly wetting Rosamund's toes. 'I have discovered thee, here in this wilderness of hobgoblins and demons. I give thanks to the lord for thy deliverance to me.'

'Rosy?' asked a rather nettled Jack. 'Who is this bloke?'

Instead of answering him, Rosamund turned to Spiggot and said, 'How does this happen?'

Spiggot shrugged. 'Here in Liöfwende coincidences

are common. They're in the normal run of things, rather than being rare. It's something to do with the magic in the air, like static electricity. If you mention someone, then you seem to run into them not long after.'

'Mention someone? Have you been talking about this bloke, Rosy? What's he to you, eh? And don't tell me he's your brother.'

The youth looked imperiously at Jack. 'I am indeed her brother, being a friar. And yet I am her father too, being a priest. I would be more to my lady than either of these, if she grants her permission.'

Rosamund said, 'This is my tutor, Jack. Solomon taught me to read and write Latin.'

Jack glared at Solomon. 'Oh, he did, did he?'

'Did not my lady just say so?' replied Solomon, looking at Jack down his narrow nose. 'Is the stripling deaf as well as a simpleton?'

'Simpleton?' cried Jack, rolling up his sleeves. 'I'll show you how simple I am . . .'

'Jack, desist,' said Rosamund. 'There will be no brawl here. We have presently escaped from a terrible fate. Should we not be grateful? Should we not be thankful? Let us go down into the village with hearts full of happiness and not bicker amongst ourselves. Solomon, Jack is no simpleton, he is a bold and resourceful squire, and thou shalt not cast insults upon him.'

Both youths glared at each other again, then Jack turned and busied himself with making sure his treasures were still in the cart. They were all three there: the green bottle, the silver shoes, the magic crossbow.

By the time they began descending towards the

glittering Standing Stones of the fairy city, Jack had
calmed a little. So this bloke had been Rosy's teacher?
She couldn't help that, could she? She probably thought
him a right twit. No reason to make a fuss over a nerd
like him, was there? Let him twitter away like a sparrow
with his 'my lady' this and 'my lady' that. It was Jack
who had won her heart.

However, she was now walking beside Solomon, who
was telling her all that had happened to him since he had
left the real world. She listened intently, clearly delighted
at being able to converse with someone who spoke her
own form of English. Jack noticed her accent got
broader and the words more medieval, as she chattered
away to the young monk. Sometimes the language was
Old English, sometimes Latin or French.

'Spiggot,' said Jack, as they walked down the white
chalk path which wound its way down, 'surely everyone
who has an accident, or suffers violence in Mortaland,
doesn't end up here.'

'I wouldn't have thought so, Jack. Mortals in
Liöfwende are rather few and far between.'

'So how come this bloke, Solomon is here?'

'It sometimes happens that one place on the Earth, is
more sensitive than others. I suspect that this man was
burned at the stake on the very spot that Rosamund
chose to throw herself down to from the battlements.'

Jack frowned. 'Yes, that would make sense, I
suppose – if anything could be said to make sense in
faerieland. Hey, Spiggot, do you – do you think he's
good-looking? Solomon, I mean?'

Kling had overheard this and said enthusiastically,

'Oh, a very fine youth, Jack. Well-chiselled jaw. Bright eyes. Nice rude tail.'

'He hasn't got a tail,' protested Jack.

'Well, it would be nice and rude, if he had one. Look how broad his shoulders are. See how graceful he is. Oh, he's a handsome one, that's for sure. Intelligent, too. Speaks very well, especially in Latin. I expect he taught her that so's they could talk to each other without her father knowing what was being said? So they could have secret liaisons, secret rendezvous. Very clever, some of these monks.'

Spiggot, with a warning look at Kling, tried to negate all this, by pointing out Solomon's weaknesses: his bald spot, his rather beaky nose, his large feet. Jack did not know whether these weaknesses outweighed the man's obvious strengths in Rosamund's eyes. He walked down the spiral path of the hill feeling thoroughly miserable now, having escaped the jaws of death only to find himself between the fangs of jealousy. It was a rotten world. One moment you were up, the next you were flat on your face.

There was an air of tranquillity about the scene below which might put peace into many hearts, were they not full of love towards a young woman, and malice towards the youth who was beguiling her with soft words from a time when the language was full of beauty.

An unexpected boggart then stepped out of the Standing Stones and began walking towards them.

Fen came up to meet them, as they descended, swinging her arms, seemingly careless of a meeting with her estranged Spiggot. She must have been waiting and watching for them, to be so timely. Without a doubt she had come all this way to see Spiggot. However, true to his faerie nature, Spiggot in his shyness blurted out the wrong thing.

'There's going to be a great battle, Fen. I am to lead a mighty army of fairies against the ulcugga. What do think of that?'

'Well,' she replied, tartly, 'you'd better go and do it, then.'

And she turned on her heel and went back down to the fairy city again, leaving Spiggot helpless and hollow.

'There *is* going to be a great battle,' he repeated, as if appealing to the others for support. 'And I am going to lead it.'

They patted him on the head and clapped hands and claws on his shoulders to show they understood.

To be continued . . .

Garry Kilworth was born in York in 1941, and has travelled widely around the globe ever since. He has written a number of acclaimed novels for both children and adults, including the Carnegie commended Bronte Sisters and the much-loved Welkin Weasels series. You can find out more about him when you visit the Atom website at www.atombooks.co.uk.

WAYWALKERS

By Catherine Webb

Sam Linnfer works part-time at a London university. He's a quiet chap with a real skill for tricksy ancient languages, and an affinity for cats. He's also immortal and the Son of Time. You might know him better as Lucifer. And with all the Gods in Heaven about to go to war over ownership of Earth, you're going to be extremely glad he's not *exactly* the person history portrays him to be.

Waywalkers is an absolutely astonishing new novel. You'll come face to face with Jehovah on a cold Moscow night, walk the Ways between Earth and Heaven with Buddha, take a hair-raising cab ride with Adam (yes, *the* Adam – only he's into denim now, rather than fig-leaves!) and find yourself trusting the one person you never dreamed you could.

Because when the gods go to war and Earth is their battleground only the devil can save your soul.

Find out more at www.atombooks.co.uk

FROM THE TWO RIVERS

Part One of The Eye of the World

By Robert Jordan

The Wheel turns and the greatest fantasy adventure of all time begins . . .

Life in Emond's Field has been pretty boring for Rand Al'Thor and his friends until a strange young woman arrives in their village. Moraine is an Aes Sedai, a magician with the ability to wield the One Power, and she brings warnings of a terrible evil awakening in the world. That very night, the village is attacked by bloodthirsty Trollocs – a fearsome tribe of beast-men thought to be no more than myth. As Emond's Field burns, Moraine and her warrior-guardian help Rand and his companions to escape. But it is only the beginning of their troubles. For Moraine believes Rand Al'Thor is the Dragon Reborn, and that he is fated to unite the world against the rising darkness and lead the fight against a being so powerful and evil it is known simply as *the Dark One*.

Find out more at www.atombooks.co.uk

TO THE BLIGHT

Part Two of The Eye of the World

By Robert Jordan

The most incredible fantasy adventure of all time continues . . .

Despite the magical aid of Moraine Sedai and the awesome fighting skills of the warrior Lan, Rand Al'Thor and his friends have been unable to throw off the foes that pursue them. Even a detour through the ghosts of the ruined city of Shadar Logoth has failed to deter the Dark One's minions. Now the companions have a Trolloc army at their rear and eyeless shadow-men, known as Myrddraal, laying ambushes on the roads ahead. Worse still, the Dark One has dispatched his most feared general to ensure that Rand will die. Aginor is the powerful magician whose dark magic first created the Trollocs and he will stop at nothing to fulfil his master's bidding. Unless Rand can unlock the secrets of his extraordinary destiny, Aginor will destroy him and the darkness will triumph forever.

Find out more at www.atombooks.co.uk

SPY HIGH

The stunning new series by AJ Butcher

Episode One
THE FRANKENSTEIN FACTORY

Somewhere in the not too distant future, there is a school that is much more than it seems . . . To the outside world, it is known as The Deveraux College for gifted teenagers. But to Lori, Jake and the other new first years, it goes by a very different name: *Spy High*. Those who pass its rigorous training program will become the world's best hope in the fight against evil megalomaniacs and crazed techno-terrorists. Those who fail will have their memories erased. *Let the lessons begin . . .*

Episode Two
THE CHAOS CONNECTION

Bond Team are back, and preparing to battle for the prestigious *Sherlock Shield*. Victory means a place in the Deveraux College hall of fame. But to win, they'll have to beat their arch-rivals – and Solo Team are prepared to do anything to stop that happening. Bond Team will have to watch their backs. And maybe everywhere else too, because in the world outside of Spy High, a terrorist organisation is about to send its first explosive announcement: *Chaos is coming!*

And look out for . . .
Episode Three: THE SERPENT SCENARIO
Episode Four: THE PARANOIA PLOT
Episode Five: THE SOUL STEALERS
Episode Six: THE ANNIHILATION AGENDA

www.spyhigh.co.uk